Soul Directive

Michael Cantwell

Soul Directive is fiction. Names, characters and incidents are either the product of the author's imagination or are used fictitiously.

DEDICATION

To my mom, Mary-Ellen

1

Few remained. The old and weak had lost their ability. Among the young and strong; few had the will. Yet it was imperative I persevered. This is my story.

Most have the luxury of choosing their own destiny. Maybe I did. I do trust everyone has the ability in freedom of choice. Only my choices were far more limited than most. It was always presented as my duty to feed our kind with stealing damaged souls. It was not until later in life, I also believed that most, if not all, deserved a second chance. Our Council had eliminated the power of restoration of broken souls long ago. My grandfather's bloodlines were chosen to alter the power of the Council and restore the power of redemption. The responsibility was now mine. However, along the way, I had lost my family as well as faith in my leaders.

My given name is Caeles Novo. I was the preeminent soul stealer on earth. I assumed I knew who my family was, and what my future held. That was until I discovered the people closest to me, never told me the truth about who I am. My mother and father did not disclose my true bloodlines to me until my natural born grandfather visited me in a hospital bed. He appeared to me with his grand visions and my future path. Sure I had been known to fight my elders, but I never could have imagined the destruction and pain that ensued.

Charon Orcus no longer owned his soul since I had just removed it. He was lying in the fetal position on the floor exactly where I'd ripped out his most prized possession. I couldn't muster up even one drop of sympathy for him. If anyone no longer deserved a second chance, it was my former leader.

After the unexpected had happened, silence fell upon the room. Three of the five elders left. I peered across the room, eyes still filled with tears. My wife and son stood like statues, where Charon Orcus cast his spell. They were not like stone but still in the flesh, unable to move. The cold marble floor started to feel even less inviting as I struggled to stand. The lone window was barely offering a glint of light as the two elders remaining in the room guided me to my feet.

"Caeles, I can assure you, no one on this Council expected this outcome. Orcus assured us your family would only remain motionless for a few moments. He told us he only wanted to scare you into backing down. I would be a liar if I stated that some of us on the Council weren't hoping for a way to remove him as our leader but no one wanted this. It all happened so quickly. Yes, there is no doubt I wanted to find a way for you to replace Charon Orcus on our Council, but removing his soul was not our first option."

"No? Then tell me, what was your first option?" I asked my grandfather.

Again silence filled the room. It was all very obvious to me that they didn't expect the outcome they just witnessed. They never dared to believe I would remove his soul. However, some on the Council did want me to start a power struggle with the man who was our leader for decades.

My grandfather spoke again. "What is done cannot be erased Cale. We will move forward from here. You have been elected as a full voting member of the Council and our new leader. Many of us are tired and have little time left on earth. It is time we pass along the responsibilities to someone with your youth. This has always been your destiny, Caeles, long before you were born." I attempted to gain a firm footing to stand alone as my grandfather continued.

"Caeles, everyone understands things have gotten out of hand. After Elder Orcus assumed his position as leader of our Council, he believed his authority was more than our laws describe. It had become a problem. However no one assumed you would use your powers to remove his soul. Even if you attempted it, not one of us considered it possible. We assumed he was too powerful. Therefore, please believe me when I tell you, what just occurred was never our intention. That being said, none of us intend on returning his soul to him."

"With all due respect, Grandfather, I don't give a damn about Charon Orcus or his soul. I only care about how to restore my family. Now, if you would be so kind in doing so, it would be much appreciated."

"Caeles, none of us has a cure for your wife and son. We don't know what Elder Orcus did to your family."

"Well isn't that just great! You bait me into a battle with Orcus and none of you envisioned what the consequences might be? On top of that, my family is lost to me and the only man who understands what he did has the capacities of a newborn, whoo hoo! Do any of you have anything to offer me other than your lame excuses?"

Stillness erupted in the room as we stared at each other. My grandfather, James Spia, the oldest of the five remaining elders with a soul, along with, Jair Rex, another elder and the grandfather to my frozen wife, looked down to the ground. The elder who was usually first to voice an opinion on the Council after Orcus, Elder Jair Rex, spoke up.

"Caeles, we all realize this was a tragic accident. We will find a solution. However, our disciples need leadership. As stated earlier by Elder Spia, who we just now find out is your own flesh and blood, we are an aging Council. Some of us, me included, should have retired many moons ago. It should be obvious for all to see that you were sent to us for a reason. You must be the one to bring back our disciples from the brink of extinction and our wicked ways."

"Thanks guys but let me say this slowly so I don't confuse any of you. I don't want to be the leader of this Council, our disciples, or even my home town city council, until my family has been saved. Can I be any more direct with you?"

At that point, my grandfather raised his voice to get my attention.

"I will not tolerate any more of your insubordination, Caeles. We will find a way to restore your family but you will lead this Council. There is a room set up here in the complex for you to rest. Once you calm yourself, you will assist us in deciding our future path, but no more childish behavior."

I'm not sure what everyone could expect from me. For as much training as I had to learn not to be emotional, it was still difficult. It is true the highest honor for our kind is to lead the Council. But I was in no emotional state to lead anyone. However, I would listen to the advice and retired for some self examination to determine what my life now had in store for me.

Sleep was difficult. Not only was I stressing about my family all night but the few times I could drift off, I would have a dream loop over and over in my brain. It contained a voice reciting, "Power tends to corrupt, and absolute power corrupts absolutely. Great men are almost always bad men." It played in my brain throughout the night.

"Elder Novo, it's time to wake." That was the next thing I heard. It was one of our disciples standing alongside my bed. "Elder Novo, please a long day awaits you."

"Who are you? Why are you in my room? And who's Elder Novo for goodness sake?"

I did my best to focus on the young man's face. I could see his confusion matched mine.

"You're Elder Novo, are you not? The Council has a long day planned. With all due respect, you need to get your wits about you. After all, you are our new leader, Sir. And to answer your initial question, I have been assigned to assist you while in the complex. My name is Peter, Peter Pascal."

"Well Peter Pascal, your first assignment is to head back out the door, lock it and don't allow anyone to enter it until I walk through it to leave."

"I'm sorry, Elder Novo. I am under strict orders from Elder Spia. I believe his exact words were; get his ass in this Council room immediately."

"Maybe so but I'm now the leader of the band around here, so what I say rules. Am I wrong?"

"Elder Novo, a wise man once said, what's in a name? I am going to conclude it applies to titles as well. I refuse to go back into that room and tell Elder Spia you decided to sleep past noon. I'm too new here. I would like to keep my job and my new title for more than a few hours. Please get up."

I didn't want my new assistant to shed tears on his first day. I got up.

When I arrived in the Council room, there were three of our disciples with their noses plastered inside the pages of old dusty books. Along with them were the five members of the Council with a soul, anxiously peering over their shoulders, as if the books contained the winning lottery numbers.

Elder James Spia, took the lead. "Have a seat Caeles. Our best historians are reading all they can to solve the issue with your family."

"Issue, you are calling it an issue?" I was none too pleased. His words and demeanor seemed almost trivial.

"Caeles, please, have a seat. There are many topics that need to be discussed. Some are of a delicate nature, but we can all agree your family is our highest priority. Now, please, we all understand you are still emotionally charged, but you are a trained professional. You've been trained for emotional situations. So calm down and get your mind right. We will fix the wrong that has happened. However, you are now on this Council. One day soon, you will be presented to our disciples as their new leader. But until that day, there are many urgent issues around the table for discussion."

I looked around the room. The five members of the Council were all seated at a large round wooden table with me. They included my grandfather, James Spia, along with my wife's grandfather, Jair Rex. It was not until recently these two men were exposed to me as more than Council members. I was hoping there would be no more surprises concerning the other three. They included, Nathan Stella, Baruch Robus and Reuel Polus. I only knew these men from coming before the Council when I was being praised or punished. Along with Charon Orcus, the previous leader of the Council, these six men had shaped my life with their decrees and words of wisdom.

There was one window I could stare out. The floor was as cold as the icy stare Orcus had in this room the previous day. The table we were using was designed as the more informal place for the Council to sit while discussing the agenda. There was also the dais where the Council sits when conducting official business, such as handing out penalties to the likes of me, when I would take matters into my own hands. There were a few scant paintings from past European masters on the walls, merely to cover up the boring and sterile qualities of the room. I was trying to focus on all the discussion around me but I wasn't interested. That was until one topic came up. Elder Stella started to speak in an anxious manner.

"Elders, we cannot continue to pretend our dwindling numbers of soul stealers is not an issue. We can no longer support all we need to support. Our research indicates that our disciples are living on average fifty years less than they were only one generation ago. This generation has been dying at an alarming rate of less than two hundred and fifty in earthly years. Our founders all survived past three hundred. Our mission on earth is far too important to allow this trend to continue."

This information was all new to me. I had noticed my own parents starting to slow, despite being barely two hundred years on earth. Why the trend?

"Ok, this being all new to me, can someone please explain why the lower life expectancies?" I inquired.

Elder Stella attempted to explain. "It is simple math, Elder Novo. When the Lord of Life bestowed upon us the ability to remove souls from humans, who no longer could appreciate all that was given to them, we were one hundred strong. Each and every one of our ancestors had the ability that the six of us have, meaning to be able to see into another's soul and remove it, if deemed necessary. Once we started to marry pure humans and thin our bloodlines, fewer and fewer acquired the same abilities. It is why now some can only remove souls and so few other than the six at this table and possibly our offspring will be able to see into another's soul. Because so many have mated with humans over the generations we have hundreds that we feed but we are down to less than thirty active soul stealers other than us at this table."

"Ok, so what's the plan? I mean you guys have been sitting around this table for decades, you musta' seen this coming? I mean if you are telling me it's all simple math then let's fix the math."

Elder Polus spoke up. "As you are aware, Elder Novo, all our bloodlines are carefully recorded. We have hundreds living now with some remaining strains of our bloodlines that we feed. However, with less than forty at least half blooded and less than fifteen full blooded, it is likely why we are dying at an earlier age. We are a dying breed."

"Why has it taken so long for anyone to do anything about this Elder Polus?"

"Would you have listened if we ordered you to marry someone other than Kalani, Elder Novo? I think I've made my point."

I couldn't believe all I was hearing. But then again, why should I have cared? I could care for myself. I could steal all the souls I wanted and keep myself in top form.

"You know what guys, this is not my problem. I can see into another's soul, I can steal, I can survive. I don't think we should really care about anyone who decided to thin out their blood line."

My grandfather spoke up. "So tell me Caeles, should you become injured removing a soul, or when you become too old or ill to remove souls, will you still wish this Council to have the same approach you are taking now?"

"You are missing my point, Grandfather. I have worked very hard to reach my goals and my position in life. If others don't care to try, why should I help them?"

"What about the ones who through no fault of their own, but only through genetics have never developed the power to steal like your father Caeles? Shall we tell him, sorry but we no longer can support you? He pays his dues to us. There are hundreds with good jobs in life who help support our cause. We should ignore them?"

"There has to be a better way, Grandfather."

"There is and it's one reason why you are now on this Council. When you risked your own life to offer redemption to Dylan James, a man who you barely knew, I knew you would one day find a solution to this issue. I suggest you start thinking."

My first Council meeting as a member disbanded. I had much to think about but my mind was still elsewhere. I walked across the hallway and sat with my wife and child, still frozen in time. I didn't care much about others shortened life spans or ones who could possibly steal, who didn't want to for various reasons, like my own mother. My mind rested with my family.

The Council sat around the table for a few more days until it became obvious that I had to continue on as a soul stealer and no one had the cure for my family. I sat through boring meeting after boring meeting with men who had led our disciples for years acting as if they were just brought into find solutions the same day I was. It was appalling to me that the ones who admonished me for years for my ideas, where now looking to me to lead. My entire world had become upside down in less than a week.

I decided that I would travel to Jamaica to visit with my old friend, Bastian "Doc" Duvaliar, who assisted me in restoring my first soul. He was in possession of a book that documented many of our secrets from the past. It had been given to his ancestors many decades ago. He taught me how to offer redemption to a broken soul from the writings stored in this book. Since many of our disciples aren't even aware of its existence, my hope is that it also stores the secrets to unlock my family.

As I departed, my grandfather was there to offer a few words.

"Cale, everyone on the Council understands the pressure you are under right now. I promise you, we will search every avenue we can to find a cure for your family. We'll also look into your idea of contacting all of our disciples to see if they want to go through some of our training again to see if they have developed powers since the last time they were tested."

"Thanks, Granddad, it seems every time I think I have life figured out, I'm on another airplane entering a new phase in my journey. I wish I could go back to being a single guy with no responsibilities to anyone but myself."

"No you don't, have a safe trip."

2

"It so nice to see you again my guut friend, Caeles. I trust you had guut journey to my island?"

"Hey Doc, yes it was a quiet flight and it's good to see you again. I trust Peter spoke with you and informed you about my family?"

"He did. Sound like Elder Orcus made sure he would be protected against any attacks from you or de Council. I tink he be two steps ahead of you."

"Whaddya mean, Doc?"

"You be smarter dan dis. What if I cannot find cure? What if your people cannot? You will be forced to restore de soul of Elder Orcus. If only he holds de key, den you must unlock dat door."

"Are you telling me I wasted my trip here, Doc?"

"No, but I'm telling my guut friend dat you must open your mind to all possibilities. Now you must go and rest. Tomorrow we begin to find you what you seek, after you meet friend of mine."

I didn't know who his friend was but after three sleepless nights, three long plane rides and layovers just to arrive in Jamaica, rest was a welcome word.

Doc woke me with a home cooked breakfast. I travel so often it was pleasant to able to sit and have a meal with engaging conversation. He had someone else sitting with us who didn't speak much. He introduced her as Carroline Clinkard, the daughter of a friend. I pressed him for more and he did say while he was ill a few years ago; her mother stepped in and nursed him back to good health. From across the table I could see sadness in Carroline's eyes. She looked to be in her early twenties with a beautiful face. It bothered me to see someone that young and beautiful radiate despair like she did.

I watched Carroline eat while I gulped down my eggs and hash browns. It wasn't apparent if she fully understood all of her surroundings. She would occasionally make a gesture with her face or utter something that Doc seemed to understand. Somehow her sad smile seemed oddly familiar to me but I could not place it. My mind was filled with my problems. Carroline was not high on my list to care about at the moment.

After breakfast finished, we moved to Doc's living room. I assumed to get to work on finding a cure for my family. His living room was exactly as it was the last time I ventured to his home. The light had many paths to enter through all the windows of his wood framed house. The paddle fan still barely spun above my head. The furniture was old but clean. Carroline sunk low in a rattan chair across from the comfy sofa I chose to sit in. Doc sat in a matching rattan chair next to Carroline as if he was watching guard over her.

"Dis de second time you travel far to seek answers from me, Caeles. I taught you much de last time you visit me, yes?

"You know you did Doc, what's your point?"

Doc tried to mask his amusement but his smirk was not so subtle. "I help you once and you return. Now you ask for my help again, yes my guut friend?"

"Spit it out Doc, what's on your mind?"

"I only want some help one time from you, for two times from me. I am simple man with simple requests. I help you second time but only after you help me one time. My friend over dere, Carroline, she is ill. De last time you visit me, you stole her soul. I know it had to be you. You were de only soul stealer on Jamaica when her life changed. I know when someone has lost de soul. Carroline lost her soul. Dat is what be wrong with her. I not pleased with you, Caeles. She was guut to me. Now, you must be guut to her and restore her soul. We both know it be much easier for de soul taker to restore de soul. When you do, I will see if I can help you."

"You will see if you can help me? You mean you're not sure you have a cure in that book of yours?"

"I am spiritual master, Caeles, but not one with every answer. But unless Carroline has her soul returned to her, de book remains locked in my safe. Do we have understanding, or no?"

"This is not something I can do on my own, Doc. I have to see what she did to warrant the removal in the first place. You know I can't just return souls without some kind of justification."

"You surprise me, Caeles. De last time you seek my help, you didn't seem to have need for your justifications. Now when I come for your help, you have rules you didn't have before?"

"Give me a break, Doc. You know my situation has changed since the last time I was here. Let me get a report from Peter. I don't want to attempt to restore her soul without more information. Allow me a few hours to do my homework on your Carroline. If we took her soul, we will have a record. Let's make sure what you are saying is accurate. She does look familiar to me, but I don't remember taking her soul."

I called Peter and a few hours later I started to read the report on Carroline Clinkard.

She was born in Jamaica to an American father and Jamaican mother. Her father, Harold Clinkard, was from North Carolina. He worked construction for a company headquartered in Raleigh. Harold's company was building a hotel in Kingston, Jamaica, where he met Carroline's mother, Raeini Stone. He was injured while working on the job and was taken to the local hospital, where Raeini was a nurse. There was an instant attraction and four months later, Harold and Raeini were wed. A year later, Carroline was born.

Harold's job was completed soon after the birth of Carroline. His next assignment was at another hotel, only this time in Houston, Texas. He promised Raeini he would set up a home in Houston for her and their child, but it never happened. The construction industry hit hard times as the global economy started to falter. Harold went from job site to job site looking for work as a carpenter. He would send money to Raeini when he could and even visited for a few days now and again. Harold supported them financially until Carroline reached her tenth year.

Eventually the letters stopped coming, as did the promises to one day move his wife and child to the United States.

Before the letters stopped coming, Carroline would get her own letters from her father. They were filled with pictures of the town he was working in at that time, with promises that one day he would show her all the places he had been. She kept every letter stored in a shoe box under her tiny bed. She loved spending time with her dad when he visited the island but those times were much too rare for her. She did her best to understand, but she was a child.

As I was browsing through the report, I would occasionally peek at Carroline. I was beginning to place her from my past. Her skin was not as dark, her hair was longer and not as manicured since the first time we met. I continued to view the report.

By the time she was a teenager her anger started to fester. She would get in trouble in school and was forced to attend school for troubled youths. Her mother did what she could to help Carroline but nothing much seemed to help. That was until she realized Carroline had a passion and skill for working on women's hair. A friend of her mother took Carroline in to work in her local shop and taught her all about the salon business. On the surface, it seemed to change her entire disposition about life.

Within a few months, she was very busy in the salon. Carroline didn't have much in the way of financial wealth but enough to live above what was considered poverty in Jamaica. She had a clean room to live and her belly was usually full. She stayed in close contact with her mother but there was always one thing they never could agree upon. "Mum, you need to file de divorce papers. De man is never coming back to you." Carroline had given up any hopes that her father would return to her or her mother and finally take them to the United States, even if it was nothing more than a long vacation. Carroline had craved that for years but stopped dreaming. Her mother however, didn't want to give up hope.

"Carroline, I want to give you a chance to step up and take on more responsibility. I would love it if you would help me with a new salon near a retirement community at Morant Bay. Carroline's boss, Jen Browne, knew how good she was with customers. "I need you to help me expand my business on the island. I will offer you a small ownership part if you accept my offer."

Caroline accepted and within a few months, the second salon was open. Caroline would now be working with mostly retired women and the occasional gentleman looking for an upscale salon. Most of the business came from a newly minted community along the water line, comprised of retired Europeans and Americans who would reside there in winter.

"Oh Dah-ling you do such a wonderful job with my hair. I so wish I could take you back to New York with me in the summers. My hair is so dreadful in the humidity."

Time and time again Carroline would hear stories about the United States and how much better she would be in moving to New York or maybe Jersey. Even the occasional Brit would ramble on about how Carroline really needed to travel abroad. "You need to see the world dear girl. I will tell you about the simply amazing places I've seen over the years."

As I was reading the report and looking at Carroline, I could feel Doc's stare burning through me.

"Doc, I don't get it. How do you really know Carroline and why care about her?"

"A few years ago, I fell and broke my heep. Her mother cared for me in my home for weeks while I recovered. She cooked, cleaned and cared for me."

"So what Doc, she's a nurse. She was being paid to care for you. Why do you feel you owe them anything?"

"Her mum came to my home even on her days off to watch out for me. Carroline would come too. Dey would clean my home and do extra tings dat I appreciated. Now her mother, Raeini, has come to me to seek aid for her daughter. She knows I am spiritual person, who understand de ways of universe. She believes I can help, sooo I turn to you."

"It still does not explain why she lost her soul. Let me finish reading the report."

As I glanced back at my laptop screen and the report, I realized how cold and calculating my job as a soul stealer had become. I would vaguely remember a name or face. Sure, a few stuck with me like Dylan James and a few scant others, but for the most part the people were numbers. I had taken so many souls, it was impossible to remember or care about them. The report continued.

An investigation had been launched by the FBI in the United States because women were dying from being poisoned. Most had particles of arsenic and other toxins in their hair. No one had associated the deaths until a detective in the New York area realized a pattern. He passed it along to the crime lab at the FBI where a Detective Nesstor was assigned the case. He had discovered at least seven women that had been poisoned in the same manner within a two year period. Five had lived in the same retirement community in Jamaica part of the year. The other two had been on cruise ships that docked in Jamaica.

It now all came rushing back to me. Nesstor and I had crossed paths a few times in the past. He knew who I was and my mission on earth. I had returned Nesstor's soul to him after it was stolen in error. We were well acquainted. Nesstor called and asked if I knew of any dark souls in Jamaica. I informed him that Carroline was on my list for removal of her soul. From that, he attempted to make the connection to the beauty salon, since the toxins were found largely in the skull area. However, it could never be proven Carroline was the culprit. I recalled all of this did happen about the first time I was visiting Doc in Jamaica. I had indeed taken Carroline's soul. The Council had voted that Carroline's soul was dark and broken and should be removed. If she had poisoned those women, only she knows. But I now remembered taking her soul

"Doc, do you have literature about poisons in any of your books in your library here in the house?"

"I am spiritual person Caeles, not one who destroys with chemicals."

"I'm not accusing you Doc, but do you have information about poisons in your house and could you always see what Carroline was doing here while she and her mother were visiting?"

"I have books on many tings. I would think you could find information about poisons, yes. Why do you ask?"

"I believe Carroline found out about how to poison people

while shampooing their hair. I think she killed at least seven people, maybe more. That is why she lost her soul. Yes, I took her soul and I have no desire to return it.

"You have no proof of dis Caeles! Carroline had hard life. She is not de killer you seek."

"Doc, her soul was dark for a reason. You are right that I have no proof but there is a lot of evidence for it. I'm sorry but I can't return her soul. I believe she is a serial killer."

"Maybe you didn't hear me Caeles, I promised Raeini I would help her daughter. You will do dis for me or dere will be no assistance from me for your family. I will watch over Carroline if you offer her redemption. If she did dees terrible crimes, I will discover why and make her whole again. I am de healer on my island, you know dis."

"No deal Doc. However, I might return her soul on one condition. You turn her over to the authorities to stand trial once she understands the charges against her."

"Sorry Caeles, she has not been accused of anyting. I will not turn her over to you or anyone else. All you have are your ancient ways and circumstantial evidence. Maybe her soul was dark because she missed her father. Maybe her soul was dark because she was lost. Maybe your Council, who you admit made mistakes in de past, made a-noder one. No, you fix her, or your family will remain where they are with no help from me. I don't like being dis way but her mother treated me very well. I owe her."

"Maybe so Doc, but I don't owe her."

Doc and I sat and had a staring contest that lasted close to an hour. I needed time to reflect and he needed to stare at me. Sitting there I knew I had to admit Doc was correct about one thing. It was possible the Council had made a mistake. I had seen it before. However returning a soul was not a simple process. The few times I had done it in the past, I had become ill for a long time. I had far too much responsibility now to be down for even a short period of time. But if Doc could help me with my family, I owed it to them to try. Being a husband and father had to come before being a leader. As I sat there in my staring contest, I was becoming angrier by the minute. Not angry at Doc, but the idea that I was now far more responsible for people than I ever wanted to be. Less than a week ago, I was a soul stealer who was happy to be a husband and father. Now I was somehow installed as leader of our group, many of whom I had never met and likely never would. Why should I put them ahead of my own family?

"Ok Doc, here's the deal. I will attempt to return Carroline's soul. However, should anyone turn up dead from poisoning who spent time in this area, I'm going to remove her soul again. As you know, once I take it a second time, it can't be undone. We can only offer redemption once. So I suggest you keep a close eye on Miss Carroline. She is far too young to have her life cut short with no hope of redemption."

"Thank you Caeles. Can we do dis right now? I have read dat should you restore de soul soon after retrieving it from the Surrounding of Souls, it lessens de time you need to restore your own body. If you remember Caeles, de first time you kept de soul with yours for weeks before restoring it to de guitar man. I think if you restore de soul right away, maybe you don't get so sick?"

"Maybe so Doc, but I didn't keep Kalani's soul for that long and I was still sick."

"Maybe so, but you love her. She is your wife. Your emotions were drained. I don't count dat as ordinary case of redemption."

"Tell me Doc, what is an ordinary case of redemption?"

"Please my guut friend, try for me. I will make sure even if she was de one responsible for doose horrible acts, it will not happen again."

We sat Carroline back up in the chair. I would now attempt to retrieve her soul from the Surrounding of Souls. Getting past the gatekeeper is never an easy assignment. Our history states that the gatekeeper takes on the earthly shape of the person the stolen soul most identifies with on earth. For Dylan James the musician, I had to talk my way past Jimi Hendrix. With my wife, I had to talk my way past myself. That was not nearly as easy as it might sound. With Carroline essentially a stranger, I didn't know what to expect.

Like before while restoring a soul, I needed total silence. No interruptions. If someone interferes with my earthly body during this experience, it is possible my soul would never return to my earthly being. I was taking a big risk with my own body every time I restored a soul. Doc would make sure I would be safe during my journey. He made sure the phones were off and the door was locked. Carroline was sitting nearby but was told not to speak. Since she barely spoke a word and Doc was not convinced her mind was completely functional anyway, it was easy for him to keep her quiet.

My mind was taken over by the spirits that would lift my soul to the Surrounding of Souls and put my soul in contact with the gatekeeper. The gatekeeper would hopefully show me the path to Carroline's soul once I could convince the gatekeeper her soul was worthy of being joined again with her earthly being. I could see my soul rise from my body in my mind. My soul left my body to enter another corner of the universe.

The light became bright with flames surrounding my soul. I could hear banging with sounds of water and people screaming then a sudden crash. A voice spoke out from behind me. It was a man dressed in jeans, a blue shirt with traces of dirt and blood, wearing a construction hard hat. He looked to be a man just past forty years of age with a worn unshaven face. "What is your purpose in coming here?"

"I seek the soul of Carroline Clinkard. Can you help me?"

"Carroline's soul is being well cared for, you can move on. She has suffered enough on your earth."

"But she is still on earth, only her soul is here. Her mind and body remain with us. I am here to rejoin her soul with her body on earth. I need you to help me. Will you help me, Gatekeeper?"

"I am not a gatekeeper. My name is Harold Clinkard. I no longer reside on earth. I reside here and protect Carroline's soul since I can no longer do it on earth."

"Why, what happened on earth?"

"I ran into trouble. Got drunk one night and was arrested for assault. They tossed my ass in jail for months. After my release, it was rough to find a paying gig. It was hard enough before but after that, it became near impossible with my record. I had no choice but to lie about my identity. I found me some work on an oil rig in the Gulf of Mexico to earn cash to support my wife and kid. Early one morning the rig exploded. I ran out to the deck and ran directly into a large fireball. My body was burned instantly beyond recognition. I fell off the platform into the cold waters. My body was never recovered. Since I was using an assumed name, no one knows I'm dead. Everyone got it all wrong. They think I ran off from my family. They don't know shit about Harold Clinkard. I wouldn't do that. So this is how I protect my kid now."

"But Harold, please, you must understand. Her body is failing without her soul. I know you think you are protecting her but in reality she is miserable inside her body. Please help me reunite her soul with her body. When I do, I will tell her the truth about you. I am sure she will want to know her daddy never left her high and dry."

"Why should I allow her soul to leave? So you can turn her over to the authorities for crimes of which she is innocent? I know all about what goes on in her life. She's innocent. They can't lock her up if they think she doesn't understand the charges against her. No, her soul stays with me."

"Harold, if she is innocent as you say, then no one will convict her. Let Carroline resume her life. She is far too young to live a life with no hope of redemption on earth. If you care about her as much as you proclaim, you must know I am right."

I had to keep reminding myself that Harold was only a vision that Carroline's soul wanted my soul to see. The spirit acting as Harold was the gatekeeper

"Harold, back on earth, there is a spiritual man, Doc Duvaliar, who has assured me he can make Carroline whole again. He can watch over her, mind, body, spirit and soul. That is more than you can do from here. If he makes her whole again, it's her path to entering eternity as she entered it. If you retain her soul, she will never have that opportunity. Please release her soul."

Instantly, my mind could envision my soul attaching to hers with spirits guiding both our souls back to my body. It happened quickly. As I awoke I could see Doc and Carroline both staring back at me. I attempted to get to my feet but stumbled over the coffee table in front of the sofa where I was sitting. Doc helped me to my feet and I staggered over to Carroline.

I connected my left hand to her right and closed my eyes. I fell to the wooden floor releasing her hand. My body was void of all energy. Doc tried to help me to my feet again, but I was dead weight and quickly fell back. I could hear Carroline yell out, "My father is dead."

3

"It took tree of us to get you back to de sofa. You been asleep for over twenty hours now my guut friend. But it worked. Carroline is guut again. Her mum sends her regards and tanks. Raeini is working but will come visit when her shift be dun."

I could barely see Doc. He was blurry. I could also see who I thought was Carroline standing behind Doc. I wiped my eyes and attempted to find my bearings. A huge headache pounded my brain. My limbs refused to cooperate.

"Slow down Caeles. Not guut for you to sit up yet. You stay dere, I get you drink. Don't let him move, Carroline."

Move, where the heck did they think I was planning on going?

A few moments later Doc returned with herbal tea. "I been reading de book about your history Caeles. Den I read oder books I have in de house. I don't see de cure for your family. I sorry to disappoint you. I keep looking and ask people I know to seek cure. I still tink maybe you will have to release the soul of Orcus. I know you don't want such path, but it maybe only way to make de family alive."

That news was certainly not what I wanted to hear. Plus I was now stuck on this sofa for who knows how long. Every time I returned a soul in the past, it took weeks to recover. However, once recovered, I came back stronger. This time since I returned the soul immediately after accepting it, I prayed my recovery time would be less.

I did my best to sleep and rest my mind. Suddenly I awoke with an eerie feeling. I was still groggy but could hear a voice and felt a shadow hovering over me. It was hard to focus but the shadow was from a petite woman in hospital scrubs. She moved away from me and towards a table near an open window. The wind was blowing the cloth curtains inward. I could only see her from behind. The small lady seemed to pick up something from the table and reversed course and headed towards me.

"I dunno know if I should tank you or keel you. Doc tells me you are da one to take my Carroline's soul. I dunno why you tink you have de right to take people's soul. Who geeve you such power? You don't look so powerful now, small man. Maybe I reep out your heart and feed to pigs down da road. You have nating to say to me little man? I know I tell Doc I am happy you return my sweet Carroline's soul, but you are evil man. Tell me why I don't keel you right now?"

"Whoa, slow down lady. I might be weak, but I still have enough energy to rip out your soul. Don't tempt me. Besides, like you said, I saved your daughter."

"Yea, so she can go back to de shop where dose womans strut around with dere fancy jewels telling my sweet baby de stories about how much better eet ees in USA? Dose womans day don't know de pain day geeve my daughter with dere stories. But don't you worry, I take care of dose womans. Day don't hurt my baby girl no more. Now I keel you like I did dose nasty womans and all will be right with de world again."

As Raeini Clinkard moved within a body's length of me I could see her raise her arm and the knife in her right hand. As she did her daughter Carroline came into the room.

Carroline screamed out. "Mum, what are you doing?"

"Dis man ees evil, Carroline. Stay back! Let me keel him."

"Mum stop, killing him doesn't fix anything. Put de knife down!"

"Dis man, he took your soul little girl. He has evil powers and will hurt more. He hurts people just like dose womans who hurt you in de shop. I will make dem pay for all de sins. De womans in your salon and now dis man who takes de souls of innocent children."

"What are you talking about Mum? Did you kill dose women in de salon? Is dat why de police came checking all de towels, water bottles and all de products we sold? They took all our stuff Mum. We almost went out business. All dat was cause of you?"

"Why, why do dis?" Carroline continued. Those ladies were my friends. I didn't care if day boasted about their places back home. Day all pay me very good monies. So what if I had to listen to dere stories, it paid my bills to listen to dem, Mum."

Carroline's mother interrupted, "Americans, day come to our island and take and take. Day tink they can come with fancy smiles and leave few drops of coins and pretend to love and tink dat is good enough. No, Carroline, your Daddy hurt me. Day hurt you and many people on our island. I make eet right."

"Mum, Dad is dead. I saw it in a vision. I thought I had a dream one night about an explosion. When my soul was restored, de vision came back. Dis man told me it was all true. He spoke with a spirit who told him what happened to Daddy. He was burned on an oil platform off de coast of Louisiana. He died over ten years ago. I believe dat."

"He lies, Carroline. Dis man ees pure evil."

Raeini lunged towards me. Her swipe missed my chest. Carroline yelled out for help. Doc ran into the room as I rolled off the sofa, attempting to evade a second swipe. I was bleeding from my arm. As Raeini lifted her arm for another swipe, Doc latched on to her and the two fell to the ground next to me. I heard a faint moan from a man in pain.

"Mum, stop, you have hurt de Doc. Stop it please." Only Raeini could stand. I no longer saw the knife in her hand, only a hint of blood on the fingers of her right hand. "Mum, go, get away now. Run."

Carroline sat on the floor and pulled Doc into her chest, to comfort him, as her mother disappeared out the front door. The two sat crying only a few feet from me. Doc whispered to us both, "Tell your mum I forgeeve her. Caeles, I am sorry I can't help you now. Be well, my guut friend."

Carroline escaped out the same door her mother had seconds earlier. I struggled to crawl along the wooden floor to the old black rotary phone across the room. Moments later, as sirens erupted, I inched back to comfort my dying friend. Blood was now coming from his nostrils as he tried to speak. I lowered my ear close to Doc's lips to hear his last gasp, "Grayson Winfield."

Two burly constables charged through the front door and immediately shackled me in cuffs. "Hey officers, I'm the one who called you! I didn't do this! It was Raeini Clinkard. Find her and her daughter and you will see I'm telling you the truth." I may as well have been talking to Moe or Larry. I started to wonder if Curley was still back at the station.

It didn't matter to the horrified defenders of the law. I was being tossed around like a rag doll by two Jamaican law enforcers who believed I just murdered one of the town's most beloved citizens.

"Who are you, what happened here?" Ordinarily I would have answered him in a calm polite manner but I was not appreciating the fact that he seemed to presume my guilt before even a whiff of an investigation. I also didn't like the idea that I was shoved into a worn out sofa and his face was close enough to mine that I could smell the liquor on his breathe while the excess spray from his words pocked my face. I don't tend to take kindly to being roughed up.

"Officer, I would beg you to start your investigation with the knife that is still dangling from Doc's belly. You won't find my fingerprints on the knife, but you will find Raeini Clinkards. I have every confidence that once you complete your testing, you will find I am almost as much a victim as the good Doc. Go round up Raeini and her daughter." The larger of the two, who seemed to be ring leader, was not taking kindly to my proclamation of innocence.

"Just answer my questions. We'll do our investigation, but you need to explain this mess. If not, plan on being a guest in our jail system for a very long time."

"Raeini Clinkard and Doc were struggling over the knife and she murdered him. That's what happened. Would you be so kind as to remove the cuffs now? I didn't do this."

The bracelets stay on. Why were they struggling in the first place?" The large officer asked.

"Because the knife was meant for me, Doc came into the room to stop the attack."

The big guy got directly into my personal space again. I could see the veins popping in his eyes. He didn't seem to believe my story. He shoved his hands into my chest and held me firmly against the back of the sofa. My patience with this guy was running thin.

Now the officers patience was running low with me. "Why was it meant for you?"

"Officer, if I told you, odds are pretty good you would want to toss me in the looney bin. I've been in this predicament many times, trying to explain what is not easy to explain. However, I will tell you that I saved the soul of Carroline, Raeini's daughter. It was not good enough for Raeini. Doc and I've been friends for some time now. I wouldn't want to hurt the guy. I will admit it was an accident, a deadly one. Now please, remove the cuffs. The longer you keep them on me, the more pissed off I'm going to get. Trust me. You don't want me being upset with you. Bad things happen when I get irritated. Now, call Agent Nesstor with the FBI and let me speak with him. He needs to know what happened here. He'll back up my story that you gents don't want to keep me in cuffs for long."

Despite my oratory brilliance and little evidence that I committed a crime, I was carted off to the local police station. I was peppered with question after question about why I was on the island and why I would want to murder Doc Duvaliar. I was still only at about half of my usual strength, so mustering up the energy to entertain all their questions was not easy. Normally, it would be easy for me to outwit two poorly trained investigators. It would not have been the first time I talked myself out of a sticky situation. However, my brain hurt. I gave up after about seven hours of being asked the same series of questions. When I refused to speak any longer they tossed me into a jail cell. It was a poorly constructed wooden cell, with no window and hard on my butt. They finally contacted Agent Nesstor with the FBI.

It wasn't the most convenient place to sit for two days but it did allow me to regain my strength. By the time Nesstor arrived in Jamaica, I was back at full working capacity. I needed him to get the Curley, or whoever was the head stooge, to release me back into society.

"Well, Soul Man, we meet again. You don't seem to be popular no matter where you land. Why can't you be a good boy and leave people alone?" Nesstor seemed pleased to see me behind bars, though I'm sure he knew I wouldn't tolerate being caged much longer.

"Gimme a break, Nesstor. Help me get outta here before I do things I don't want to do. I've got work to do. Raeini Clinkard admitted to me that she poisoned those ladies using her daughter's water bottles in the salon. She was upset because she assumed her husband had abandoned her. She knew the salon catered to mostly foreigners and wanted a warped sense of payback. Her daughter is innocent and so is the salon. Now stop sitting there with that stupid grin on your face and get me out of here, will ya? You're enjoying this way too much."

"Ok Novo, I'll talk with the police chief. But what really happened with Doc Duvaliar?"

"I was telling them straight, Nesstor. I really was. The woman got all crazy and was trying to 'keeeel' me. I know you were already updated, get me out of here! I don't think the great investigative minds in the other room even bothered to get the prints off the knife, or look for either woman."

"Alright, I'll obtain your release, but you owe me one, Novo and likely the Chief too."

"Owe you one? I gave you the biggest case you ever cracked and now I handed you a serial killer without you even breaking a sweat. Plus, let's not forget I risked my own life getting your soul back. If anything, you owe me, Mr. Big Shot FBI Man."

Nesstor wasn't completely buying my explanation. "You only got my soul back for me after your wife stole it, Novo. Let's not forget that part."

"Well I guess the lesson is not to mess with a wife who can rip out your soul."

"Maybe so", Nesstor said with a smile. "How's the wife doing these days?"

"Don't ask. It's the reason I was here searching out Doc. It's a long story that involves stuff you would find hard to believe. I don't need you looking all cross eyed at me again like the time I tried to explain to you and your wife that I had just restored your soul. Kalani and my son are not well, but I'll find a cure. Now please, get me outta here."

An hour later I was walking out of the station. The arresting constables grumbled as if a guilty man had just walked free. I darted back to Doc's house. I searched high and low for the book with the history of our people that Doc's family had been in charge of storing for years. It was not in his home.

I was under orders from the Inspector to stay put in town for more questions. But since I had multiple passports, there was no way I was going to hang around. I couldn't risk even the slightest possibility they would try to pin a murder charge on me. I didn't know what obligation Nesstor granted to release me, but I was not going to hang around long enough to find out. Like I had so many times in the past, I disappeared into thin air.

4

"This Council has some explaining to do. Why did I have to once again restore a soul that was not dark enough to steal? This is the second time I've had to do this. How many other times have you all screwed up that I don't know about?"

My grandfather attempted to calm my nerves. "Caeles, the Council takes every step to make sure only broken souls are taken. We are not perfect. It is possible in the case of Carroline, we saw her mother's soul and we took Carroline's in error. It is possible they were both dark enough to steal and her mother's was not on our radar yet. Our resources are becoming more limited by the day. Just because Carroline was not the one who murdered those women, does not mean she had a clean soul."

"Maybe so, Grandfather, but after she had her soul returned, she seemed to be a very likeable human."

"For one thing Caeles, when given a second chance most humans do change for the good. For another, you saw her for what, one day, after restoring her soul? From what your report tells us, you were not at full competence the entire time you saw her, post redemption. So I would not be so quick to assume our haste in taking a soul. You have always had this streak in you, to rush to judgment. I recommend you dampen your accusations. None among us is perfect, Caeles, including you. I encourage you to listen to the advice of a dying man who has nothing to gain in misleading you. "

"I will, Grandfather. However, the idea of souls being stolen in error is not something that I can easily forget. Now what can any of you tell me about a chap by the name of Grayson Winfield?"

You would have thought the local restaurant stopped offering the early bird special at half price. Instantly, five old men turned sour. Elder Nathan Stella spoke up after a few moments of eerie silence.

"Elder Novo, we no longer speak his name in these chambers. I suggest you forget you ever heard that evil name. Besides, where did you hear it?"

"They were the last two words Doc spoke to me before he died. I think Doc was telling me he had a way of curing my family. I refuse to forget his name, unless you all have a really good reason. Do you?"

"He is born from the Devil himself, Elder Novo", Elder Stella replied. "He has attempted to destroy our mission on earth. I implore you, as does the remainder of the Council, to never speak his name or contact him, ever!"

"I'm not afraid of him. If he can help me find a cure for my family, I intend to seek him out."

"Elder Novo, you do so at your own peril. Our mission is clinging to its last moments in history as we speak. Should you contact Winfield, it could be our last breath of survival."

I would be the first to admit my judgment was clouded with my determination to repair my family at all costs. I also had confidence in my abilities I never had in the past. Since it was widely believed that Charon Orcus was the strongest among us, and I had beaten him, a task no one believed possible, nothing could stop me. I would not rest or allow five dying old men make me fear another on earth. Maybe Grayson Winfield wouldn't have the answers I was seeking. However, stories of devils and old tales spun by others who no longer had my skills would not stop me. I commanded my assistant Peter to dig up all the information he could about Winfield.

"Elder Novo, those records are sealed. I did my best. I did discover that nowhere in our records can I find Grayson Winfield as being part of our bloodlines. I don't believe he is one of us. But may I remind you, your records were erased as well. I did find one note that Winfield is a family doctor who works in Lubbock, Texas. I am sorry, Elder Novo, but that's all I can tell you."

"Thanks Peter, I'll be paying this guy a visit."

"Please don't Elder Novo. There are only six files that are sealed and his is one of them. Your trip will lead to danger. Please listen to the Council and find another way to assist your family."

"Thanks Peter, but do you see my wife and child frozen in time? None of our scholars have been able to free them. If this Winfield guy has any clues, I have to try. I will be careful."

Three days later I found myself in the medical office of Dr. Grayson Winfield, a local family physician, specializing in terminal diseases. There was nothing special about his office. It was at the end of a quiet suburban street, in a building that also was home to the local dentist and a cardiologist.

A beautiful woman with auburn red hair, green eyes, a figure normally reserved for women's magazines and a distinctive beauty mark just below the bottom corner of the right side of her lip, met me just inside his office door. She informed me Doctor Winfield would see me soon. I took a quick peek at her soul, not a bad mark on it. Her outward appearance matched her beautiful soul. It was rare any woman could catch my attention since Kalani, but this woman had a certain appeal that was hard to miss. She didn't flaunt it, but there was a confidence in the way she acted that was very attractive.

"Doctor Winfield will see ya now," she said with a slow Texas twang. My legs buckled as I tried to stand and walk towards this Southern beauty. She led me down a small hallway and into a back room. The small room was decorated with one desk, two chairs, three diplomas on the wall, outdated fake wood panel covering and deep pile shag carpeting. I thought I turned the clock back forty years walking into the room.

Behind a large cherry desk with papers strewn all over it stood Doctor Grayson Winfield. "Doc Duvaliar called and told me to expect ya'll. Rumor has it that you killed Doc. Then again, why wouldcha? Unless you feel you didn't need the good Doctor's services any longer and wanted his little book?"

"I can assure you I did not kill Doc. As far as a book, I have no idea what you are talking about."

Winfield took his seat behind the desk, waved for me to be seated and responded. "Ok, Novo, you can come here and visit with me, but the moment you take me for a fool, you can git your ass outta my office. I know all about dat book. I also reckon you ain't got it. So let's cut the crap and get down to business, shall we? I know why you're here and yes, I can help ya. But it comes at a cost. Always does."

I sat back in my creaky, wooden chair, scratched my head, and wondered if maybe I should have listened to the Council. This guy must have done something they are afraid of, or regret, for his file to be sealed. I had to think about how to proceed with him.

"Ok, Doctor, let's both cut the crap. Why are your records sealed in our files? Why was I warned to stay away from you?"

Winfield laughed. "'I didn't realize my name was so worrisome to you boys, Caeles Novo. Please due tell me more about my sealed records. I'm just a local physician who fights the good fight in keeping the locals healthy. I reckon I wouldn't have any idea why you boys would have a file on me, let alone sealed."

He sat further back in his chair and rubbed his chin. In poker, we call that a tell. He was acting as if he was strong in his choice of words. He paused. He then moved forward and stared at me. A fatal error and another tell. He now told me he was lying. I suspected he was, but his icy stare confirmed it. This guy was dangerous. Bells and whistles were going off in my head, informing me to leave. My ego wouldn't allow it. I refused to be beaten by this guy before even trying.

"Eh, what do I know, Doctor? I'm just one of the minions stealing souls. I do what I'm told and I'm good at it. I haven't seen your file, nor do I really know if one exists. I only know what I'm told. Now tell me what you know about my wife and child."

"Caeles Novo, or should I bow and call you, Elder Novo? You

waltz in here and try ta play me like I don't know who you are or what you're after. I know exactly what powers you possess, as well as your new title. Now, can you stop pretendin like I just bounced off the turnip truck? If not, once again, git your ass outta my chair and return back to whatever persona you're playing today. I'm growing weary of you already."

"Funny, how you know so much, for being a local physician, I mean."

"Last chance, cowboy. Doc told me all about you and I know all about your people. But the only thing I know bout your family, is what he told me."

Grayson Winfield sat forward in his chair and stared at me. How many lies was this guy expecting me to believe?

"Please tell me what you know about my wife and son, Doctor Winfield."

"Now, that's better. A little respect goes a long way in these parts, El-Dar Novo. But I need to see your wife and son, to be sure about my diagnosis."

I interrupted immediately. I knew he would never be allowed in our compound.

"I am so sorry, Doctor Winfield. They are being housed in a secure area. No one is allowed to enter where they are staying. We will have to find another way. It would prove impossible for me to get them here in their current state. You will have to offer your best advice without seeing them."

He gave me a wicked smile as if he knew my response before I stated one.

"Ok, cowboy. I'll do my best without seeing em. I heard another rumor that possibly you took the soul of a good ole boy by the name of Charon Orcus. I kinda like that fella. I'd like to see you return his soul. When you do, you'll get your answer."

"No frigging way, Winfield! I have no guarantee that you even have an antidote. I go and bring back his soul and then you do the same thing Doc Duvaliar did to me and not know the answer. Try again, that's not happening."

Winfield calmly sat back in his oversized chair and ran his fingers through his salt and pepper hair. He wasn't a particularly good looking guy. He appeared to be a man in his mid to late fifties, slender, a taller than average man with a tanned face. I would assume he was a golfer with the few knickknacks on his desk along with one photo of him and other golfers on the wall. He took close to a minute before responding.

"Trust works in both directions, cowboy. I'll tell you what. I'll offer you a small hint that I know what your family suffers from, as proof I have the cure. Then, you'll do something for me. When your task is complete, I'll tell you anything you wanna know. How's that, El- Dar Novo?"

His tone was one of pure intolerance. He peered at me as if I had no other option. I had options, but none as good as his at the moment.

"Tell me what you want me to do. Then I'll decide if I even want a hint, Doctor Winfield."

"Glad you asked. That good looking lady that led you into my office, well, her name is Taylor Simon. She's worked here for going on six months now. We've become, let's say, friendlier than some bosses do with their employees. She seems like such a caring young lady but one night I woke up with her next to me and realized she had a knife under her pilla. Now, I be fixin to stay on this earth a long time coming. That sweet thing sure does know how ta treat a man. But I surely don't like surprises with my boots parked under my bed. I've been told that you have an expertise in searching people out. You find out what you can about that beautiful creature, and I'll tell you what you came here for. Do we have a deal?"

"Let me get this straight. I follow her around for a few days and give you a report on why she had a knife under her pillow and then you will tell me how to cure my family?"

"That's right, cowboy. And in good faith, I'm gonna give you that clue. I suspect your wife and kid were drugged with a heavy dose of a sedative; like the ones we give during surgery. Only, they got a special batch of it. It's all in that book you pretend like you don't know about. Only the part you don't know, the longer they stay sedated; their internal organs start to deteriorate. I can hear that clock ticking now, tick tock. Tick tock. Listen closely, you hear it too? Now, she struts that purty ass of hers outta here at five thirty on the nose every afternoon. It sure would be an awful shame for you to rescue that purty wife of yours, only to find out her mind has turned to cow dung. Now, don't be too slow, tick tock. Course, you can restore Orcus, since he's the one who did it to her. It's all on you now, cowboy?"

This all seemed too simple. Why would he help me just for following someone around for a few days after only moments ago wanting me to restore Orcus, or else? Then again, one of the first tips in negotiations is to ask for something you know you can't get and when turned down, ask for what you really wanted all along.

Was he playing me?

"Ok, Winfield, I will follow Miss Simon around and try to get your answer. But I warn you. If I get your answer and you don't give me what I want, I'll rip your soul out so fast, it won't make it in one piece to the Surrounding of Souls. You got me, cowboy!"

"Listen here, El-Dar No-vo, don't come round these parts threatening a good ole boy like me. And never assume I give a damn bout my soul. I know exactly where I'm heading my last day on earth. Now, you run on along and watch your tongue. She'll be fixin to leave here in about two hours' time. Tick Tock."

My patience was running thin with fool's errands but I had little choice. Even if I restored the soul of Charon Orcus, there was no guarantee he would cure them, or in fact confirm he was the one who cast the spell. In truth, there was no real reason to believe Winfield knew the answer. But what was I to do? I could follow Miss Simon for a day or so, report to Winfield, hope he was not a total liar, then get out of Texas.

Sure enough, promptly at five thirty she left the office. She loaded into her shiny sports car and started up the road. I followed her for ten minutes until she turned into an apartment complex in an upscale part of town. I followed her into the building where she headed up to the second floor. I dashed up the steps at the end of the hallway while she took the elevator. I made it up to the top and opened the stairwell door just in time to see her enter her personal space. I walked down the hallway to notice the number on the door, Apartment 222. This was just what I wanted to be doing on a Friday evening, spying on some poor young woman with a clean soul.

I stayed outside her apartment building in my car for a couple of hours but I didn't see her leave the apartment, so I went back to my hotel room. The stress was wearing on me and I needed some rest. While sleeping, my old friend, Mikeal Sano came to me in my dream. It was not the first time he invaded my thoughts while asleep. "Three Caeles, not one, think of three, not one," was all he said over and over until I awoke.

Early that morning I went back to Miss Simon's apartment. I parked within a bird's eye view of her car. All I could think about was how I should be back at the compound with my family as well as discovering a way to get more soul stealers. Our kind was dying out. And me the best soul stealer remaining, was playing errand boy, watching the car of some hot looking nurse for a guy I was quickly learning to despise, who didn't want to get caught with his boots off in the wrong moment. This was plain wrong. Just as I figured there had to be a better way, I witnessed Miss hot to trot, only looking like the local mortician. Her long auburn curls were in a tight bun and her curvaceous body was being covered up in a long dress and a sweater two sizes too large.

I followed Taylor Simon to the local library of all places. I waited patiently outside for over an hour until I wandered inside to see what was taking her so long to leave. I found her in the children's section, reading a book to a few children who weren't knee high to the head librarian. Miss Simon had a huge grin on her face as she meticulously turned each page with great care, reading to a handful of eager listeners. The session went on for thirty minutes. Soon after, she got up and started to refill the stacks of returned books to their rightful spot. I must have gotten too close to her or hung around her row too long. She approached me and starting to ask questions.

"May I help find a special book for you, sir? I noticed you've been sitting in the same spot for close to an hour now. I've never noticed you in here before. Are you new to our fine area?"

Not only did she not remember me from the day before, she didn't have an accent. If she had one at all, it was more of an eastern US dialect, certainly not the twang she had in the office not twenty four hours earlier.

"Yes, I moved into the area a few weeks ago. I do not know anyone around here. I thought I would come and check out a few books. I love the classics.

She smiled gently. "Oh, I love to read too. It's one reason why I volunteer here. I love being around books and people who can appreciate the written word. My mother taught me to appreciate a book when I was a child. I try to read as often as possible."

I was still perplexed. She didn't seem to recognize me at all. Plus this was not the same woman from the doctors' office, yet I knew it was the same person. Her beauty mark was in the same place as was her smile. I decided to continue the conversation.

"You sure have that big Texas smile I see on many around here, but your accent tells me you are possibly new to the area as well. Am I correct in my assumptions?"

"Well, yes you are. I moved here six months ago, from Maryland. I was a school teacher back east but they closed my school. My parents have both passed on, so I decided it was time for a fresh start in life. I'm still looking for a teaching position, but in the mean time, I spend my time here in the library. The people here are so nice."

"Well it was nice to meet you, I should get going. By the way, my name is Caeles. But I have taken enough of your time, and besides we are starting to get glares for talking so much in the library."

I extended my hand hoping maybe she would offer a name before leaving.

"The pleasure is all mine Caeles. You have a unique name. Maybe one day you can tell me where it comes from? My name was given to me by my daddy. He always told me one day I would be a queen. So I was given the name, Isabella, though he always called me Bella. Come on back and join us anytime, Caeles. We are filled with classic stories here. You only have to know where to look." With that, we gave each other a passing smile and I found my way back into the shadows.

5

I settled back in front of Taylor's, Bella's or whoever she truly was, apartment. A few hours later, the person I spoke with at the library arrived. Nothing seemed suspicious. I sat outside until late in the evening. My eyes were growing weary and I wanted to close them, when I noticed my subject appear from her door. This time she was fashioned in clothes the exact opposite of what she was wearing during the day.

She had a short tight red dress on that left little to the imagination. As she hopped into her car near the street light, it was obvious how little imagination I needed to have to see what was under that dress. Her body was bursting through it, with every curve in perfect form and location. Her long auburn locks of hair were free flowing and even from a distance her rosy red lipstick would be hard to miss. If this was a typical librarian and nurse, I need to read more medical books in libraries.

She drove a few miles to the same hotel where I was staying. I kept my distance, but since I was a guest, it was easy to sit in the lobby and not draw attention. She sat alone at the small hotel bar until someone approached her. They acted as if they knew each other. He gave her a quick peck on the cheek. Soon after, they made their way up to the third floor via the elevator. I sat in the hotel bar for just over an hour, until she showed up in the lobby again.

Every lock of her hair was still in perfect condition as were the curves in her dress as she made her way to the bar. She sat two seats to my left. I thought if she were to say hello and recognize me, I could be honest and let her know I was a guest of the hotel for the evening.

She sat alone until a man in a cowboy hat and jeans made his way to the seat to her left. She didn't seem to be easily amused with his small chat. I could overhear his weak attempt to cozy up to her. She didn't even look at him until she splashed what was left of her drink towards his face and moved to the seat next to me. "Sorry cowboy, but you have the wrong impression. This is my boyfriend." She pointed at me. "We had a scuffle earlier this evening, so I moved a few seats down. I don't think he'll take too kindly if he knew what you asked me. Now, move along, little boy."

The man in the cowboy hat gave me a stare as if he was going to ask me to step out for an old fashion alley fight. I had heard about them but had never taken part in one. Just then, the bartender spoke up and told the very fit looking man in the hat and jeans "Move along before I call security." I was just as surprised as the young guy as to what was happening. I sat there not saying a word until he left the bar area. The person I knew as Taylor and Bella started to speak with me.

"Sorry for all of that. I don't know why a girl can't come for a drink without some ape thinking they have a right to act like an idiot. I didn't mean to put you on the spot, sugar."

She acted like she had never seen me before. I was starting to think this was some sick joke Winfield was pulling on me. For a third time in less than two days, this beautiful woman pretended like we'd never met. I decided to play along with the ruse.

"It's fine. Women refuse to allow me to drink alone too. I can hardly walk into a bar and not have a beautiful lady, like you, make a lame excuse to sit next to me. My name is Caeles, nice to meet you."

She giggled. "Nice to meet you Caeles, I'm Rose. Again, I'm sorry if Rose put you on the spot but she didn't feel like messing with that chucklehead. She gets so tired of boys in big hats thinking they can flash some testosterone in her face and tell her what to do. If there is one thing she is not, it's easy. He's lucky he got off with only a few drops of Jack Daniels in his face."

I let out a half hearted laugh. "It's all good Rose. I was getting ready to head off for the night, so it was fun to add a little excitement before I finished my day. Besides, I lied. I rarely get approached by pretty ladies no matter where I am."

"You seem like a smart man. It's so hard to meet a nice man round here. They all want the same thing. Even after Rose explains to them that I am a Rose, no man has been smart enough yet to figure out that if you get too close to a Rose, eventually you get the thorns. But now Rose is rambling. What's your name again and where you from, sugar?"

"Caeles, but most call me Cale. I'm from everywhere really. My home is in California but I travel a lot."

"Well Mr. Cale, Rose should be heading home. If you plan on staying round these parts for a few days and want to see if you can smell the roses, here's Rose's private number. She refuses to go out with just anybody. But Rose does like smart men. Her daddy was a smart man. He liked to smell the roses, but eventually like most men, he got the thorns. If you know how to treat a lady real special like, maybe you can avoid the thorns. Call me." She got up from her seat and the beautiful Rose wandered into the shadows of the evening.

The following morning while enjoying a quiet breakfast in the downstairs restaurant, paramedics went flying through the lobby doors. They hit the elevator for the third floor. By the time they came back down with a body on the gurney, the local sheriff had arrived. I tried to see what I could find out about the body from the sheriff.

"Nothing to see here, pal. Some guy croaked with a heart attack in his room. Why do ya ask? You know sumtin I don't' know?

"No, Sheriff, it was only curiosity getting the best of me," I replied.

"Well take that curious mind of yours back to where you came from, before I suspect you do know sumtin I don't."

The last thing I needed was to have the local sheriff crawling up my butt. I went back to my table and finished breakfast. I spent much of the day watching football and the Miami Dolphins give the Buffalo Bills one of their twice a year thumpings. It gave my mind a day off from all the stress.

The following morning I made my way back to speak with Dr.

Winfield and the multi-dimensional Miss what's her name.

"Ok, Dr. Winfield, it is one thing to ask me to do something, expecting your help in return. But to send me chasing all over town for the weekend to find your young lady out there acting as three separate people, well that was just plain cruel. My family is as you say, tick tocking their way to the end of their lives, and you do this to me? What's going on here? I demand some answers!"

"Whoa, slow down, cowboy. I swear on my mamma's grave, I ain't got a clue what all the hooting and hollering is about. I asked you to folla Miss Simon round for a few days, but I swear to ya, I don't know what you're going on about."

The guy actually looked sincere. I wasn't sure what to think. There wasn't even a tiny hint of a smile on his face. He really was expecting a different report.

"If that is true, Doctor, then you have a genuine whack job working in your office. She was three very different people. The strange part was she didn't seem to know me, except as the persona she was at that moment."

Winfield sat back in his chair, scratching his head. We both seem perplexed.

"Novo, I really don't know what to tell ya. She might be a fine looking filly, but she's not smart enough to pull off being three people. She's got enough troubles being one. In fact, she ain't even a nurse. I couldn't find any record of her holding a nursing license. Now mind you, I don't let her near a real patient in need of medical help. I let her answer my phone, hold my charts, and look as purty as she can. Hell, she wouldn't know how to take your temperature. But she sure can make me smile. So, tell me what you really found out about her."

"Call her in here, Doctor. Ask her what she did all weekend." He did. Miss Simon bounced in with the same wide smile and curvy shape she had on Friday.

"Nurse Simon, honey, did you venture outta your apartment this weekend and bump into Mr. Novo here? Don't fib to me now. I wanna know what your purty self did all weekend."

"I was home with a sore throat, Doctor Winfield. I didn't leave the apartment once. On Saturday, I slept most of the day. On Sunday, I watched the Cowboys game on TV. Then I did my nails. I'm feeling much better now. Why do you ask, Doctor?"

As she was talking, I again searched her soul. Nothing new was registering as a dark spot. The girl really did believe she was telling the truth.

Winfield asked her again. "You sure you didn't see this man all weekend, honey?"

"No, Doctor Winfield, I didn't see him. Not unless he was hiding underneath my bed?" She giggled. "Is that all, Doctor?" He winked at her. She offered a giggle and one last smile before leaving the Doc's office.

"I think your detective skills need some work, ole boy. That girl is honest as she is purty. She's never once given me a reason to think she was leading me down the wrong path. So whatever you think you saw, think again."

"I'm telling you Winfield, that girl worked in the library during the day on Saturday and she was working something else in the evening. In fact, I believe she had something to do with that man showing up dead in the hotel over the weekend. Maybe you saw it in the news? Some out of town guy died of a heart attack. I suspect your darling nurse was in the same room just hours before his heart stopped beating."

Winfield moved forward in his seat and started to laugh. "I gotta hand it to ya, cowboy. You had me going there for a few minutes. But if you think I'm gonna give you what you want because of a story like that, well, just forget it, Novo." He paused and sat back in his chair again.

"All right, Doctor Winfield, I still believe it's possible you know more than you're letting on right now. Heed my words, pal. If my family dies because you're playing some kind of twisted game, I'll rip out your soul and the soul of every person that carries your family name. I will find the truth. You have been warned!"

"This is the second time you've come into my little ole' office with that tone of yours El-Dar Novo. I suggest very strongly you don't make a habit of it. Now, you mosey on outta here and find me some real answers. I do hope you can do a better job this time, cause I hear that ole clock justa ticking away, tick tock."

I don't think I had ever heard a cackle more sinister, than his. I knew I had to act quickly. I hurried over to the library to speak with the head librarian.

"Hello, my name is Caeles Novo. I met a young lady here the other day. I am trying to get in touch with her, can you help me please? She told me her name was Bella or Isabella."

"I'm terribly sorry sir, but I can't divulge information about people who work here. I'm sure you can understand."

I knew I had taken a bad approach with the librarian but I tried again. "But she does work here? She was so helpful the other day. I wanted to thank her personally."

"All of our employees are quite helpful. May I help you with anything? Bella is a fragile young lady. I would appreciate if you stay away from her. She comes here for some solace from society."

This was not going as well as I had hoped. I could tell the woman was very protective of Bella, not just in her words, but her now aggressive stance towards me. It was time to change tactics.

"That's fine. I am not looking to hurt her. I'll come back on Saturday and see if she's around then. Sorry to have disturbed you."

The librarian took another step towards me as I turned for the door. It was as if she was shoving me out. "You can try on Saturday, but Bella is a volunteer. She arrives and leaves on her own schedule. We never really know when she will be here, but she is a big help when she does arrive. Please, allow the young lady to have some peace and quiet. She has a very hard life, leave her alone."

I left the library and called my old friend Special Agent Nesstor. I asked him to run checks on anyone born in Texas with the name Taylor Simon, and anyone in her twenties with the name Isabel or Isabella from Maryland, who may have been a school teacher. I also asked him to see if Doctor Grayson Winfield had any issues with the law. I then went back and followed Miss Simon back to the apartment. I sat there till midnight and went back to my hotel room.

The following morning I received my report from Nesstor. "What do you have going on now, Soul Man? First of all, there are only three people with social security numbers in Texas with the name Taylor Simon, in their twenties and early thirties. Two are men. Our records show the female died in an auto wreck when she was nineteen."

I stopped Nesstor. "Did you check for professional licenses too?"

"Cale, I do appreciate you giving me the heads up with some dangerous people, but I'm not your personal secretary. I had the boys run a full report. We don't have full reports on people the way you seem to have, but we do try."

"I'm sorry Special Agent Nesstor, please finish what you do have."

"We did find an, Isabella Bernard from the Ocean City Maryland area, who has a teaching certificate. She's twenty eight. Her parents died in an accident in their home. There was a gas leak. They died in their sleep. There's not even a traffic ticket on Miss Bernard. I have no indication if she is in the Maryland area any longer or not. She has not filed a tax return since her parents passed away. As far as the Doc, he's a well respected guy in the community. He's been written up in medical journals as an expert in rare diseases and gives a ton of cash to charity. I doubt he's on your list. Now, I gotta get back to work. You owe me one, again. Be well, Soul Man."

I was running out of time and options. Maybe the lady in the office didn't want anyone to know she was really Isabella Bernard? Maybe she was running from her past? Maybe she had a knife under her pillow because she didn't trust Doc? All I knew was I was going to give it one more day and if Winfield would not accept my report, I had to find another way.

I decided to try something off the wall. I called the number Rose had given me in the bar when we met. The person who answered the phone had the same voice as the nurse in the office. She had the giggly Texas twang in her voice. "Hey, who's this?"

"Hello, I am a friend of Rose, is she available? I would like to speak with her, please."

"I think you got your numbers crossed up mister, ain't nobody here named Rose."

I waited for a moment and responded, "Well can you take my number anyway? If you do find Rose, please have her call me."

"I'll take your number mister, but you ain't likely to get a call. Hey, do I know you? You sound familiar to me. Did you come to Doctor Winfield's office recently?

"Yes, I have been to his office. But I am looking for Rose. She gave me this number when we met the other day," I responded.

"Well, my name's Taylor, but you already know that if you met me in the office", she giggled. "I still don't know why you're calling this number to find Rose, but if you really want me to write this number down, I will. It's really spooky how many people call here looking for Rose. Her number must be close to mine."

I explained to Taylor who I was and reminded her of when we met. She agreed to take my number and leave it by the phone.

Two hours later my phone rang. "I hear you're looking for the

Rose, sugar. What can she do for you?" This time the voice was deeper and more sincere in tone.

"Good evening, Rose. I was thinking about what you said the other night about either smelling the roses or getting the thorns. I wanted to know if we could discuss that over some coffee."

Sugar, you called Miss Rose cause you wanted coffee? Well now, it's not too often that she gets an invite out for plain ole coffee. Is that what you call it from wherever you said you were from? Coffee? Rose does tend to enjoy some sugar in her coffee, sugar."

"I can assure you Rose, coffee means coffee."

"You can call it whatever you like, sugar, but it'll still cost you five hundred dollars to sip Rose's fine blend. Like coffee, she is a rich commodity. Rose will be in the same spot we met the other night in forty five minutes. If you're not there, Rose will be gone to you, forever."

Exactly forty five minutes later, a magnificent vision for the eyes appeared in a green strapless dress usually reserved for Hollywood premieres. Rose glided across the room, every male's head twisting her way in the upscale lobby. Every inch of her perfectly constructed body dripped with sexuality.

She sauntered over to the dimly lit table in the corner of the bar and sat in the seat closest to me. "Rose enjoys it when her men are on time. She is all yours for an hour, sugar. But before we sip any coffee, Rose sure would appreciate an expression of just how happy you are to see her in the form of five Benjamins or whatever combination of green stuff you got in your wallet. Rose doesn't take plastic."

Rose was not the same personality as Miss Simon back at Winfield's office. Not even close to the personality of Bella Bernard in the library. I needed to figure out who this person really was so I could give Winfield his report and be on my way back to my family. I peppered Rose with a series of basic questions until she became a bit agitated with me.

"You weren't kidding ole Rose, were ya, you really did want to drink coffee. Rose is not to be played with, sugar, she's meant to be enjoyed." Her mood shifted. She became interested in my past, if I had a family or children. She wanted to know if I had a daughter and, if so, where was she. I answered all her questions honestly, until I started to ask her questions again. Time was of the essence. This was an expensive cup of coffee, sugar not included.

"Tell me, Rose, where is your family?"

"Rose's family doesn't exist. She moved here a few years ago and that's all that matters to Rose now. And you got just twenty five minutes left to sip some pleasure from Rose's coffee cup."

She ran her tongue along her top lip and ended with a smile. As delicious as she was, I kept my focus on the task at hand. "Tell me about Isabella Bernard, I think you know her."

"Izzy is a worthless child. She never could take care of herself. Rose makes sure no one touches her. If they do, they pay the price of getting the thorns. Now, Rose has had enough of these questions and you have nineteen minutes. Maybe Rose should reach under this table cloth and find out if you really only want to ask questions or take her to your room and smell her perfume. You still have time to prove you are man enough to hold a delicate Rose."

"I want to stay here Rose. I can smell you just fine from where I am. I paid for my hour and I expect Rose to honor her word. Now tell me about Taylor Simon, I believe you know her too."

"I don't know any Taylor. Rose keeps to herself most of the time. So, you can take your last fifteen minutes of time and stick em up your ass, cause Rose is done with this conversation. If you make a fuss about her leaving, that bartender over there will take you outside and rip you limb from limb. Don't call Rose again. And if you decide to go near Izzy, Rose will have her steel thorn slice off a piece of your manhood; she surely thinks you would wanna keep. Rose would like to say she enjoyed her evening, but it would be a lie. Good night, and thanks for the coffee, little boy."

The next morning I charged back to Winfield's office. I wasn't going to investigate into his nurse any longer. Either he was now going to help me, or I was moving on to another option. I was greeted by Nurse Simon in the waiting area.

"Hey, are you the one who called my place last night, looking for Rose?" She didn't say it in anger but more of a laughing way. "I sure wish I knew why men keep calling my apartment asking if Rose is available. Why did you do it?"

"Taylor, I wish I had time to explain it to you, I really do. But right now, I need to see Doctor Winfield. The only thing I can tell you, I met Rose, twice now, and she gave me your number. Now please, take me to see Doc Winfield."

I allowed Miss Simon to take the lead down the narrow hallway to Doc's office. She certainly had the same shape as Rose from behind while she walked, but Taylor's step was lighter, with less purpose. Rose made every step count.

Winfield could not be bothered to stand and greet me as we entered his office. Nurse Taylor Simon excused herself from the room quickly. I enjoyed one last peek from behind as she left the two of us alone in the room.

"Doctor Winfield, I will admit I am not a mental health specialist but I did some research last night. After following Miss Simon around for several days now, I believe she needs medical attention. I believe she is suffering from a condition called Dissociative Identity Disorder. You being a medical man, I would think you have heard of it?"

Again, he let out a sinister sound, "You really are trying to sell me a pile of horse manure, aren't you, Novo? You folla her around for a few days and think you can make some medical prognosis? Tell the truth, Novo, you tried to get in that purty girl's panties over the weekend and she turned you down. Now you wanna come ta my office and have her committed thinking I'll fall for it and make her pay. Plus you get your answer. Son, you don't know ole' Doc Winfield very well."

I sat there flabbergasted. I looked at this man who by all indications was a brilliant physician, but wouldn't even attempt to open his mind to my conclusions.

"Doctor Winfield, I believe your Miss Simon is three distinct personalities. I don't think your nurse is her real persona. I believe she is a person named Isabella Bernard from Maryland. Something happened in her past that made her move to Texas. I think she is escaping that reality by day as Taylor Simon and at times at night by Rose, who is a prostitute. I think Rose protects the real identity of Isabella from harm. Now I highly suggest you seek medical help for this young lady and keep your distance from her until you can see if I am correct or not. I think you made a date with your nurse and you woke up with Rose."

"Cowboy, you are a funny one. I'll tell you what. Since I do believe you really do believe this horse hockey you are flying my way, I'm gonna give you a clue to fix your family. I don't believe one word of your story, but I will call a friend of mine and have it checked out. Plus, I'm really tired of having you hang around my office and my nurse. I saw you stare at her purty backside as she waltzed outta here. I don't trust ya round her much."

I stopped him before he sounded even more ignorant, if that were possible. "Doctor, as purty as she is, and as alluring as Rose can be, I never once tried to do anything but get you the answer you were seeking. Now, if you are a man of your word, I gave you my true thoughts. I would appreciate it if you live up to your end of the bargain."

"Ok, El-Dar Novo, I've heard you're an honorable man. So here's your answer. From where I'm sitting, you have three choices. You can find that missing book a yers, restore Orcus and hope he'll assist you, or learn it the way Orcus did. I know all about the training ya'll go through. I know there's a wall you've seen, Novo. On the wall is scribbled your answer. Now, I've been way too kind to you, considering the cow dung you offered me for my services. Git outta my office and please don't return till I call for you."

"Call for me? I know you are joking. I do not answer to you. And I did what you asked. I don't owe you a thing for telling me what I already knew days ago."

"Oh, I will be needin your services, cowboy, and you will come when I call you. Now scoot."

61

I walked down the narrow hallway in need of a paint job and new carpet but stopped by to leave a parting thought with Taylor. "I won't be returning Miss Simon. It was nice to meet you. Please give my regards to Rose and let her know she needs to keep an eye on Doc Winfield. I do think he is hiding something in his past."

She tossed her hair back from her face with a flick of her neck, giggled, and said, "I do wish I knew who this Rose person was. I truly do. Please bring her by the office so I can meet her." Her walk instantly changed as we moved towards the door. She came closer, locked herself into my personal space, then walked her fingers down my back, from my neck, to my waist line, and said, "You take care of yourself now, sugar, Rose will take care of everyone round here."

6

"Caeles, this Council begged you to stay away from Doctor Winfield." Those were the first words from my grandfather's lips after returning to the compound to check on my family. "He's capable of horrible acts."

"Grandfather, I have no reason to see Winfield again. However, I am curious how he knows about our training to steal souls? Why are his records sealed, even from me?"

My grandfather let out a huge sigh. "Caeles, Doctor Winfield was at one time, one of our brightest. There was a time we believed he would one day lead this Council. He shares our unique bloodlines, unfortunately that is all he shares with us now."

I would like to say I was shocked, but I wasn't. Winfield seemed to know too much not only about me but also our inner workings. I sensed he was holding back some information. Or was it possible he assumed I knew of his past?

I was again frustrated with the lack of information my grandfather seemed to drip oout at his convenience. "So what happened then? What led to his files being sealed?"

"Caeles, I'm sorry for my sins. I will one day pay my penance for my lies and half truths. But for now, I'm trying to leave this Council and our disciples in better condition than we sit currently. Destiny is often a misunderstood term. Some would say it means, predetermined. In my youth, I would have agreed with that definition. However, as I've aged, I realize you create you own destiny. Your life was no more predetermined for you, than mine was for me, or Winfield's was for him. Our Council has lost their way, stop worrying about Winfield and look deep into what is going on around here."

I was waiting for the next revelation to come from my grandfather's mouth. He and I had few of these conversations, but they always ended one way. I would be offered crucial information withheld from me for years.

My focus became sharper as he continued. "You made your destiny, Caeles and I am so very proud of the man you have become. You became a wonderful husband, a father and our best soul stealer. You will now take your place as a great leader, one Grayson Winfield never could become. This Council trusted Dr. Winfield would be our leader, once Charon Orcus no longer had the ability to continue. Doctor Winfield chose another path. The vote was six to zero to ban him from our compound and stop all his education in our secrets. Even his own father, Elder Charon Orcus voted to remove him from our ranks."

And there it was; the missing piece. These five dying men allowed me to walk right into his office knowing this information, yet once again refused to tell me all I needed to know, before confronting a member of the Orcus family. I wanted to heal my family and leave this place forever. I was so tired of being mislead or ill informed by people who were supposed to be allies. It made no sense to me. I was furious and let me grandfather know it.

"Don't you think that was a valuable piece of information to know before proceeding to meet him, Grandfather? I'm growing very weary of this Council's either ineptitude or total lack of respect for my well being. If this happens again, I will leave this place and never return!"

"Caeles, you're not totally innocent here. We warned you to leave Winfield alone. If we had the power to forbid you to go, we would have. Once again, you disobeyed our words and went there knowing it could be dangerous. Now you stand here like a child and accuse me and this Council of wrong doing. Grow up and take responsibility for your own actions."

Maybe he was correct. I did have a history of failing to listen to my elders. "Ok, Grandfather, you made your point. But why was Winfield removed from our ranks?"

"Like most within our ranks, he was offered an opportunity to become a member of society in a profession he chose. He determined he wanted to be a medical professional. We paid for him to attend medical school. Like the others who we pay for, he worked in the compound as our staff physician while he worked on his training to be a soul stealer. Once he became a licensed physician, he refused to finish his training as a soul stealer. Because of his pure bloodlines, it would near impossible for him not to have the ability to steal. But we don't know if he has the ability or not. We also don't know if he has the ability to see into one's soul. We suspect he does, but we have no solid evidence. Once the newly minted doctor declined to finish his obligations to us, his father became furious with his son. Doctor Winfield claimed he was a healer not a taker."

I heard this story before. He would not be the first in our ranks to have the ability to steal and not take of advantage of the power. I didn't understand why he would be banned for refusing to steal. I know we had others who elected not to finish their training.

"There must be more, Grandfather. What else happened to have him banned from our compound and our ranks?"

My grandfather became very uneasy. "Caeles, this information is only known amongst the Council. However, if you are truly committed to being our leader, then you must know. Are you ready to become the leader we so desperately need?"

Why all the pressure? Why couldn't these people realize my one and only priority was to save my family? But what would become of me, beyond my family? I was being offered our highest honor for weeks and all I could do was run around the globe chasing air.

"I am, Grandfather. I will accept the responsibility of leadership."

"Don't let us down Caeles. Here is what we suspect. Doctor Winfield specializes in rare diseases. He is one of the world's leading experts in his field. Don't let his tiny office in Texas mislead you. He possesses a brilliant mind and a larger ego. As you know, our bloodlines are immune to most earthy diseases. It is our belief that once his father showed his displeasure in his son's refusal to finish his training in removing souls, Doctor Winfield developed a chemical compound that destroys our ability to see and take a soul. Many of our disciples became ill and their life expectancy became shorter while he worked in our compound. He was barred from ever entering our sacred home again. We believe he is the reason for our sudden decline."

"Well now, isn't that just great, Grandpappy! We have a percentage of our people, who refused to even try to steal. We have a Doctor, who is potentially destroying the few of us who still can steal. We have an aging leadership, the leader's soul who I took a few weeks ago, and a remaining population of us who can't survive unless we continue to take broken souls. The same Council, who keeps most of this secret from our population, and they are now looking at me to fix this chaos. Does that about sum it all up here?"

"You always were one for theatrics, Caeles. What's your master plan to fix it all?"

At least my grandfather followed it with a chuckle.

"Caeles, my dear boy, you stood before this Council for decades, practically berating us, informing us as to how you knew better, you had better ideas than our archaic ways. Leadership isn't easy. There's a price to pay for it. The time's upon us for you to step up, pay your dues and realize decisions are not always easy and they do, at times, have unintended consequences. We have changed. You need to change us back to our old ways."

I never enjoy it when others use truths to make a point. It can be so darn difficult to dispute. This was one of those times. It was time to take the role of leadership. But one task was still at hand.

"Winfield spoke about a wall. I have seen so many walls in my time. Do you have any idea what he was speaking about?" I asked my grandfather.

"He can't be trusted, Caeles. When will you understand?"

"I think he was trying to tell me something. I did offer him my assistance while I was in Texas, and I do believe he offered me a small clue about finding a cure for Kalani and Nic. I need to find that wall, or the book."

"Stop with the book! There is no book. It is pure nonsense that all our secrets were stored in a book and eventually smuggled to Jamaica. I know you want to believe there is a cure somewhere. If I were you, I would feel the same way. The time has come for you to realize, your family is gone Caeles. As hard as that might be for you to come to grips with, they are dead. Now, help us find a way to restore our disciples."

"You're wrong, old man! I refuse to accept the premise that there is no cure. Winfield believes there is a limited time and the clock is ticking away. I will accept my responsibilities of leadership, but I have a responsibility to my family. Until every option has been exhausted, I need to find that wall. And by the way, I have seen the book. It does exist. That's just another example of your poor vision."

My grandfather had a sad look in his eyes. "Maybe you saw a book, true. So what? Any fool can author a book and think it has merit. I'm starting to think you're not ready for the heavy burden being placed upon you."

The tired man was wrong on so many levels and I would prove it. He may have been accurate in stating anyone can write a book, but not about my wife and child.

Immediately after visiting with my grandfather, I ventured to our library to find the journal from my training. Each of our kind, who goes through our training, must keep a record of all that was attempted and accomplished during the process. Thankfully, I have always been very detail oriented. My journal, though tedious to read, was no different. It took less than an hour to find what I was searching for, the wall.

Despite objections from the remainder of the Council, I was off to Australia. While studying there, I remembered a cave wall many of our people wrote as a remembrance of our time spent in the northwestern section of the land. We purchased some of the out of the way land where we could sit and be solitary as part of our training. I was willing to bet, I would find a clue in the cave.

It took three days to arrive at my destination. The land was far from most of civilization. It sits on the edge of the Great Sandy Dessert. I enjoyed seeing the abundance of stars in the sky once more, but the red dirt all over my clothes was irritating. I studied the walls for hours. The heat from the day was exhausting. As the sweat poured off me, I discovered a cryptic math problem. Below it were the initials, GW. I was never one good at chemistry but the more I stared at it, possibly it was a series of chemical compounds.

The light was poor where I found the markings. Some of the markings were partially destroyed from the bat droppings that covered part of the cave. I scribbled down as best I could all the markings I could read. I took a digital image of it as well but even with a flash it was hard to read the wall. I had to guess on two of the potential compounds. Once back near a population base, I forwarded the information to Peter. I asked him to have anyone of our disciples who understood chemistry, to have a look at the compounds for me.

I flew back to California to my home, rarely seen in recent months. It was a cold empty place without my wife and son. The following morning, Peter contacted me. "Elder Novo, I'm sorry but I don't have any good news for you. None of our chemists could make anything out of the scribbles left on the wall. Yes, they were compounds as you suspected but our experts couldn't find any correlation between them. I wish there was better news."

My patience had run out. Winfield would help me or I would destroy him. Against all objections from the Council, I was going to confront Grayson Winfield again. I booked the next flight back to Texas.

"Good morning Miss Simon. I didn't expect to be back so soon but I have urgent business with Doctor Winfield, is he in the office today?"

Nurse Simon just looked and me and stated, "He's expected in shortly, please have a seat."

Something seemed out of place. The smile on Taylor Simon was missing. The bubbly personality that was Taylor's was subdued. I sat patiently in the waiting room observing her every move. It was methodical. Her playboy shape was still intact but her persona wasn't that of Taylor Simon. Was there now a fourth personality in her damaged mind?

"Is everything ok with you Miss Simon? You seem ill in some way. Is there something I can do to help you?"

"I have been feeling depressed lately, that's all. Thank you, but I'll be fine. The doctor has returned and will see you now."

This time she only opened the door to the hallway in need of a paint job and new carpet but moved back to her desk. There would be no escorting to his office. There was only a deep sigh and a very sad look from Taylor as   moved past her, to the back of the building.

"How'd you like my filly now, Novo? You're so predictable. I told ya you'd be back and here you be. I'll give ya credit for finding that wall quicker than I thought ya would. But those chemist's of yours, did ya really think they'd figure out my notes? I kept my end of the deal, Novo, the answer is on that wall. I can't help it if your boys ain't smart enough to find what you wanna know. So now you're back once again looking for my assistance."

"I'm over this Winfield. You give me what I want or I leave with your soul. Yes, that *is* a threat." Despite my blood pressure rising with every passing moment,   attempted to sound calm in my delivery.

"Oh, sit down, Novo. Go ahead, take my soul. For one thing, you can kiss that purty wife of yours goodbye if you do. For another, do you think I really fear you? Those boys back in the compound musta told ya sumtin bout me by now. I can't figure if you're downright stupid, or have half a brain.

Winfield offered a mocking stare my way.

Tell the truth, Novo, did someone tell ya bout that wall or did you find it on your own? Oh hell, it don't matter much. Sit down and listen to me carefully. You got one chance at doing this right. The way my calculations work up, your family's got about a week before their organs start to chemically break down inside their bodies."

I had to stop him right there. "How do I know all this is even true, Winfield? It could be another wild chase around the globe to make me look stupid."

"You don't, cowboy, that's the beauty in all this for me. Don't you see that? I have the new leader of the Council, of my former people, doing the Texas two step at my command. Sorry if you don't see the humor in all that, I surely do."

Again Winfield offered his mocking stare.

"Now, you listen up here, cowboy. That beauty queen out in my office, she made one fatal error. She caught your attention. She's now my back up plan. I figured since your own family wasn't gonna be enough to shove you into gettin my daddy's soul returned to me, she'd be my insurance policy. You'd come charging back in here on your big white horse and here you be. I'm a generous man, Novo. I'm gonna give you a three for one swap. You git me back the soul of Charon Orcus and you can have that purty one outside in my office and your wife and son. Three for one, Novo, take the deal."

What was this guy talking about now?

"Unless I'm missing something here, Winfield, I don't want Miss Taylor. Besides, the last time you offered to help if I followed her around, you promised me a cure. Give me one reason why I should trust you a second time?"

"Cowboy, I wouldn't give a pile of cow dung to restore your family. I surely would not. But I do want that good ole boy Orcus back in one piece so I can expose him for the fraud that boy is. I'm guessing by now you know he's my daddy, though I don't usually admit it. You took him from me, Novo, before I was dun with him. I want him back with all his senses so I can ruin him right and proper the way he ruined me."

I sat there listening to him talk about his time growing up as one of us. His story was not matching up with much of what my grandfather had told me about him before I left. Winfield continued on about after he received his medical license and his time in the compound.

"I'll bet you heard a nasty rumor bout me wanting to destroy our kind with some blood breakdown. Did you hear that story from the Council, El-Dar Novo?"

"Yes, I did."

He laughed. "I'm here to tell you, cowboy. I took an oath to heal, not destroy. I've spent my life attempting to find cures for rare blood disorders, like leukemia and other horrible diseases. Why would I want to hurt my own people? I wouldn't. I'm gonna let you in on a little secret, cowboy. My daddy was a total fraud. Oh hell, he probably took a soul from a rat to pass his test like all the others, but have you ever seen any recordings of him taking a real person's soul. No, I bet you ain't. And how do you know he could ever see into one's soul? He never could. He lied about it all. See, them boys on the Council, they had it all planned out for him to be the leader of that band from the day he was born, just like me."

There was a pause by Winfield. For a brief second, I thought I even witnessed a small tear drop from the right corner of his left eye.

"My daddy didn't wanna let his daddy down or the Council, so he lied about all his abilities. What, you think you took his soul cause you were better than him? He didn't take your soul that day cause he couldn't. He didn't take it from your wife and child, cause he couldn't. He stole my journal and figured it all out on his own."

"Whoa, stop for a moment Winfield. You expect me to believe the guy who was making all the decisions for the Council about which broken souls would be stolen had no idea if they were broken or not?"

"No, cowboy, as you know, every soul is voted on by the entire Council, not just him. I'm willing to wager you that if you read the minutes from the meetins' you'll find he second's most of the motions to steal, or just voted along with the others. Nah, that boy fooled all them other boys, for years."

"Here again, Winfield, how do I know all this is not another of your lies?"

"You don't. I'm telling you that once my daddy realized I knew all about blood disorders, he wanted me to find out why he had direct bloodlines but couldn't steal. Let me refresh your memory, cowboy. All of us are descendants from the original one hundred people permitted to steal from the Lord of Life. It was the Lord of Life that gave our people the power to steal and see into another's soul."

"You are wasting time, Winfield. I know our history as well as anyone."

"Well if you know it so well, El-Dar Novo, then you would realize my daddy should have that ability. After all, he is a full blooded descendant. He shoulda had the ability to steal and see, yet he claimed to me, he didn't. He didn't want anyone else to know about it. So, being a good son, I worked on the mystery in the compound, in secret. It was all in my journal. In the process, I found a way to stop a person in their tracks by stopping their blood flow in short spurts. My daddy knew about it after he stole my journal. He practiced on some poor fool and the Council thought he took a soul."

"This all seems too hard to believe, Winfield. What would be your plan if I did restore his soul?" I asked, waiting for another lie to flow from his lips.

"Novo, I don't like you. Not sure why, but I surely don't. But what I'm telling you is the truth. I want that good ole boy's soul restored so that I can have him admit to the Council and the ones who remain who will listen that I don't have nuttin to do with your people dying off early. I want that fraud to admit he never could see into another's soul. And I want him to tell the Council, he made up that lie about me entering poison into the bloodlines to eliminate our people. That's why it's very important to me to have him restored."

His story sounded plausible. However, if he was working with Orcus and really needed his soul restored for more destruction, I would be jeopardizing all of our disciples.

"Ok, Winfield, but what did you do to Miss Simon?"

"I had her soul removed, of course. Like I said, if you wouldn't help me cause of your family, I wanted to sweeten the pot. I wanted to prove to you that I can have a soul stolen as easily as you. I know you're a sap, Novo. I can keep you're boney ass busy restoring souls you don't believe should have been stolen. I also know you might be the only one left who can actually restore a soul. You plan on letting that good looking filly walk through life without a soul? Come on, cowboy. Do your magic and let me have my office girl back smiling."

"How did you have her soul removed? Did you do it?" I asked.

"Tick, tock, tick tock, I done answered all I'm answering today. You gonna swap three for one, or as you think, two of your family and three of her for my daddy? Yes or no, tick tock?"

"I'll do it, Doctor, only this time it's by my rules. You want your daddy restored so badly, you give me the chemical breakdown to restore my family first. Once they are better, I will restore your father's soul and Miss Taylor's. Not before."

When Doc Winfield laughed, it had a friendlier tone to it this time. "You know what Novo, you are many things, but not a liar. I'll trust you'll honor and your word."

Doctor Winfield grabbed a pad of paper reserved for writing prescriptions and scribbled down a few compounds. He handed me the paper with an egotistical sneer and a few words. "Don't know who still knows much about chemistry back at that sacred compound of yours, but they shoulda been able to figure it out from the notes on the wall. The last two were reversed, that's all. Send it to em, cowboy and be quick about it. Sometimes my math is not always the best. I'd hate to see that purty wife of yours already be rotting away."

I ran outside and sent an email to Peter on my phone. Hopefully this would bring my family back to life. If not, I had every intention of ripping out Winfield's soul without offering him a third strike. I went back inside to sit and wait making sure Winfield didn't try and dash out the back door. On my way back into Winfield's office I noticed Nurse Simon reading a book at her desk. I stopped to inquire.

"What are you reading there, Miss Simon?"

"I'm reading the Great Gatsby, I love reading the classics. Did you call me, Miss Simon?"

"Aren't you the doctor's nurse, Taylor Simon?" I asked inquisitively.

"I'm Bella. I'm sorry but you must have me confused with someone else. Hey wait, I know you. I met you a couple of weeks ago. You told me that you were new in town."

I looked at Bella's soul, there it was. It was still pure and intact. As I was about to ask Bella another question, Winfield yelled from the back room.

"Nurse Simon, honey, kindly escort Mr. Novo back into my office. He needs to allow you to git back to work."

The woman seated at the desk, reading her book, slowly stood, her smile erased, let out a long sigh and moved towards me. She patted me on the backside and whispered in my ear, "Rose has it all under control here.'

We moved down the corridor to Winfield's office. Once we reached Winfield's office, I asked the woman, who I assumed was Rose, to stay with us for a moment. I looked at her soul. It was gone. What was going on here, I thought. "Rose, would you like to sit with Doctor Winfield and me for a moment?"

The doctor never allows me to sit in his office, at least not during working hours."

"That will be all Nurse Simon, you can return to your work now," Winfield stated in an impatient way.

"Whatever you say, Doctor." The woman turned and walked back down the badly lit hallway.

"Winfield, I am telling you, that woman needs medical help and she needs it now."

Winfield just smiled, "What she needs, cowboy, is her soul."

7

The ticking of Winfield's clock on the wall was driving me insane. It was all I could hear for what felt like days but was actually just over an hour. Winfield sat behind his desk shuffling papers back and forth and making the occasional telephone call. I did my best not to listen but I had nothing better to do. Finally a text message arrived on my phone. It read.

"One of our doctors has forwarded a prescription to the local drug store. Will advise further once we have the drug."

The clock's ticking continued until my brain couldn't take it any longer. At every beat all I could hear was Winfield's voice in a low murmur, reciting over and over, tick, tock, tick, tock. While he was setting up his Saturday tee time for a round of golf, I nervously paced up and down the corridor, until I needed to sit. I took a seat in the waiting room away from the ticking sound and the doctor's boring phone conversations.

I sat tapping my feet against the stained carpeted floor for two more hours, watching as two patients came and went from the office. Nurse Simon handled the patients, but she wasn't her usual good natured self. I looked for her soul but it was missing. Finally another text arrived.

"They are awake but very weak. Doctor is examining both now. Kalani asked for you."

I couldn't remember the last time I wept but I instantly started crying. I didn't realize how much I had been crying until I heard a voice.

"You ok over there, Mr. Novo," I heard with that Texas twang that could only be Nurse Simon.

"Never better," I replied.

I marched back into the doctor's private office. "Thank you, Doctor Winfield. Whatever your notes told the chemist, it seems to have worked. I am heading back to the compound to see my wife and son now."

"Not so fast, cowboy. Your part of the deal was to restore my purty girl out front and my daddy. I do hope you don't plan on slipping out so quickly, El-Dar Novo?"

"I will honor my word, but in case you are not informed about how restoration works, I can become ill for a period of time, if the missing soul is not restored quickly. It is much better for me to be near the person when I retrieve a soul and restore it quickly. The first time it was days before I could restore the soul back to its owner and I became ill for many days after restoration. If I can restore it quickly after obtaining the soul, I can recover quicker. When I return to the compound, I will restore your father's soul. Then I will return and restore the soul of Miss Simon."

"Novo, do ya think cause I don't use all the proper words like you, I'm some kind of mental midget? Did you really think you were gonna waltz outta here like I did nuttin for you? You got one week to deliver my dear daddy to my doorstep or your purty wife and cute kid will go back into their frozen state."

"What the hell does that mean, Winfield?"

"Means what it says, cowboy. Oh, they'll recover for a few days, but after that, they'll start to get sick again. They will appear frozen in time again and soon after their organs will start to shut down. You want me to fix that, than you bring my dear ole daddy to me. Tick, tock, Novo, you best be on your way now."

This guy truly was a monster. How could I trust anything he would tell me? I caught the first flight back half way across the globe. I was receiving updates about my family every few hours in short text notes. From what I could surmise from the notes, they were recovering nicely.

Some I had met in my travels assumed I could teleport from place to place. This was certainly a time I wished they were correct. It took over thirty hours in travel time to get back to the compound. I hopped on three flights, had two layovers and waited in line for a car rental. I knew it would take almost as long returning to Texas, though we would pick up a few hours in the time differences. This left me about four days to restore a soul, recover and convince Orcus that he had to return with me to Texas and confront his son.

Once back at the compound, I visited alone with Kalani and Nic for a few hours. They seemed in good spirits. Kalani's sense of humor returned. I expected nothing less.

"I really need to rethink this entire idea of being married to you," my beautiful wife Kalani remarked. "I lose my soul, now I'm told I was frozen for days and days, and all the while you're traveling the world like a frigging tourist. Couldn't you have waited till we thawed out before you gallivanted all over the world there, Mister Elder Novo, leader of the soul disciples?"

"Yea, it's nice to see you too. But let's get the record straight here, Miss Hawaiian Tropic. You lost your soul because the Council thought you were stealing unauthorized souls. Had the Council not been punishing you, we never would have been in the compound. And secondly, I'll travel anywhere I darn well please." Then with two very large smiles and a passionate kiss, I felt whole again.

Speaking of traveling, I have to return to Texas. Not only do I have to return to Texas, I am obligated to take a healthy Charon Orcus with me. I bargained with Winfield for the antidote for you and Nic. In that agreement, I must return to Texas with Orcus in tow."

Kalani gave me that look I hated to see. "You can't do that Cale, we need you here with us. Besides, what good can come from offering Orcus another chance to destroy us?"

"I don't believe Orcus can hurt anyone, especially you and I, Kalani."

"Oh, really, than why did me and Nic just lose several days of our lives frozen in time?"

She had a point. But I didn't want to tell her that it was a possibility her healing process was only temporary. She was going to have to trust my judgment, something that never came easy to her.

After spending time with Kalani and Nic, I called our chemist, Doc Chamoun, who worked up the antidote. "What can you tell me, Doc? Winfield has led me to believe the antidote is only temporary, is that possible?

"I wish I could give you a definitive answer, Elder Novo, but I can't. I've never seen anything like this before. The pharmacist was very skeptical about even making the antidote for us. If not for the fact he is one of us, I don't think he would have done it. I would think it's a fifty-fifty proposition at best they remain healthy."

My options were again limited. I could refuse Winfield in restoring his father's soul and have faith my family would remain healthy, or take the chance Winfield would honor his word once he got his vindication. That is assuming that truly was the main objective in escorting a healthy Charon Orcus to his doorstep.

I went to my grandfather for advice. "Caeles, we both realize no matter what I advise, you're going to do what you deem appropriate. I've learned over the years you are strong enough to take on adversity and defeat it, but Winfield is not your average person. Not only is he of our blood and familiar with many of our ways, but he is blessed with a brilliant mind. My advice is to never speak with the man ever again. Plus, even if you do offer Elder Orcus redemption to atone for his past sins, do not deliver him to Grayson Winfield."

"And I should watch my wife and child die?"

"You don't know they will. Winfield can never be trusted."

My grandfather was correct on two levels. Doctor Winfield was not your average mind, and I rarely listen to anyone's advice, even when I seek it.

The sound of Winfield's voice repeating tick, tock, would not stop permeating my brain. Action was needed. Unless the odds of a full recovery were one hundred percent for my family, I couldn't sit by and trust they would continue to recover. I decided to restore the soul of Charon Orcus.

I was locked in a small room next to the library with my new assistant Peter at my side. It was essential I wouldn't be disturbed during the process. Since the soulless Charon Orcus was two doors down, I was hopeful I could restore his soul quickly and not have a long healing time. My only trepidation was how Orcus would react to all that had changed since I removed his soul.

I called on the spirits to again take over my mind and lift my soul to meet the gatekeeper of the Surrounding of Souls. I heard the sound of cannon fire and men screeching horrific cries of pain. From the haze, a man who looked very similar to George Washington was standing in front of me. He had a commanding presence and stood over six feet tall. However, he looked weary. He turned away long enough to offer commands in a soothing but authoritative voice. He focused his attention back in my direction.

"Are you here to join us in our battle against the mad king?" The general inquired.

"No, General, I'm here to bring one of your souls back home."

"Impossible! We are a small army with a daunting task. Every soul is needed to combat the evil that surrounds us. You are commanded to either join us in our fight to wipe out tyranny or remove yourself from this battlefield. Our mission here is too important to return even one of our souls."

Engaging an irritated Charon Orcus was one thing, standing in front of our Council and attempting to talk my way out of another mishap was yet another. But a verbal exchange with General George Washington? This was an experience I hadn't expected.

"General, as much as I can empathize with your cause, I can't stay, nor can I leave without the soul I seek. I too am a leader of men. One soul under your command is vital in assisting me with my leadership. I beseech you, as one leader to another, to assist me with my own crusade against darkness."

"Son, we all have our own personal crusades to wage. But our objective in life is to win the war and not one battle. If I were to allow every soul to leave a single battle because of a personal trauma, I would be an army of one. Permission denied."

I could now see why George Washington was appointed to the leadership command he was centuries ago. Failure wasn't an option in the here and now.

"General, the soul I seek is not a foot soldier. If I were to promise to replace one soul with ten for your army, would you release the one I seek?"

General Washington moved closer. His war-torn face was now evident. His uniform, covered with emblems only a commanding officer would dare wear, was dirty and ripped along his right leg. The steely glint in his eyes was one of resolve. The harrowing screams in the background stopped. The drumbeats were silent. He took hold of my shirt collar and leaned into my left ear to ensure I would hear and respect every word.

"I will offer you what you want in good faith, from one leader to another. However, should you let me down in your promise to return ten souls for one, I will personally strike you down the next time I see you. Do we have an understanding, sir?"

How do you turn down a man like Washington? "Yes, General Washington, we have an understanding."

With that, the soul of Charon Orcus was attached to mine and the spirits lifted my soul back to my physical body, my mind released back to my control.

Once I was fully awake, the heaviness of his soul was too much for me physically. I had to return it as quickly as possible. Peter led me into the room where Orcus was seated. He was frail looking as he gazed out the window from his chair. Orcus had not spoken since I took his soul. None of us were sure he even knew his name or was aware of his surroundings any longer. I walked across the room and took Charon Orcus by the hand.

"Elder Orcus, I am returning to you a special gift. I trust you will use it for good and eradicate the evil still remaining." My body trembled as I fell to my knees. It was as if I was experiencing the worst migraine headache one could ever imagine. Two men dashed into the room and moved me to my private quarters.

Hours later, I awoke with Kalani sitting patiently next to my bedside. "Sure, take another nap why don't you? Some fearless leader you are; one small task then off for another siesta." It was good to see she hadn't lost her dark humor while frozen in time. I was starting to wish I had some of that magical elixir she was given for times I wanted her to not be so boisterous.

"That's me, leader of the broken soul brigade, lying around doing nothing again. I am happy at least one person on earth understands I need my rest, like the rest of you bums." My wicked humor could never match hers, despite my efforts.

"Now if you would, my ever so dear and loving wife, go round up Elder Orcus for me, will you? He and I have many topics to discuss."

"I really don't think you are ready for visitors my sweet husband," Kalani quipped, showing the patented stare she provides, when she thinks I'm wrong.

"Kalani, my dear, I realize you may have missed much of the news while you were on hiatus for days on end, but I am the boss now. Maybe not in our house, but in this compound, I am the leader. Now, go do as I ask because Peter gets on my nerves when he follows me around like a lost puppy dog. Sometimes, I swear, I think the guy is actually spying on me."

Another long stare from my wife followed. I was sure she didn't appreciate my tone but she left the room without me having to make another request. A few moments later, Charon Orcus, Kalani, the other five members of the Council along with my assistant Peter, all entered my now crowded chamber. Now I had eight people staring at me. It was time to seek the truth from all of them.

I began the conversation. "Elder Orcus, I am not aware of how much you have been told about what occurred while you were without your soul but I did visit with your son, Grayson. He informed me that you never did have the power to look into or steal a soul, is there any truth to his words?"

I really didn't trust him any more than his son, but he did surprise me.

Orcus started to speak, "Caeles." I quickly cut him off.

"That would be Elder Novo to you, Elder Orcus. I offer you the name Elder out of courtesy. However, I have now earned the right and will expect you to offer it to me out of respect for my title."

Another stare, I should have been used to them by now. Orcus began again.

"My apologies, Elder Novo, of course, please disregard my lack of manners. As usual, my son speaks in half truths. I did have the power to see and steal like anyone on the Council. I had it for decades. If you check our documents, you will find that when I came to the Council, it was an aging group, like it is now. I went from training to being on the Council with little time to steal souls. That is why there is no record of me removing a soul other than during my training period."

Elder Polus spoke up, "That is an accurate statement."

Orcus continued. "When my son started to experiment with blood work, it was to be a famous medical man. He had wild dreams of being known as the man who cured cancer. However, in his experiments, not only did he find his potion to freeze people in time, he also informed me that he could extend my life for many decades, if not centuries. He disclosed to me that I could rule the Council well beyond any previous expectations."

Orcus stopped for a moment and took in a deep sigh before continuing with his version of the story. "I was washed in desire to maintain power. I was driven to rule this Council long after my contemporaries had vacated this earth. My son assured me he could make that happen for me so I would rule our disciples and this Council for a century, possibly longer and he would have time to wipe out many ills on the earth."

The others in the room had looks of disbelief on their faces, not me. I was more surprised that the others seemed surprised by his comments. Orcus continued as the others stood in silence.

"I would like to tell you all it was an experiment gone wrong. Maybe I will never know the truth. I drank what my son told me would extend my life. I felt stronger for weeks, almost indestructible. Soon after the feeling of the high I was on, I started to feel depressed. I became short of breath after long meetings. My legs no longer had the strength to move me through my day without constant breaks. I couldn't blame it on the common flu, since none of our full blooded kind ever come down with the flu. My son told me the effects were not staying in my bloodstream, but he would fix it."

Orcus moved closer to my bed and sat on the edge. This put not only me on alert but the others in the room as well. What evil would Orcus attempt to commit now? But he was not the same man as he was before his soul was stolen. The fire in his eyes was now just tired sunken remnants of what they were when he ruled the Council. His shoulders slouched as he sat on the corner of the bed. I sat up higher however, just in case he tried anything unexpected. This was a man who tried to destroy me for years, I had to remain guarded.

"Elders, I didn't know what to do. Over time I had lost my abilities to steal and see into another's soul. I tried for years to regain my power. My son claims he did all he could to restore me. I would like to believe Grayson. He was such a well intended son. But, to this day I don't know the truth. I don't know if his intentions were to always destroy us, or to find a way for me to rule for decades. But it is true, I no longer have the ability to see or steal. I kept that from you all for many years. I'd like to repent and live out the remainder of my life in quiet solitude. I will offer guidance when asked, but I will not stand in the way of allowing others to rule."

"Not so fast, Orcus, you have amends to make before you wander off to your life of solitude. You are going to journey with me to see your son. Then you can do whatever you like."

Charon Orcus stared at me like I was crazy. I was growing weary of those stares from just about everyone.

He answered back. "Why would I ever want to see him again after what he did to me? Besides, no doubt he is still very upset over his lifetime ban from ever returning to our compound."

I wasn't about to know no, for an answer. "I am not at liberty to speak freely in front of others, Elder Orcus. However, it appears to be the only way to make amends for poisoning my wife and child."

However, Orcus would not go easily. "Unless I am mistaken, Kalani seems perfectly healthy and I saw your son earlier. You managed to heal them without my assistance. Now if all of you would excuse me, I need to catch up with the news from the past couple of weeks."

Was this idiot joking with me? Did he really think he could walk away from me without repercussions?

"I don't remember anyone allowing you to leave the presence of the leader of the High Council, Elder Orcus. Yet again, I highly suggest you find your manners. I wouldn't dare to leave a Council room before being excused, the roles have reversed now."

Elder Orcus, along with my grandfather and wife, were now glancing at me with that same wicked stare I was about to ban from anyone looking at me with ever again without serious repercussions to their health. I knew this was my first real challenge as leader.

Orcus slowly turned back towards me with that same sneer he had just before I ripped out his soul the first time. One wrong step by him and there might be a second occasion to remove his soul. I was not going to tolerate his insubordination.

He dared to speak in an evil tone. "Novo, I never once liked you. I tolerated you at times because we needed you. My time left on earth is limited, so do whatever you like to me. Go ahead, take my soul. Without being the leader of this Council, I'm dead anyway. There is nothing more you can take from me. Say hello to my son for me."

8

"Cale, what is really going on between you and Orcus? Why are you so upset he won't return to Texas and face his son?"

"Kalani, you know I would do anything to protect you and Nic, don't you?"

Of course I do. Now tell me what is really going on here?"

I didn't want to tell her but persistence was one of her strengths.

"The antidote you and Nic received might only be a temporary fix. No one knows, not even Orcus. Winfield claims he offered me a temporary fix long enough to get his father back to Texas. I only have two days left and it takes that long to travel back to Texas. My only option is to face him alone. I had hoped Orcus would have more remorse than he is showing, but then again, he never was a compassionate man."

"I feel fine, Cale. I don't want going back to Texas. Doc Chamoun told me he was working on a solution. He didn't know you hadn't told me yet. He begged me not to tell you, but I'm pleased you were honest with me. Doc Chamoun is a good man, he'll figure it out. Please, Cale, don't go back to Texas."

"I must go, Kalani. Taking Orcus was only half of my assignment. Somehow Winfield took the soul of an unsuspecting woman in his employ. I need to restore her soul and find out how he did it. If he can steal souls, I need to take away his power. If one of our disciples stole it for him, I have another challenge to face. Either way, I need answers. Running from Winfield is not an option."

The two of us sat holding each other for over an hour, without a sound, our hearts in total harmony. I couldn't remember the last time the two of us had this much time to hold each other. My determination wouldn't allow it to be the last.

Three hours later I was on a flight to Texas. I had Doc Chamoun and two others working on the chemical compounds to ensure a permanent solution for my family. I also had two guards stationed with Charon Orcus. He was confined to a small area of the compound. It was the same area in which he had imprisoned me years earlier. He wasn't going to have his peaceful existence and freely roam the globe, not while I was leader of the Council.

Once back at Winfield's office there was a strange woman working in the reception area. I inquired where Nurse Simon might be. "She called in sick a few days ago. I'm working here until she returns. Would you like an appointment to see the Doctor?"

"Tell him Cale Novo is here. I can assure you, he will see me right away."

Within seconds I was being escorted into Winfield's office.

"Why you seem to be a person short, El-Dar Novo. I never took you for a dishonorable man, but I do believe you were sposed to return with my daddy. So, unless he's sitting in the waiting room, I suspect he ain't here. You mind telling me why, cowboy."

"Doctor Winfield, my apologies. I did all I could. I restored your father's soul and pleaded with the man to come here to face you. However, I did bring a document signed by all the Council members proclaiming that you had nothing to do with our disciples becoming ill. It also claims Charon Orcus did not have full power and hence proper authority to rule the Council."

Winfield took a long breath, closed his eyes and rubbed his forehead with his right hand. He then scratched his chin and opened his eyes. Those same eyes were now glaring at me with a tension that made me uncomfortable.

"Well, El-Dar Novo, seems here you failed me. I would assume in reading this worthless piece of paper, nowhere will it state I'm welcome back home, now does it? What did my dear daddy really tell you after you did your magic, cowboy?"

"He claims that you were working on an elixir to extend lives. He said you both had your reasons to extend your time here on earth."

Again, Winfield scratched his chin. "Ya'll really are dumb ole sons a bitches in that compound. I dun told ya, my daddy stole my notes. He made the potion, Novo, not me. He made the drink that took away his power. He wanted to rule for centuries, dumbass. I wanted no parts of the politics of running you takers. I done told ya, I'm a healer not a taker."

Here we go again, back on the merry go round of lies and deceit. As much as I despised Winfield, I have yet to be able to prove he ever lied to me. His father had a record of attempting to destroy me, not Winfield.

"Doctor Winfield, it's your word against his. Your father is locked down in the compound. He will live out his last days there. He will have little access to the outside world and has admitted he was a fraud for many years while serving on the Council. You have your document claiming your innocence. I have done all I can for you."

"Really, cowboy? If that paper meant what it says, why is it me who still can't return home? Why is my good ole daddy living peacefully in that blasted compound of yours, while I sit half a world away being treated like I dun wrong? Do you believe I'm innocent, Novo?

Now I was the one scratching my head and rubbing my forehead. "I wish I knew what to believe, Doctor Winfield, I really do. But you sent me across the globe, later chasing your nurse for days, and finally forced my hand at returning your father's soul, knowing it was the last thing I ever wanted to do. Does that sound like a healer to you, Doctor?"

Winfield frowned at me then declared, "It sounds to me like a desperate man wanting to have the record clean before his daddy died cowboy. I do believe it would sound the same to you if you were sitting behind my desk. Even so, cowboy, you got another errand to do for me. My nurse, she's been gitting ill since you parted. I do believe she's gone missin her soul. It's time you do your magic and git it back for her."

"I'll do it, Doctor, but what about the status my family? Can you pass along the cure so I can rest easy knowing they will continue to heal?"

"For a leader, cowboy, you need to look around more. What did my daddy do before joining the Council? Hell, you don't know a damn thang, do you, El-Dar Novo? You think I was the first to head off to medical school in our family? My daddy went there long before me. You might want to dig up the old archives. I'll be willin to wager a herd of my finest steer that you asked Doc Chamoun to break down the compounds, didn't ya?

"I did. So what?"

Winfield let out a loud belly laugh. "Course you did, Novo. He's the head scientist for your people. He also went to medical school with my daddy, was his lab partner for a while too. Hell, Chamoun knows if that mixture fixed your family or not. After my daddy stole my journal, I got no doubt Chamoun assisted him in making that drink. They know how to fix your family. I gave you what I thought would fix them the first time. I may not care about your family or you, but I am a healer, cowboy. I dun told you this a few times now."

"I will find out the truth, Doctor. If all this is true, I will make it right. But why can't you be happy with your career as a successful medical man and find that cure for cancer your father told me you wanted?"

"Think about it, dumbass. I was raised the same as you. I was told from the time I was knee high to a cotton weed that I was part of a very select group on earth. I was one of the privileged. My daddy was the ruler of em all. I was given a good education, played by all the rules and one day got kicked out cause my daddy dun wrong. Everyone, including you now, the new leader of your people still believes I'm a criminal. What do you think that does to man who lived his life wanting to heal people? I want my good name back, El-Dar Novo. If you are the man to do so, then I sure would be obliged."

"Like I said, Doctor, if all you have told me is the truth, I will restore your name amongst our disciples and bring you back home. I still don't know how you stole Miss Taylor's soul, but for now I'll get her soul back."

Winfield let out another laugh. "You better learn real quick who you can trust in that compound, Novo, else your time as leader will be a short one. Now go fix my girl, least thing you can do since you didn't drop my daddy at my door step."

I needed to restore the soul of Taylor Simon and return to the compound. Winfield was correct about me deciding who I could trust, or my tenure as leader would be very short indeed.

I checked back into my hotel room and called the phone number I had for Taylor's apartment. "Hello, I am looking for Taylor, maybe I speak with her please?"

"Sorry but Miss Simon seems to be not feeling so well. She's not been herself for days now. Can I help you with something?"

"Who am I speaking with?"

"Well, sugar, if that was any of your business maybe I would tell you. Now what business is it of yours to be speaking with Miss Simon?"

I knew I had to handle this in a delicate manner. "Rose, this is Cale, we met a couple of times last week. It is very important I speak with Miss Simon. I believe I can help her feel better. Please, let me speak with her."

There were a few silent moments awaiting a reply. "Sugar, I do remember you. But I also told you that Rose would handle things. I'll make sure Miss Simon gets your message but Rose knows how to take care of Taylor. Now, if you want to see Rose and finish our drink, that can be arranged, assuming your wallet's filled again?"

"Rose, I know you do a wonderful job protecting Taylor and Isabella, but you cannot fix what is wrong with her. I can. I need to see her as quickly as possible or she will not get better anytime soon, no matter how much you care for her. Please Rose, you must trust me."

"Rose will see what she can do. But if Rose finds Miss Simon for you, Rose sure would like another cup of coffee, only this time with real sugar, sugar." With that, the phone clicked in my ear and I sat patiently by the phone.

While waiting for Taylor Simon to appear to me, I called Peter so he could dig up the archives of Charon Orcus and Jeremy Chamoun. I needed to find out if Winfield was telling the truth about them having a history together in medical school. I also asked him to find Winfield's training journal. I assumed it would be under the name, Orcus. Doctor Winfield informed me that he changed his name once he moved to the United States and applied for citizenship. His wife Janet Dickinson, a surgical nurse he met while interning at the hospital in Dallas, Texas suggested the name. He took the name and her to be his bride.

Winfield claims she died of breast cancer three years after they were married. It's the main reason he devotes his life to finding a cure for cancer. I would like to believe his story, but when Peter returned with his updates for me, there was no mention of Winfield ever being married. It was around the time he was banished into exile from our people, so his story might be true. I asked Peter to follow up and research Janet Dickinson's records for me.

"What else can you tell me about the relationship between Doc Chamoun and Elder Orcus, Peter?"

"The archives don't have any record of those two being friends in school. Yes, Elder Novo, they are the same age and indeed attended medical school at the same time, but in speaking with both, they went to different schools entirely. They weren't even in the same training classes in the compound. They both admit to knowing each other since we are a small society, Elder Novo, but both men claim they have never been close friends."

None of this made sense. Was Winfield this warped that he would constantly make up his lies to keep me off guard? Everyone warned me about him, but his soul wasn't that dark.

"Peter, keep Winfield's journal for me. Put it in my chambers and don't allow anyone to touch it."

"Will do, Elder Novo."

I sat in my hotel room through the evening and into the next day. I was about to venture over to the apartment where Miss Simon resided when my phone rang. "Hello Mr. Novo, this is Taylor Simon. There's a note here on my desk that you called. I don't remember you calling me? But I've not been myself lately. I do hope I didn't ignore you somehow?"

"No, it's fine Nurse Simon. I heard you have not been well and I think I can help you. I would really be pleased if you could meet me in the park near your apartment in one hour. I noticed a park bench near the large swing set, we can meet there."

"I dunno Mr. Novo, Doc Winfield claims I have the flu and I should be resting till I git ta feeling better. I don't reckon there's much you can do to help me."

"Please, meet me in the park in an hour. I assure you, I know what is ailing you and can make you whole again."

It took another five minutes attempting to ensure her all would be ok, before she finally relented. If she didn't show up, I would have to search her out because once I found her soul; I couldn't keep it long. It was imperative my mission end quickly.

I locked the doors to my hotel room and called the front desk. I asked not be disturbed until further notice. Once I retrieved Taylor's soul my only challenge would be get back to my room in case I should pass out and need recovery time. I called upon the spirits to lift my soul once again to the Surrounding of Souls. I landed in a spot that was very familiar to me, since my family home in California was only a few miles from Yosemite National Park. I had hiked the area around Half Dome, the image my soul was imagining.

A grey haired gentleman with a short salt and pepper beard and dirty overalls was standing next to a large view camera. He waved me over. "What brings you to this beautiful site?"

"I am in search of the soul belonging to Taylor Simon, Mr. Adams. Nothing would please me more than to stay and walk this wonderful gift of nature with you, but my time is limited. Can you please release Miss Simon's soul to me?"

"I agree this is a wonderful place and normally I wouldn't let Miss Taylor leave so easily but we both know it was not her time to rest. But before I release her, you need to make me a promise."

Why did everyone want something from me in order to make things right with the world? I was getting frustrated with the long list of favors, but hey, what could Ansel Adams want from a guy like me other than to buy up the remaining inventory of Kodak sheet film for him?

"What can I do for you Mr. Adams?"

"You have many contacts, including a congressman by the name of George McAdams. I want you to pay the congressman a visit and ensure he will push legislation to provide adequate funding for our national parks. If you promise me this, you can take Miss Taylor's soul. Besides not being Miss Taylor's time to arrive here, her soul isn't whole. I knew when it arrived. There must have been a mistake. It seems to be misidentified. Our records show this soul belonging to an Isabella Bernard, yet marked Taylor Simon. Put it back where it belongs and when the times comes for this soul to return, I will care for it."

The moon rose over Half Dome. Mr. Adams ambled slowly back under his black sheet to look through his viewfinder. A peaceful feeling came over me as the spirits guided my soul and Taylor's to safe return back to my body. When I awoke, my mind felt scattered. Maybe my body was fighting off the effects of having the broken soul of a multiple personality inside me. I didn't know, but I didn't want to waste any more time tempting what damage could happen to me personally. After all, I didn't remove Taylor's soul, which meant it should take longer to recuperate after restoring it.

As I peered at my time piece, I was more than aware Taylor Simon was ten minutes past our scheduled meeting time. It's hard enough to get one woman to be on time, but I was asking three of them. What would I do if Isabella or Rose arrived and not Taylor? I had too many pressing issues in front of me. I couldn't waste a lot of time hoping the proper personality would arrive. Then she appeared. In any personality, she was a physically stunning woman despite being mentally damaged. Her once obvious smile was now hidden underneath her confused persona.

I wasn't quite sure who it was sitting next to me until she spoke. "I'm sorry I'm running late Mr. Novo. I've really been struggling to get myself together lately. Doc Winfield keeps telling me it's just the flu and to stay inside, but this here, it ain't like no flu I ever had before. I was fixin to go to see my old doctor, but you said maybe you can fix me. I figured I'd let you gimme an opinion, before I make an appointment later today."

"I am very happy you came to see me Nurse Simon. I do believe I can help you. We have little time to spare, please, take my hand and close your eyes."

She gently placed her hand in mine and closed her eyes. I closed my eyes and felt the breeze wafting in the park blow through my hair. My body shook as the palm of her hand became moist. Taylor took a deep breath and exhaled slowly. We both opened our eyes.

"Whoa, Mr. Novo, I don't know what that was, but I sure wish I had a boyfriend who could do that for me once in a while." Taylor Simon giggled as a huge smile ran across her face.

"I think you will be feeling back to your old self in no time. Here is my private number, Miss Simon. I want you to call me immediately if Doc Winfield has any strange people asking to take a photo of you, or asks to touch your hand."

She turned to me in a startled way, "That's what happened before. I mean the Doc, he's always trying to sneak a picture of me when I visit him at his house. But, well you know, those are more private type photos. But a week or so ago, he had some man take photos and by the next day, I was feeling like I had this flu bug. How did you know that's what happened?"

"Miss Simon, listen to me. Do not under any circumstance allow anyone to take your photo or ask to hold your hand if you don't know them. Don't let Doc take any more photos of you, even if you think they are cute. I also think it's wise you find a new job."

Her startled look turned to one of puzzlement. "Why would you think that, Mr. Novo? The Doc has always been very kind to me. He would never hurt me."

"Miss Simon, you are a big girl, you do as you please, but call that number if anything seems odd to you."

My body started to shake violently. I attempted to stand to make my way back to my hotel room. I knew I couldn't be found passed out in the park. I asked Nurse Simon to assist me across the street and back to my hotel. We made it to my room where I stretched out across the bed. The room went dark.

I don't know how long I was out but when I awoke, someone was in the room with me.

"Awe sugar, Rose was really starting to worry about you. It's not often Rose sticks around to see if her man wakes up from a deep sleep, but this time Rose is happy one did."

9

Searching for the truth can make even the strongest weak. It seemed every time something made sense to me, the other side seemed more logical. In speaking with Doc Chamoun, he and Orcus both denied all what Winfield had stated about the two of them mixing up a batch of the elixir that froze Kalani and Nic. "Grayson created several bottles of it years ago. It was under lock and key until Elder Orcus asked for it," were Chamoun's exact words to me.

"Doc, at this point, I do not care who made the potion, I want the remaining bottles destroyed."

"I have no idea where the remaining inventory is any longer, Elder Novo. Like I said, I gave it all to Elder Orcus a few weeks ago. What he did with it, is not my concern. I take orders from the elders. I do as I'm told around here."

This was upsetting news. I kept thinking about what Winfield had told me, about if I don't know who to trust, how good of a leader could I be? With so many issues at hand, the remaining inventory was not high on the list. Even if Orcus had it stashed away somewhere, he was under guard, so the likelyhood of him using it, was slim to none.

After another restless night, I was sitting in the Council room with the five other leaders discussing our urgent need to establish more soul stealers. The most frightening aspect to the conversation was that with a group as small as six, we could not even agree that more were needed.

Elder Baruch Robus pleaded his case to remain a small group of soul takers. "We have all lived a healthy and secure life. Our kind who can't steal, support us with their money to continue our mission and in return we continue to steal and provide them a longer life. If there are fewer of us who steal or lead this Council, then we have fewer who need to share our riches. Why can't you see, Elder Novo, the fewer of us remaining who can steal and lead have more riches to keep among ourselves? The less off us there are, the more luxury we have around us."

I couldn't believe what Elder Robus allowed to fall from his mouth. "Elder Robus, with all due respect, our mission was never to see how many fine suits we could wear, or fancy houses we could obtain, while doing our mission. Our original mission on earth was to remove broken souls from those who no longer could see the beauty of life and offer redemption to those souls who later repented. Nowhere in our mission statement does it include a reference to a shopping list at Cartier for a nicer watch."

It was obvious the longer these leaders stayed in power, the less they cared about our mission. A few only cared about living out their lives in a comfortable fashion with little regard to ensuring our mission would endure. The five members couldn't agree on anything. There seemed to be factions within our group. The meeting ended with no solutions and one large headache which now seemed endless.

Because we had less than thirty approved soul stealers and even fewer who could see into other's souls, I was still assigned broken souls to steal. Even though I was now leader of the Council, a title I was learning was assigned more because no one wanted it, than a real honor, it was imperative I kept up a busy schedule. Leaving my wife and son behind again was not something I wanted to do, but they were acting completely healthy. Kalani, who was also still a registered soul stealer, was feeling so well she wanted to resume her duties.

I spoke with our assignment chief, Brandon Bink about putting Kalani last in line for a future assignment. "Even if I were to do as you ask Elder Novo, Mrs. Novo would be given an assignment within days. Our soul stealers are in heavy demand, with so few working. I really don't appreciate the Council always trying to reschedule assignments. My job is difficult enough without you political types telling me how to do my job."

I assumed he would give me a response like the one he did, but even a few more days would be helpful. Brandon was always an independent thinker. He was not much on following commands. Was it because he reminded me of myself, that I allowed Brandon more leeway with his occasional belligerent tone directed at me and the elders?

Kalani was not pleased when she learned she was put at the end of the line. But what else was new? She didn't like the idea I watched over her ever since her accident on the side of the road soon after we met in Hawaii. She may not like the fact that I watched over her, but I was effective at it.

After bickering with Kalani about her spending a few more

days in the compound, as well as calling me twice a day with an update on her condition, I started to read the report on my latest assignment. I think Bink knew I was a baseball fan since my time spent chasing Johnny Joe Jackson and others in the Chicago area many years ago. I loved spending an afternoon at Wrigley Field or other ball parks when I was working in the States. I was assigned the case of a baseball family from Oklahoma. It was the perfect assignment for my frayed nerves. Brandon knew he stepped over the line with his tone to his leader. I took the afternoon to read about my new case.

Cliff "Lookout" Owens was born in Enid Oklahoma in 1975. His parents were lower middle class people with a love for sports. His mother raised six kids, including Cliff. She worked as a bank teller and still had time to run the little league baseball snack bar every little league season. Cliff's father, John, was a plumber who worked hard and played hard. He drank too much beer but it didn't stop John from coaching little league for all his boys. In the winter, John Owens was a champion bowler, on the local lanes.

The entire family loved to go camping and enjoyed a two week vacation fishing and hunting at a different location in the Midwest every August. It was a tradition started the first year his mother, Miriam, and dad, John, were married. Cliff was raised a rough and tumble kid. He had three older brothers and two sisters. He was the fifth child born in the Owens brood. Only his sister Patricia was younger. All four boys were not only expected to try out for sports teams, it was almost required they spend more time playing sports than doing school work. The two girls also played sports in the yard with their brothers. But the girls were not pressed to achieve athletic stardom.

Since Cliff was the youngest of the boys, most of his clothes were hand me downs. He had to occasionally fight for any extra scraps of food he could find at the dinner table. He never left the table under fed by a wide margin but it was not always easy feeding six kids. His parents did their best to raise a good family.

By the time Cliff was three years young, his dad and brothers had him in the yard tossing around a football, baseball or bouncing a basketball. It was a rare day indeed, unless the family was camping, not to have at least one or more child in the Owens household being involved in some athletic practice or event. For Cliff, it was only natural for him to have sports be a major part of his life growing up.

His dad would make a habit out of letting the boys all know, "I seen the Mick play ball here in Oklahoma when I'ze growin up. He played high school ball with your uncle Danny. I know I'ze told you boys bout the Mick. They only made one like the Mick. I'd be proud as I could be if one of you boys ever come close to the likes of Mickey Mantle." The boys would hear it over and over from John Owens about how he wished he could see their name in lights at Yankee Stadium, just like the Mick.

Cliff was not an angry kid but was one who stood his ground. Even at a young age, he would not be pushed around. His three older brothers made sure he could use his fists maybe better than his wits. His parents were called into the school office more than once before Cliff was ten years old, due to talking too much in class or rumbling in the school yard with classmates. His mother would attempt to punish Cliff but his dad's response was usually the same, "Boys tend to act up at his age."

In his first year of little league baseball, Cliff would play two innings and get one at bat per game as the rules stated. Despite his dad being the coach, he made Cliff earn his playing time. There would be no favorites. Cliff usually played right field.

It was now the last game of the season. Much to Cliff's surprise and joy, he was called to the pitcher's mound. Win or lose his team was not going to make the playoffs, so his dad wanted to see what Cliff could do as a pitcher. The score was tied at six runs each in the last inning.

Cliff's first two pitches were wild high, showing off his nervous energy. He could hear his dad bark from the dugout, "Let em hit it, Cliff. Throw the ball over the plate." The next pitch hit the outside corner of the zone with the umpire throwing out his right arm, "Strike one." It offered Cliff some assurance he could do this. The next pitch was in the exact same spot, the umpire again raised his right arm with a called, "Strike two." Cliff looked into his catcher with a sudden rise in self confidence and hurled the ball as hard as he could over the heart of the plate and watched the batter take a mighty swing, only to see the ball land in the catcher's mitt for strike three. Cliff instantly knew his path in life.

The next batter was much easier. The overmatched kid in the batter's box struck out on three pitches all right down the middle with three long swings. Two outs and the score still tied. The next batter was young Tommy Canata. Tommy was the source of many a school yard tussle with Cliff. Tommy was a year older than his adversary on the pitcher's mound. He enjoyed pushing Cliff and his friends off the school yard basketball court during recess. This was Cliff's chance at retribution.

Tommy stepped to the plate awaiting the first pitch. He dug his back foot in the hole already made by many of the players from earlier in the game. Tommy offered Cliff a wicked smile. Cliff was not going to be intimidated. This time there were rules. This time, no one could push him off the mound. The first pitch was high and close to Tommy's chin. You could hear the coach along the third base line yell out. "Look out", as Tommy dropped to the ground. Cliff walked off the back of the mound acting as if the pitch got away from him, it didn't.

Tommy wedged himself back into the batter's box, only this time with less enthusiasm. The next pitch was a perfect strike on the inside corner. "Strike one", you could hear the umpire yell out. The next pitch was a ball, just wide of the plate for ball two. Cliff took a deep breath and delivered a pitch right over the heart of the plate with Tommy taking a mighty cut but missed. "Strike two", the umpire bellowed for the crowd to hear. Tommy dug a little deeper into the ground as Cliff glared back. Cliff reared back and threw it as hard as he could. He watched Tommy start his swing through the strike zone and hit the ball safely into centerfield for a hit. Tommy ran to first base flashing a huge smile. As the ball was retrieved and given back to Cliff on the mound, he could hear Tommy yell over to Cliff, "I knew I would get a hit off of you. I own you sucka." Cliff was none too pleased.

The next batter stepped to the plate. Cliff's dad offered the instructions from the dugout. "Get this batter out so we can get our chance to hit, Cliff. Don't worry about the guy on first, focus on the batter." That was not so simple since Tommy was still making comments from his position standing on first base. Cliff delivered the first pitch. It was hit directly on one hop back to Cliff. Rather than making an easy toss to first for the last out, he threw the ball towards second base. The ball nailed Tommy Canata right in the small of his back, several feet from his teammate waiting on second base for the toss.

Tommy slowly got his feet back under him and stood safely on second base. Cliff could see a tear fall from Tommy's right eye. The third base coach ran over to check on Tommy. As he rubbed Tommy's back, both Cliff and Tommy knew it was like rubbing salt into an open wound having to stand there garnering extra attention. Cliff's dad walked out to the mound to have a few words for his son.

"That's not the way we play ball in this league son. If you gotta gripe with that boy, you take it outside this fence, not on my ball field. You can't go round plunking every kid who gets a hit off ya. Now settle yourself down and get this next batter out or I'm taking you off this mound. You won't ever pitch again."

Cliff knew his dad didn't know half of the story but he knew it was a losing battle. After getting a warning from the umpire, Cliff struck out the next batter. His team scored a run in the bottom of the inning to win the game. The next day in the local paper, the small clipping read, "Winning pitcher, Cliff Owens." It wouldn't be the last time Cliff Owens saw his name in the newspaper.

The following day at recess, the chatter wasn't about Cliff hitting Tommy in the back, but for throwing one under Tommy's chin. They loved seeing Tommy's backside hit the dirt around home plate. His best friend, Ryan was retelling the story.

"Cliff I don't know if you saw me sitting in the stands or not but my game on the other field finished early. A few of us from my team were watching the end of your game. When you threw that heater at Tommy, all we heard was his coach yelling, looookooouuttt. I saw Tommy hit the ground and I was laughing, so hard. I loved seeing him eat dirt. It's about time that jerk Tommy got his paybacks."

The following winter, Cliff had grown a couple of inches and put on some weight. Come spring, he would be one of the bigger players in the league. Cliff developed into a very good pitcher. He would also play the infield when not pitching because he was also the team's best hitter. He never knocked down Tommy or anyone else the entire season. He would throw the ball high but on the inside part of the plate just enough to intimidate the other kids. The umpires and coaches really couldn't stop it because he never hit anyone. But his teammates would yell, "Lookout" every time he threw one high and tight on a batter. Cliff had amazing control of where his pitches ended up for a player his tender age. At the end of the season, Cliff was selected to the all-star team. In the program listing of all the teams and players in the tournament, Cliff was listed as "Lookout Owens", not Cliff. The nickname would forever be embedded in everyone's minds.

Cliff excelled in basketball and baseball. He was selected to the all star teams in both sports during his junior year in high school. His reputation was growing to such an extent that major league scouts started to come to watch him play. Colleges were also lining up to offer scholarships. His dad seemed more enthusiastic about the attention than Cliff. John Owens had a way of running his mouth where it wasn't appreciated.

One day while Cliff was pitching in his junior year, a scout with the Philadelphia Phillies was in the area to watch Cliff's team play another top team. The scout was not only there to see Cliff but a catcher from the other team as well. After the game, Chet Ullrich, the scout with the Phillies walked over to introduce himself to Cliff. Chet wanted to let Cliff know the Phillies had an interest in possibly drafting him in the future. Standing only a few feet away, John Owens popped off to the scout, "That's all very nice indeed but my son will play with the New York Yankees or he ain't playing no ball. He won't be playing no ball for a second rate team."

Cliff was horrified and shouted at his dad to go back to his seat. Cliff was hoping the Phillies scout missed the stench of beer emanating from Owens senior. It wasn't the first time Cliff had been embarrassed with his dad's comments. However on the plus side, if not for his dad pushing him so hard to work on his game, it was unlikely any scout would ever have noticed Cliff. However, it was a tightrope Cliff was losing his patience with as he grew older. After John Owens waddled back to his seat, Chet Ullrich would only tell Cliff, "You do realize that you don't pick the team you want to play with, right? It's a draft. If you are fortunate enough to be one of the few drafted, I would encourage you to get your father to understand there are other teams in the league, besides the New York Yankees."

"Yes, sir, I do understand. My old man is a lifelong Mickey Mantle fan. Sometimes he gets a little crazy with his mouth, that's all. Me, I'm not into much more schooling and I'd love to play for your team or any other team that would be willing to draft me. I wanna pitch in the big leagues, don't matter much to me which team. He's the Mickey fan. I'm more a fan of Greg Maddux and Randy Johnson. Them guys, they know how to git guys out. I just wanna git guys out for my team, any team.

"That's good news Cliff. There is a good chance we will see each other again in the future. Good luck finishing up your school work." With that Chet Ullrich grabbed up his notebook and headed off to the parking lot. Cliff headed over to his dad and insisted he stop running off college and pro scouts who don't have a Yankees logo on their caps.

In his senior year in high school, Cliff made the Oklahoma all state team for baseball and received an honorable mention for the all state team in basketball. He had multiple offers for college scholarships all across the mid west. His dad wanted him to accept the offer from University of Oklahoma but Cliff was leaning towards University of Texas and their rich tradition of baseball excellence. After talking it over with his high school coach and guidance counselor at school, he decided he would enroll at the University of Texas for the fall semester. His only comment to his dad was, "I know it weren't your first choice but Coach O tells me that UT is the Yanks of college ball."

If Cliff thought he had issues with his college choice, his real problems didn't start until the late spring of his senior year in high school. He was drafted in the third round by the Florida Marlins. The Marlins not only didn't have the rich tradition of the New York Yankees, they didn't even exist as a big l league club yet. They were an expansion team in major league baseball and wouldn't exist as a major league team for another year. Cliff's dad was dead set against the idea of him playing for an expansion team.

"Cliff, they don't play in a real baseball park. They play in a frigging football stadium, I forbid you to sign a contract with that team." This was not what Cliff wanted to hear. He had enough of school and in truth really didn't want to travel to Texas and play college ball. He put up a fight with his dad about what he could and couldn't do with his life.

"Dad, you're missing the big picture with this Marlins thing. For one, they're just making a farm system yet, which means I'd be one of the first to play for em. It should be easier for me to make a mark with a team like that, than a team like the Cardinals who are full of pitchers like me in their minors. This is a great opportunity for me, Dad." His logic didn't faze John Owens.

"Dad, schooling and me don't mix so good. I can't play at Yankee Stadium or any other stadium one day, if I'm sitting behind a desk in college. I'm signing with the Marlins. I could go back in the draft next year but there's no guarantee the Yanks would ever draft me. They ain't never even sent a scout to look at me. I'm gonna play ball for the Marlins."

John Owens was seething. "Oh, you're all grown up now and think you can handle what it takes to be a man, huh? Ok, big man, you take your fancy ass contract with some two bit team that don't even play in the big leagues yet but don't come back round here no more. Your mamma and me will no longer welcome you in our home. I know it's been your dream to play in the big times. It's been mine too, to have a son play pro ball. But not like this, Cliff. You can go to college for a year or more and then see what happens. I know your mamma and I never pressed the books on you like maybe we shoulda but this, nah, this is bull crap, Cliff. You're only doing this to spite me and you know it."

Cliff got right up in his dad's face. "Spite you? You're not making any sense now. I love you and mamma for all you done, but I'm tellin ya, this schooling thing ain't for me. Getting some punk to swing and miss at my best fastball, that's my life now. I'm bored with learning bout how many hours it takes to get some train to go a hundred miles traveling at some speed I don't care much about in math. I'd rather be on the train with my teammates. I love you, Daddy, but I'm gonna play ball with the Marlins."

10

Cliff reported to the rookie league in Florida soon after the major league draft. His ego took an immediate shot to the gut, once he realized, like himself, everyone on his team was an all star back home. Some were even older in age and had played at a higher level in college ball. This was now Cliff's profession, not practice and games after school. Coaches were expecting him to work harder and longer than he ever had previously. To add to the situation, he had already completed his senior year in high school having pitched more innings than he ever had before. He was worn down. He had to adjust to his new life and fast.

The other major adjustment was living conditions. Cliff and his teammates were barely being paid enough to survive financially. He was forced to live with three others in a small apartment. The college aged players had a small advantage having lived away from home before but the high school players had much to learn. As tough as Cliff's adjustments were, one of his roommates was from the Dominican Republic. Not only was this his first time away from home but also Edwin Martinez barely spoke a word of English.

Every game, it was the same thing being pounded into Cliff's brain by his pitching coach. "Son, you can't throw that ball past most of these guys like you did in high school. You gotta spot your fastball and use your breaking ball or you might as well get on the next bus back to Oklahoma." That was usually followed up with his coach either patting him on the backside or spitting a wad of tobacco juice next to Cliff's feet, depending how upset the coach was at that moment.

The rookie ball season was short. It was fifty games. Cliff pitched in nine games and pitched well enough to be assigned to A ball in Viera, Florida the following March. However, this was only September and he had nowhere to live. The team arranged for him and a few others to live with older married couples in the area, near Viera. Cliff took a job at the local grocery store stocking shelves to pay for the minimal rent he was being charged. He learned one thing that fall and winter; he was going to do anything and everything he could to make sure he didn't have to spend many more off seasons doing manual labor.

Cliff called his mother every Sunday and would occasionally speak with his siblings. His father was still upset that he chose not to go to college. His mom would tell him that even though his dad was upset, he would called the Viera newspaper every day during the season to hear about Cliff's team. Since John Owens would not speak directly with Cliff, it was the only way he could follow the team's progress from his home in Oklahoma.

March and spring training couldn't come fast enough for Cliff and his teammates. He stayed in close contact with the few he knew from rookie ball who were in the area. They would work out at the team's complex a few days a week along with a few of the big leaguers. Some from the major league team would take the time to explain to Cliff and his mates what it takes to make it to the "Show". One of the grizzled veterans on the team, who lived in Viera in the off season, took a shine to Cliff and would offer advice.

"Youngin, it takes all you got to make it to the show. You gotta learn how to prepare yourself for the long season. You gotta care for your body and your mind. You gotta eat right, keep your legs strong and I suggest to you, read some good books. Your mind gotta stay as sharp as your body. I been round this league and been to every stadium there is, but I gotta tell you, ain't nuttin like playin in the Series for the ring and to be called World Champion. But you gotta prepare this time of year and listen to the coaches and the guys who've been round a few years. You do that and one day if you're one of the lucky ones, they will be sizing your finger for that golden championship ring. But you keep that nose clean, keep your legs strong, and keep your mind right. Ain't nothing in this world I wouldn't give to win the last game of the season. There is only one team every season who wins the very last game. That's the game you wanna pitch, younging."

Cliff soaked it all in. He had never even seen a major league game in person, yet here he was working out with the same players he had watched on television as a kid. When he called home to tell his mom about meeting some of the major leaguers, his dad still wouldn't come to the phone. He told his mother and brothers about his experiences. He was living the dream.

Spring training finally arrived. His team was made up of players ranging in age from nineteen to twenty five. They came from several countries and different cultures. But they all had one goal in mind, to be able to practice earlier in the day with the big league team and make the major league roster. But there were a few things Cliff was not expecting on his first day of practice. For one, there was not one or even two teams on the fields, but over one hundred players all dressed in Marlins uniforms. His path to the majors wouldn't be an easy one. The second thing that happened took place while walking back to the clubhouse. A teenage boy, only a couple of years younger than Cliff approached him.

"Uhm, Mr. Owens, please, will you sign this card for me?"

Cliff was shocked. He had no idea he was even on a baseball card, let alone the idea someone would actually recognize him.

"Where'd you get this card? You got any extras," Cliff asked the nervous kid.

"It's part of the new minor league set that came out this week. Yea, I got like ten of yours. If you sign them all for me, I'll give ya one."

Cliff didn't know whether to be upset or laugh at the kid's moxy to ask for nine autographs at once. "Sure, I'd be happy to sign them all." He signed his first autograph on his first baseball card, well nine to be exact. Right after that, Cliff and one of his buddies ran over to the local card shop. They bought up all the remaining boxes that might have their minor league card hidden inside. He sent a few home to his family, put one in his cap and started a scrap book with the last one.

As it happens in spring training; it rained. Only this time it rained with the major league game only completing four innings. The field became wet but the team didn't want to stop the game and have to refund all the ticket money. The big league manager asked for a few of the minor league players to finish out the game with a few of the remaining major league players. Morning workouts were complete, so many of the older players with more experience had already finished their work outs and were sent home. Only Cliff's team and a few others were still working out after the rain had stopped. A few including Cliff, were sent over to play with the Florida Marlins big league club.

Cliff sat with the pitchers along the railing, too nervous to utter a sound. He was torn between wanting to pitch and being afraid the other team would tattoo his best fastball all over the park. Then he heard it.

"Owens, get loose, you're pitching the 9th inning."

The blood instantly drained from his head. Cliff thought maybe he should attempt to stand and stretch his legs and pitching arm. He stood slowly. His knees wobbled. As he stretched, all he could think about was his dad and what he might think when he finds out that he, Cliff Owens, was about to play in a game against bona fide major league players. Owens was about to pitch against the Los Angeles Dodgers. Granted the Dodgers were playing many of their bench p ayers now too, but not all. He completed his stretching then made several tosses to his catcher. The signal came from the umpire, time to make the walk to the pitcher's mound. The public address announcer came over the loudspeaker, "Now entering the ball game for your Florida Marlins, number eighty three, Cliff "Lookout" Owens, Owens now in the ball game." Cliff was terrified, yet exhilarated all at once.

Eight wobbly tosses to home plate by Cliff and the inning began. It was from the same spot where Orel Leonard Hershiser, "The Bulldog" was standing only a couple of hours earlier. Orel was one of Cliff's idols. The first batter, Tom Goodwin, came to the plate. Cliff walked around the mound trying to gain his composure. For some odd reason Cliff peered into the Dodger dugout, where Tommy Lasorda, manager of the Dodgers, staring back at him. He took a deep breath and delivered his first pitch.

The ball sailed five feet over the batter's head. Lasorda yells out, "Lookout, the rookie can't throw strikes." Cliff was embarrassed. Never had he thrown a ball so poorly in all his years of pitching.

His catcher brought him out a new rubbed up baseball and told Cliff to throw an easy one over the plate. "Throw your get me over fastball." He did. Goodwin hit the ball close to four hundred feet. Lucky for Cliff, the fence was four hundred and two feet. His teammate Scott Pose ran the ball down for out number one. Cliff walked around the mound again. He looked at Lasorda who was laughing at the rookie trying to gain a shred of composure.

Cliff walked back up to the pitchers rubber and scratched the ground a few times with his new cleats. He put a scowl on his face and delivered his best fastball to the outside corner of the plate for strike one. He then threw another pitch in the same location for strike two remembering his pitching coach imploring Cliff to "hit his spots." The catcher put two fingers down asking for Cliff to offer up a breaking ball. Cliff snaps off a perfect curve ball with the batter buckling his knees and watching the perfect pitch for a called "Strike Three", by the umpire. There were now two out to the inning with no damage done.

This time Cliff looks over into his own team's dugout and notices a small smile on the Marlins manager's face, Rene Lachemann. Cliff's attention shifts to the next hitter. Nothing else mattered. He no longer hears Tommy Lasorda chirping about not being able to throw strikes. He found his zone. He rears back and tosses another perfect fastball, this time crossing home plate on the inside corner for strike one. Next pitch was a perfect changeup with the batter fouling it off into the crowd for a souvenir. His catcher tosses out a fresh ball. Cliff looks at Lasorda then throws a fastball high and inside making the batter jump out of the way. This time Cliff knew exactly where he wanted to throw the ball. It had a purpose. He wanted the world to know he had arrived. Cliff took his time, shook off the catchers sign for a fastball and makes him change it to the curve ball. He released the ball perfectly from his fingers and watched the ball dance perfectly across the outside corner. Strike three, ball game over. You could hear Cliff's sigh of relief all the way back to Oklahoma.

His teammates all walk to the center of the diamond for the end of game handshakes. The Marlins manager stops to offer a quick tap on the back and offers, "Nice job kid" and walks away. Cliff was on cloud nine. Yes, it was not a game that counted in the standings but he entered a real major league game and left unscathed. He found his way back to the practice fields behind the stadium, only this time Cliff had a confidence he didn't have when the day started.

The next day his mom called. "Cliff we looked at the roster for another Owens who pitches for the Marlins. We didn't see one. Your dad saw the box score in the paper and noticed an Owens pitched one inning yesterday. Do you know the guy?"

"Yes mom, it was me." In all the excitement of the day, Cliff never thought about calling his family to let them know he played in the game.

"Oh my goodness, you pitched in the game and didn't think to call us!" His mom exclaimed.

Cliff spent the next thirty minutes on the phone telling his mom and oldest brother all about the experience. His mom claimed his dad was out on a job and wasn't home. Cliff knew better.

Cliff's first full season of pro ball went better than expected. He led his team in wins as a starting pitcher. Plus all his other meaningful statistics like earned run average and strikes to walks ratio were all better than the coaching staff had set as goals. He had done so well that Cliff would be promoted the following season to AA ball in Portland Maine to play for the Sea Dogs.

During the offseason, Cliff's mother begged Cliff to return home for the holidays. "Please come home at least for Thanksgiving Cliff, for me. We all miss you round here."

"As soon as Dad invites me, I'll come home. Till then the people I live with here in Florida, the Gibson's, they take good care of me. I'm staying with them till Daddy realizes I'm a man with my own life now. Till then, I'll work out and get ready for next season."

Cliff called home on Thanksgiving and Christmas but only his siblings and mother would come to the phone. He would hear his dad in the background, but John would never come to the phone. As much as Cliff had a heavy heart, the Gibson family treated Cliff as if he was their own son. They went to every home game the previous season and were his big supporters.

Spring training arrived quickly. For the first time in well over a year, Cliff was on the move. He was sent to Portland, Maine to play for the Sea Dogs, a minor league team for the Marlins. He would also be playing against stiffer competition. But that didn't deter the younf right hander. He was going to do whatever it took to make it on the major league roster.

His new team was very good. Cliff and the team were having a good season until a couple of his teammates were moved up to the major league team in South Florida, but not Cliff. He finished out the season with the Sea Dogs. He kept in contact with one of his teammates who made the jump to the big leagues. The Marlins were fighting for a playoff spot.

The Marlins were doing very well and went all the way to the World Series. Cliff got four tickets to sit in the upper decks in Joe Robbie Stadium to watch the Marlins compete against the Cleveland Indians in game seven. He invited Rob and Betty Gibson and their son Trey to the game with him. He wanted to experience that moment with his father but John Owens refused the call. He only heard in the background when speaking to his mother, "Florida is too hot for me."

Cliff's mother kept assuring him that his father would one day take his calls since, "Your father called the paper in Maine every few days to see how you were doing, Cliff. You should see our phone bill." It bothered Cliff but then again, he had actual teammates, who had started the season with him in Maine, now playing on the field in game seven of the World Series. Not only that, he had worked out with many of the other players in the off season in Florida. They were no longer just people on his television screen. These were people he knew; he sat on long bus rides with and had developed actual friendships.

It was not the same sitting in section 405 in the upper decks of a stadium designed for football as opposed to being on the field in uniform but Cliff felt a sense it was his team too as he watched the Marlins win the World Series that night. The next morning, he was allowed to visit the clubhouse and tour the stadium with the Gibson family before heading back to Viera. He wished it could have been his own family.

Next spring arrived and with it, another season back in Maine. Cliff was told to develop a better changeup before he could ever make it to the next level. He did just that and had a good season for the Sea Dogs. The Marlins had traded away many of their top players and Cliff now had a real shot at reaching his goal of becoming a major league pitcher. He did so well, after that season, he was invited to spring training as a member of the Marlins with a real chance at becoming a member of the Florida Marlins pitching staff.

He worked hard the entire off season. Cliff didn't work any job in the off season other than to prime his body for another long grueling season. He saved enough money to pay rent to the Gibsons and still had enough to live on during the offseason. His legs and mind were ready for the upcoming spring. He could taste it. One day after working out and reflecting on sitting in the stadium, watching the Marlins beat the Indians in game seven, he told a teammate, "I think I'd give my soul to be the winning pitcher in a World Series game." His buddy responded back, "I think every player would give up something, but your soul is asking a lot, Lookout."

11

Another spring began with Cliff in top form. This would finally be his year. He did all the drills and pitched his bull pen sessions in preparation for his first appearance of the spring. It would be against the New York Mets in Port St. Lucie, Florida on your average sunny Florida March afternoon. Cliff was scheduled to pitch in the third and fourth innings against the Mets. He made it through the third inning not allowing a hit but walking one batter. He came out for the fourth inning when his life changed.

He allowed a single to the first batter. Cliff paced around the pitcher's mound tossing the rosin bag around in his fingers. He discarded the bag back to the ground and wedged his right foot along the pitching rubber. He came to the set position and looked back at the runner on first base. He looked in for the sign from the catcher and let loose with his best fastball. Before his ninety two mile an hour fastball could travel less than sixty feet, a pain exploded in his pitching elbow. A pain Cliff had never experienced. He danced around the mound pretending like it was nothing. He looked back at the trainer to have him stay in the dugout. Again he stood ready for the next pitch. He let it loose and so did the tendon in his elbow. His season was over.

Three weeks later while sitting in the surgeon's office awaiting, "Tommy John Surgery", Cliff started to question why him. He worked for years to get into the position of reaching his dream and just as it was about the happen, he was injured. All the stress on his elbow finally revolted. Cliff Owens was staring at fifteen to eighteen months of rehabilitation. His career in baseball, for the first time, was now in jeopardy. His mother begged him to come back to Oklahoma to recover but Cliff declined. He wanted to go back to the Gibson home to recover.

The current season was lost as was half of the following one. Cliff worked mostly alone for month after grueling month to get his elbow and body back to form. He used the minor league complex but was mostly ignored by the Marlins and the coaching staff. He would get an occasional call to check on his progress but for the most part, he was on his own.

Eighteen months after his surgery, Cliff was working his way back into pitching an inning or two in minor league games. He had lost nearly two seasons off his career. The Marlins had decided his future might be better suited as a relief pitcher. Cliff was not pleased and asked to be traded or released. The Marlins refused his requests. His agent convinced him to do as the team asked. He needed to prove he was healthy. He was still under the teams control for another two years. Cliff wanted to make the major league roster more than he wanted to be a starting pitcher, so he relented and worked as a relief pitcher.

He pitched out of the bullpen for the remainder of the season in the minor leagues. Cliff worked on developing his changeup and restoring the accuracy on his fastball. By the end of the season he had regained confidence in his ability to pitch at the highest levels. However, Cliff felt he was now just one of the extra pitchers in the Marlins system. In the amateur draft the following spring, the Marlins drafted a pitcher with ten of their first eleven picks. The minor league system was now loaded with pitching prospects.

Cliff "Lookout" Owens did whatever he could to stay within the system. He made himself valuable as a top relief pitcher. His specialty was being able to get out batters from both sides of the plate.

By the middle of the 2003 season his goal was finally realized. Cliff "Lookout" Owens was called up to the Marlins big league club. He had no desires to return to long bus rides and marginal food allowances. He called his family to give them the news but they didn't want to travel to Miami. "We will never know when you're pitching Cliff. It's not like you're a starting pitcher and we know the day you will play, it could be a week or more before you pitch. I'll get your father to get the sports package on the TV so we can watch your games. It's the best we can do." The Gibson family made the drive from Viera, Florida, the night Cliff was called up from the minors.

The first game Cliff was on the roster the Marlins were losing in a lopsided game 8-1 in the top of the 9th inning. Cliff was called in to pitch the last inning. Who was the first voice he heard as he made his way to the top of the pitcher's mound, none other than Tommy Lasorda. Cliff was summoned in against the Dodgers and Lasorda remembered, "Lookout". "Watch out for that first pitch Rickey, this guy doesn't know where it's heading." Cliff got the first batter to hit a lazy fly ball to centerfield before striking out the next two.

As the season wore on, Cliff's confidence rose to an all time high. The team's confidence in him did as well. He started to pitch in meaningful games in a pennant race. By the end of regular season, Cliff had become a valuable member of the pitching staff. He was no longer just another pitcher in the organization. He helped the Marlins reach all the way to the World Series against the venerable New York Yankees. Cliff "Lookout" Owens would be part of a team playing the World Series in Yankee Stadium.

Tickets for the members of the team were limited. People lined up requesting them. Cliff offered them to his family for the games at Yankee stadium and the Gibson family for the games in Miami. He felt it proper to include the Gibson family. Much to his surprise, his family accepted the tickets for the first two games at Yankee Stadium.

This would be the first trip to Yankee Stadium for Cliff and many of his teammates. The grass seemed greener, the seats closer to the action. Cliff would later comment to his friends, he heard the echo of Mantle, Ruth and Dimaggio, whispering in his ear during batting practice.

After practice, the team had time to wander the outfield and see all the monuments. Cliff wanted so much to share that moment with his father but his family wasn't scheduled to arrive until the next day.

The team met with all the media about the upcoming games. The New York media wanted to know how Cliff got his nickname. Lookout reminisced about Tommy and the little league game. He hadn't thought about that story in years but enjoyed reliving the moment with the few members of the press who cared to listen.

The following day was game one of the World Series. The Yankees were heavy favorites. Most dismissed the Marlins as mostly upstart players, with no chance of defeating the twenty six time World Champions. The team was understandably nervous. Cliff took his spot in the bullpen far away from home plate in the outfield. He wasn't sure his family made it for game time. Cliff curiously scanned the crowd where he thought the seats were as he stood for the playing of the national anthem. Unfortunately, all he saw were throngs of people donned in famed Yankee caps.

The game had spectators on the edge of their seats. The Marlins had a one run lead late in the game when the call came down for Cliff to get warmed up. He would be pitching in the World Series, inside the historic Yankee Stadium, with his father possibly in attendance.

He took the long walk in from the outfield. Bob Sheppard, the public address announcer, read Cliff's name. "Now entering, Clifford Owens, Owens now pitching." Cliff thought he heard a cheer coming from the upper decks but he was so nervous it could have been his imagination. He blew on his fingers. It was a chilly New York autumn evening. First pitch was high and tight on the Yankee hitter. Cliff could hear ribbing from his own dugout, "Lookout is in the house that Ruth built." He looked into the dugout to see his team laughing it up. It was enough to calm his nerves. He managed to get out of the inning without a run being scored. The Marlins had won game one of the series 3-2.

Early morning was creeping in before everyone had given their post game interviews and showered up. The bus was leaving for the hotel in twenty minutes. Cliff walked outside of the player's clubhouse to find his ride to the hotel. He could hear people calling his name over near the fence. It was his family. Cliff walked over to find his mother, sister and two of his brothers, all wearing Marlins caps.

"We're all so proud of you Cliff. Could you hear us screaming for you when they announced your name? Lucky for us we were sitting with the other families from the Marlins, cause we were the only section rooting for ya."

"Thanks Mom. Pop couldn't make the game? I always thought it was his dream to see his kid pitch in Yankee stadium?"

"I'm sure he's watching the game at home. We didn't want to upset you and tell ya. Your father suffered a minor stroke but he's getting better. One day outta the blue he lost his speech and fell to the ground. It was a shock but he's recuperating. He can speak some but it's coming back slowly. Don't you worry bout him though, you go and beat those Yanks. Your father is a hard man, Cliff but I know deep down he was so proud when you made it to the big leagues. I would catch him peeking at your games. But don't you worry bout nothing, Cliff, he's going to be just fine."

Cliff didn't know what to say. He tried to find a place to allow his family inside the gate but it was locked. They spoke for a few minutes then met up at the hotel for lunch the next day. The Marlins won the World Series in six games.

After reading the report concerning the Owens family, I thought if I removed the soul of every disgruntled dad, I would have a never ending supply of souls to feed our kind. I was beginning to believe this was the goal of the elders. Were we getting easy assignments to rip out the souls of tired old men so we could move on to the next victim? Was that really our mission on earth? What really passes the threshold of a broken soul? Did a pissed off dad really meet our criteria? Was I getting an easy assignment on purpose? My original assignments all involved killers, rapists, brutal dictators. Did we evolve into taking the souls of grumpy asshole fathers because our kind was dying out and like a common junkie we needed a quick fix?

I barged back into the office of our assignment coordinator Brandon Bink to get some answers. "Elder Novo, I'm given a list of names from the Council and I assign the cases. It's all I do. I'm given a report with a name and number. We have hundreds of backlogged files."

"Are you telling me you don't peek inside even once to see the type of person who is losing a soul, Bink?"

Brandon lowered his head and replied, "I did once and Elder Orcus found out. I was banished to the solitary cell for a week. I won't make that mistake again. I don't question the Council's judgment."

My next step was to find the other members of the Council. They were all lounging in our dining hall, enjoying a nice buffet stuffed with the finest foods from around the world. "Excuse me gents but I need a word," I proclaimed in a nasty tone. "It's time to add oversight on stolen souls to the list of items we need to fix."

Elder Polus spoke up. "Elder Novo, I've listened to your rants since you were starting out as a soul stealer. You think you have all the answers, yet the few times when you sat in on Council meetings, you were mostly silent. It's so easy to criticize leadership until you hold the power. You have one vote, like the rest of us. Please take your objections and toss them in the suggestion box on your way to Oklahoma, because quite frankly I'm really tired of your terminal whining."

How dare this old man stuffing himself on lobster, accuse me of running around criticizing others without an idea. Well, I didn't have a master plan yet, but I wasn't gorging myself on fancy foods and wines while thinking about it. Either way, I wasn't about to back down to some old fool who should have been on forced retirement decades ago. I started a brisk march in his direction wanting to rip out his soul when Peter grabbed my arm. "You're wiser than the old man, Elder Novo. Removing his soul will only lead to more responsibilities for you. Now would not be the time as overburdened as you are now, my leader."

Peter did have a point. Besides, I could remove the soul of that weak being anytime I chose. I decided to let my temper calm and head off to Oklahoma and pay a visit to John Owens. If I couldn't persuade this group of old codgers to see things my way, possibly I could persuade one broken down plumber with a bad heart and dark soul to abide by my ruling.

Two days later I was sitting in the living room with John and Miriam Owens and their youngest daughter, Patricia. It didn't take much to make my way into their home. I told Miriam I was sent over to check on John's health. I hated to take advantage of an older lady like that, but it was for the best. After a few pleasantries and with a cold glass of lemonade at my side, I started in with my real reason for traveling to see John.

"Mr. and Mrs. Owens, I am not normally direct with people in your situation. The people I deal with don't know who I am, or my mission. You see, I am a soul stealer. I have been assigned to take John's soul for his many years of not speaking with his son, Cliff."

I took notice as Patricia left the room and Miriam sat up in her chair with her eyes now glued on me. John gave me that stare I have learned to despise, as he turned his attention back to "Days of our Lives" on the television. I was trying to have a real conversation with this guy and he wanted to watch his daily soap opera. Obviously this guy needed to treat me with more respect.

I tried again. "If I were in your situations, I would think I was a nut job too. But I am telling the truth about my mission. I am required to leave with John's soul. Personally, I would rather him pick up the phone and call Cliff. Please, John, do us all a favor and call your son. It will save me the aggravation of having to go and retrieve your soul in a few months when Cliff finds me and asks for redemption for his father. Be a sport, John, make the call."

Miriam looked at me, looked at her husband, looked at me again and started to mumble. At first I couldn't decipher a word she was saying. She looked again at John, then back at me before speaking again. Only this time her words were very clear.

"If you are who you say you are, git on with your business, then git outta my home. I prayed this day would come. John's been abusive not only to Cliff but me and most round him for years. Plus, he did more than fix Shirley Johnson's kitchen sink. I would assume others with leaky pipes too. He's a miserable sad excuse for a father and husband. Take his soul! Do it! Then git outta my house. Be quick about it too, I gotta nice a fine roast in the oven and I don't wanna burn it."

Well this is another fine mess you have gotten us into Ollie. Here I was thinking I was sent on an easy assignment where I didn't have to take a soul but now I am being begged to take it. Was she serious or thinking this was all a joke set up by Cliff? John remained almost comatose, sitting in his overstuffed lounger with the stuffing coming out of the seat.

"Mrs. Owens, please understand. This is not a joke. It is very real. I can remove your husband's soul in a matter of seconds. You should value his soul more than it seems you do. I cannot tell from his reaction if he understands all that is going on or not?"

"He ain't said much going on bout three years now. The Doctor tells me he knows everything going on but since he had his second stroke few months back, he ain't good for much else but taking up space in that ole chair. He won't miss his soul much. It's a small price to pay for all the crap he's done to this here family."

Just when I thought it could not get any weirder, Patricia came bursting into the room with a shotgun pointed directly at my skull. "You git your ass outta this house, mister, fore I splatter your brains all over this here livin room."

"Now, now, Patty, this man is here to help us, or so he says. Put that gun down fore someone gits hurt."

I sat there thinking, oh yea, real easy assignment, cowboy. I took a moment to peer inside of the soul of one, John Owens. It was black as the heels of his worn out cowboy boots sitting next to his lounger. Maybe I had misjudged the Council and Bink's schedule of assignments. Could the Council be doing a better job of reviewing cases before sending them over to Bink? I needed to rethink my position but first I had to deal with a shotgun four feet from my head.

"Uhm, Patricia, I surely would appreciate if you would listen to your mother and put the gun down. I don't want to hurt you or your mother. Your father will be given a chance at redemption before his earthly body takes its last breath. But for now, please, lower that gun."

Patricia didn't take directions well. "You listen to me, Mista, dunno who you are or where you come from, but you ain't hurting my daddy. Now, kindly remove your skinny ass from our home and maybe I'll let you keep your head on top of ya shoulders, where it belongs."

Miriam darted over to her daughter and grabbed the gun from her hand as if it was not the first time she had performed such a feat. "Gimme that rifle and go check on my roast, girl. I done told you a million times not to touch your daddy's rifles. Besides, they work better when they loaded. Now go do as you was told."

Miriam turned her attention back to me. "Now tell the truth. How much is Cliff paying you to be here?"

"Mrs. Owens, I mean no disrespect to you or your family. I have never spoken with any of your family, nor has anyone paid me. I know it must be very difficult for you to understand. This is why I rarely approach anyone. I take from the shadows. But I can see now, your husband has much to repent. Cliff is only a small part. Mr. Owens must have done some other things that maybe he is not proud to admit."

I was on guard not knowing what Miriam would do, or if her daughter would show up with another rifle pointed my way, so I wanted to steal John's soul and get out of there as quickly as possible. My original intent was to leave his soul intact if he made amends with his son, however I could see I was assigned this case for more than a family squabble. This man had a very dark soul.

John was now sobbing as he shifted in his chair. With a very weak voice he spoke, "I neva claimed to be a perfect man. I only wanted a good life fer my family."

Miriam bent on one knee beside her husband and took his

hand. "Ssshhh, it's all ok, my dear, none of us are perfect, not even the man who lied to me to get into our home. You rest now and enjoy your program."

Miriam then looked at me. "It seems here, Mr. Novo, you really don't have any miracle cure for my husband. You entered our home under false pretenses. I suspect it's bout time you turn tail and leave, please. I prefer not to call the sheriff."

"My apologies, Mrs. Owens, I never said I could cure your husband. I only said I wanted to check on his health. If I told you the truth on the porch steps you might have shoved that shot gun in my nose and asked me to leave before I could ever see your husband. I really did come here in the hope John would make peace with his son, not only for his sake but the entire family. I will take my leave now with my apologies. I wished I were able to save your family from anymore pain."

With that I took my last sip of the homemade lemonade, gave a nod of my head to Miriam Owens and put my hand on John's shoulder and removed his soul. He slumped farther down in his over sized lounger. I made my way as quickly as I could to the exit of their home in case removing John's soul gave me a seizure. Plus, I didn't need to give Miriam any time to find ammunition for the weapon still glued to her aging fingers. Patricia slammed the door behind me as I jumped into my rented car and drove as quickly as possible to the local outdoor park, where I could recover unnoticed.

12

The ensuing weeks were spent back in the compound attempting to find answers to why our soul stealers were claiming to have lost their ability to steal. This had been happening at an alarming rate over the past few decades. Also, there was the issue of why some among our ranks had the ability to steal but chose not to do their duty.

This was never a question for me, as I was growing up. I would become a stealer of souls. It was our highest calling, short of serving on the Council. Were they now afraid of the endless travel or the danger in the line of duty? Our mission is to rid the world of evil and despair. Is there a higher calling? I think not.

The Council droned on for hours about how Doctor Winfield was obtaining the names of the remaining soul stealers and intentionally poisoning them to remove their ability to steal souls. It was assumed, since he was banned from our people, he would seek to destroy us. I disagreed with the rest of the Council for several reasons. I had looked into Winfield's eyes several times over the past few months. Winfield insisted he was a healer over and over, to the point where I thought there was truth in his words. Oh, Doctor Winfield had an evil streak, no doubt, but I found it difficult he wanted to wipe out our ability to steal.

Another topic at the Council meetings was how to fund our operations. To support our lifestyle, the Council would recommend a yearly budget and tax. Anyone in our bloodlines who refused to take souls, or couldn't for any reason, would be taxed. It's how we finance our operations. It was rumored, though never confirmed, that in the last century, some who refused to steal, or pay the tax, disappeared from our ranks. Once one loses the ability to steal and is dependent on us to extend their lives, it is imperative they support us in the form of taxation. Collecting the tax became an easy proposition once the few who refused to pay were never found.

Our system of finances had been set up and fine tuned over several generations. It came down to simple math. Every time anyone of our disciples takes a soul, it adds strength to our lives. But it's a finite amount. The more the stolen power is being spread out amongst our disciples, the less each of us gains from taking a soul. Our strength, derived from soul stealing, adds days to our lives. If we have no one taking souls, our body strength and time to live diminishes.

When the original one hundred were chosen, each had to agree to extract souls before accepting the gift of soul stealing. In return for stealing, the original one hundred would survive more than three times longer than your average human. The power derived from stealing souls would be distributed only to the ones with the power to steal. They shared their power, each time any of the one hundred took a soul. However, in recent times, our bloodlines have thinned out to the point where too many share only a percentage of our bloodlines. Many have lost the ability to steal souls, yet still share in the benefits of a longer life cycle, when we are stealing in high numbers. It is believed to be our ability to remove souls is in decline because our bloodlines have been thinned out by mating with pure humans.

Because of the longevity and thinned blood lines, we now have over one thousand of our disciples receiving the benefits of gaining strength each time we take a soul but less than thirty soul stealers actively taking souls and empowering all. Each time we take a soul, it now barely keeps our life cycles extending beyond one hundred years for new children. Our power from soul stealing is being spread too thin among non soul stealers. It affects the youngest among us, since their life cycle will be far less than the older of our people. It's been in recent times our life cycle has been rapidly deteriorating. We need new soul stealers among our ranks to survive or find a way to cut off the others from our benefits.

I can't claim to be a wealthy person financially, but paying my bills has never been an issue. All of my living expenses are paid with the taxes collected from non stealers. I fly first class on airplanes. Our home is usually slightly more than the cost of your average home in the area where I reside. I wear nice clothes, though admittedly, some of the Elders wear custom fitted, expensive suits. The system has its flaws but it has worked for generations. But we can't continue spreading our power amongst a thousand from thirty soul stealers. We will all perish and our mission will end.

My recommendation to the Council has been to offer incentives to the others who can steal but refuse. I suggested we distribute a survey and discover why they refuse to steal. For those who refuse to steal, yet have the ability, we raise their tax.

We need to encourage those who refuse to steal to use their full capacity to steal and help us to survive as a race. For those who have grown tired and weak, but who have served as stealers; reduce their tax. They've done their service and deserve a rest. For those who come from thinned out bloodlines and have attempted to learn how to steal but can't, keep their tax rate the same. However, encourage them in finding a mate within our ranks. Should they have offspring with another of our kind, it should increase the likely hood of their offspring developing the power to steal. Let's reward them with a lower tax rate, should they mate within our ranks and fortify our bloodlines once again.

I took these ideas and others to the Council meeting, only to watch one or two of them sit and stuff their faces with fine food and wine and dismiss all my ideas. I was starting to think it would be much easier to go back to stealing souls full time and leave the politics to others.

Elder Polus, in particular, always seemed to revel in destroying my attempts to alter our tax system. "Elder Novo, our system has worked for many years before your grandfather disclosed your true identity, which allowed you on this Council. I still say under false pretenses, but for now, I'll drop that complaint. However, changing our tax code won't result in more of our kind offering their services. We have a system that works, deal with it."

"Really, Elder Polus? How can you be so certain since you relics, identified as leaders are afraid to change your lunch menu, let alone our tax code? All I know is that we are losing our ability to remove souls at an alarming rate, while you all sit here and delight behind the shady secure walls of our compound. Well, guess what, I have the ability to take as many souls as I like, so I will be just fine. But, I assumed since we are the Council assigned to rule more than just our six, maybe, just maybe, we should do our best to fix what ails us."

I was getting irritated in being told to come to our Council meetings with fresh ideas, yet when I did, they were dismissed with little discussion. It was time to do what I did best. It was time to take another soul. I abruptly removed myself from the Council chambers and went to seek out Bink for my next assignment.

"We are sending you back to Washington D.C, Elder Novo," Bink explained. "You will remove the soul of an internet blogger who can't seem to report the truth."

"Only one who can't tell the truth? Or can I take a few dozen while I am in town." I asked Bink, although he didn't seem to enjoy my humor.

"Pay attention Elder Novo, this isn't your common journalist. No one will admit in knowing him or where he works. No one claims to know his true identity, yet he is read by over a million daily readers on his blog. He leaks classified information. No one seems to know where he gets his information, yet many of his stories are pure propaganda for his political point of view and the government's agenda."

I wasn't buying Bink's point of view. "We can't take his soul because of his opinion, Mr. Bink. There are many labeled as so called journalists, who are merely puff piece writers and story leakers, for powerful government officials. There has to be more to him than being a yellow journalist."

Here came that stare again, the one that drives me up a wall when I see it. "Elder Novo, please go to Washington and find this creep. People assume he lives in the area, since his expertise is in politics and he writes as if he was in the room of some important government meetings. He could be an elected official as far as anyone knows. Stop questioning your assignments and do your job."

"Bink, I should have your reprimanded for your tone with me, but you are about the only one who works hard in this compound. Give me the file on this journalist and let me read it."

Jason Mendace was the name used by my target. Since I was fluent in Italian, I assumed it was a pen name. After all, mendace means false in Italian. I assumed he knew he was printing false information just by the name he uses. But that's speculation on my part.

My first stop in Washington was with an old friend, Congressman George McAdams. I originally met George at a fundraiser for his reelection campaign in South Florida. A few months after that, he asked me to work with the CIA to remove the soul of an African dictator. It was a very dangerous mission but since the dictator was on my list anyway, I worked with the government on a covert operation. Because of that, I was calling in a favor from George.

We met in a park near the Potomac River away from cameras and the bustling crowds. But McAdams was still being careful about who could possibly see or hear us speaking.

"Not sure how much I can tell you, Cale. This guy has Washington upset over the information he leaks out. I've heard the rumor he's in the President's cabinet, but it's not been verified."

I pried McAdams for more. "What do you think though,

Congressman? Is it possible he works inside the government somewhere and really he's a rube to pass legislation with his leaks? After all, many times what's being released is damaging to the President's foes."

"Cale, don't' quote me, but this President Morrison, he's not a good guy. I can't tell you why right now, but I think he's dirty. It wouldn't shock me at all if he has someone inside the White House is leaking classified documents. Don't breathe a word of this, but he told me that if I drop an investigation I'm working on, he'll make sure it's easy sailing for me to win the Senate seat in Florida, next election. He knows how to get what he wants."

"Sounds like maybe the President will be on my list soon", I stated with a smirk.

"Don't laugh Cale, between Morrison and the Speaker of the House, they are dangerous people. I don't trust either of them."

"Well, what about the blogger, George? Do you really think he's working directly for the President?"

"Morrison is out to destroy anyone who opposes his agenda, even inside his own party. So, yeah, I do think it's possible there is a direct pipeline between Morrison and the writer."

I could tell the Congressman was hesitant to offer much more information. "Well George, after I discover who this guy is and rip out his soul, I would like to come back for some advice from you. I am new at this politics game and the people I am supposed to be working with don't want to listen to anything I have to offer."

"Hey, get in line, Cale. I'm trying really hard to find out about some money being funded to the secret service. The funds have been on the books since the time of Lincoln, but no one will come clean and help me. I had no idea politics would be such a dirty profession until I came to Washington. I can't decide if I want to do my best to clean it up or head back to Florida and get back in the investments game. I started working with Dylan James and a few others buying up commercial property back in Florida. Are you interested in joining us?"

"I am not into investing much, but as you know my parents live down there, I'll call my dad and ask him if he's interested if you don't mind. But either way, I will contact you once I find this guy. I do want your advice about politics."

"Sure thing, Cale, I owe ya one for taking that mission in Africa. I can only imagine how rough it was staring down more than one rifle pointed at your head. But for now, I've got a vote to place back on the hill, so I gotta be running. Take care, Cale."

It was time to turn my attention to Jason Mendace. My starting point would be to research all the articles Mendace had written over the past two years. I would see what the information involved and did the leaked information come from an open hearing on Capitol Hill or a closed door meeting. I would attempt to find any similarities as to any government official who may have been present in all of those meetings. The defense department seemed to be a popular theme of Mendace's stories. The budget process was another.

During the next few weeks, I went to any open meeting I could enter and make notes of anyone in the crowd, as well as any government official behind the dais or in the room. It was a tedious process but one I thought necessary to find a common thread.

There are so many reporters that cover news coming from Washington. More than one of the same reporters seemed to be at the majority of meetings I covered. This avenue of attack seemed pointless. The other way to investigate is always a popular one, follow the money.

I ventured my way over to the internet provider where Mendace had his web site and blog hosted. I pretended to be there for an interview in the accounting department. I snooped around until I discovered the name of the person in charge of signing checks, Tim Walsh.

I searched the building until I found Mr. Walsh's office. On his desk was the usual family portrait with Tim and the family. I now knew what he looked like. I waited in the parking lot until he was on his way home for the evening. I still had my credentials from an earlier case when I was disguised as Special Agent John Latens. I flashed my badge quickly at Walsh.

"Mr. Walsh, I need a moment of your time. My name is Special Agent John Latens with the FBI. I am investigating the identity of a blogger, Jason Mendace. I would like to schedule a time tomorrow to review your client list."

The guy actually laughed in my face. "Look here, dip shit. I don't know who you really are, but the real FBI wouldn't meet me in a parking lot. I know his identity is important to a lot of people. But if you think I'm going to tell you cause you flashed a badge at me, you're a fool. Now get outta my face before I call the real police."

It was quickly apparent this guy was no ordinary pencil pusher. Plan B would be put in place, once I decided what Plan B would be. I had to think fast since Walsh was digging into his pocket for his car keys and ignoring me.

"Mr. Walsh, as odd as this may sound; my mission was given to me from an authority higher than your boss and even the President. By the photos on your desk, it seems you have a nice family, so I really don't want to hurt you. But I posses a power only a small handful are blessed with on earth. It is meant to rid the world of evil, like what Mendace is doing by spinning his tales to an ignorant public."

Before I could finish my thought, Walsh stopped me. He now had his car door open. "Look pal, I'm sure I'll be seeing you in the next X-Men movie with your special powers, but here in reality land, we do our jobs and go home to our families. If you got a beef with one of our clients, you take it up with management. It's not my job to be the editorial censor of our web sites. I write checks, pay bills and go home, end of story."

Before Tim Walsh could get all the way into his car and pull his door shut, I grabbed hold of the car door. "You are making a huge mistake in underestimating me, Walsh. I will get the information I am requesting from you, or you will lose something very valuable."

I let go of the car door. Walsh flashed that stare at me which now only upset me slightly less than the Miami Dolphins losing to the Oakland Raiders in football. He drove off quickly but I did notice he glanced into his rear view mirror at me more than once, before he was out of view.

I went back to my hotel room and scoured the notes about the meetings I had attended. I again tried to match them with reports being written by Mendace, as well as others in attendance at those meetings. There was not one government official at all the meetings but there was one office represented at the majority of them, the Department of Agriculture. Why would someone from that department sit in on defense hearings and many budget hearings? My curiosity was peeked

Joe "Spud" Kile was named Secretary of Agriculture soon after President Morrison was elected. I had Agent Nesstor pull his file. Not only did Secretary Kile grow up in the same neighborhood as the President, Kile was an official visitor of the President an unusually high number of times. He visited the White House fifty-five times. The Vice President and the Speaker of the House didn't enjoy that many visits combined.

I approached Nesstor about the high number of official visits and asked him why that didn't set off any red flags with the FBI? "Cale, sometimes you can do your job so well, it gets you fired. Finding the leak isn't my case, but I can assure you, there are times you don't wanna know." Maybe Nesstor's superiors didn't want to discover the leak inside the White House, but I was required to uncover the real identity of Jason Mendace and remove his soul.

In my early soul stealing career. I was allowed time to search out my target and not put myself in harm's way. Looking back, maybe that's why the Council wasn't strict with time requirements. I was offered easy assignments compared to now. The Council was allowing me to hone my craft of being a top soul stealer. But as I aged, my patience ran thin with people who refused to answer simple questions or refused to accept me for who I am. I've earned respect and worked hard to obtain my abilities. Playing spy and searching out mysteries doesn't offer me the excitement it once did, even a mere decade ago. I wanted to finish my task and go home.

The next day, I perched out at Kile's office until I watched him leave. I followed him down the tired hallway until we were the only two in a small elevator car taking us down four floors to the bottom.

"Mr. Secretary, my name is Caeles Novo. I do not work for any government agency and quite frankly my job is not to discover why someone is leaking classified information to the media. However, I am assigned to discover the real identity of Jason Mendace. I think you can help me with my assignment. Please do not waste my time with lies, Mr. Kile. Like you, I am a very busy man and I desire to return home to my wife and son."

Kile, who stood a slender six feet, with wire rimmed glasses and a polished suit, peered back at me lowering his glasses near the tip of his sturdy nose and replied, "Say another word to me and the armed guards at the bottom floor will have you arrested."

The remainder of my thin patience was gone. "Mr. Kile, let me slowly explain this to you one time. I don't want there to be any misunderstanding. Many with larger guns have attempted to stop me. Your one guard at the door who should have retired years ago is no match for me. Don't you think I have already thought out how I intend to take you with me until I get the truth? I want the truth or you will regret your next sentence."

The elevator car reached the bottom floor. When the door slid open, Kile immediately called for the old grey haired gent, barely able to get out of his chair, to arrest me. The security officer looked stunned as if no one had ever asked for his assistance in the past. He slowly approached me. "Before you attempt to arrest me, please tell me the charge. And if you dare attempt to detain me long enough to let Kile out the door, you will regret it."

The old man looked at Kile, "What's the charge, Mr. Secretary?"

"Harassment of a government official, now arrest him, or I'll have your job," Kile boasted.

I offered one last warning. "Neither of you want to go this route. I will ask you one last time Mr. Kile, tell me what you know about Jason Mendace and I will leave peacefully. If not, both of you will regret your decision."

Kile looked again at the worn out officer, who now looked as scared as he did weary from a long day. "Arrest this idiot, McCarthy, or find a new security job in the morning."

Officer Bo McCarthy came closer as Kile made his way towards the front door. As McCarthy pulled out his hand cuffs, I yelled at Kile to get his attention. He turned back as I calmly stated, "Take one more step towards that front door and this will happen to you too." I touched the wrist of Officer McCartney and watched him fall to the ground.

Kile made his dash for the exit. I quickly followed him, leaving McCarthy to fend for himself on the cold floor. Kile was quickly out of breath as he stumbled down the cement sidewalk in a mostly vacant side street. Despite my aching knees, Kile was easy to run down.

"Come on Mr. Secretary, I have asked you politely more than once to tell me what you know about Mendace. It is not a big secret you have known the President for many years and are likely friends. It has also come to my attention you have been to see President Morrison more times than his own Vice President. Maybe you are not the leak but tell me what you do know."

Kile finally stopped trying to avoid me. "What did you do to McCarthy? He didn't deserve to die. The poor fella was about to retire. Who the hell are you and what do you really want from me?"

"I already told you, Mr. Secretary, my name is Caeles Novo. My job is to discover the real identity of Jason Mendace and have him pay for his evils. Lies are being told about the President's opponents in the upcoming election. I believe you are Jason Mendace. Come clean with me and one day, when the time is right, you will be offered redemption but not unless you tell me the truth."

My body started to shake as Kile began to speak. "I'm not the guy you are looking for, I swear it. Just don't hurt me."

I was having a difficult time keeping my composure. "If not you, then who? I know you're keeping information from me. Speak now or you will be without a soul."

Kile suddenly looked relieved. "My soul, hell, I lost that the moment I moved to this town. Is that what happened to McCarthy? You think losing my soul is supposed to scare me? Please, get outta my way."

I could now hear the police and ambulance sirens reaching ever closer. My body was now convulsing from taking the security guards soul. I arched my back against the side of the building trying to brace myself but it was no use. I slid to the ground as Kile darted off around the corner.

13

The following day I made my way back to the office where Tim Walsh worked. My patience had run out with these jokers. Someone was going to tell me the true identity of Jason Mendace or the few remaining souls left in this town would all be removed.

As Walsh left his office around lunchtime, I followed him to a local deli where he was in line to order food. "Walsh, if you read local paper, you will notice a small story about a security guard dropping to the ground after being assaulted by an unnamed man. The paper even has quotes from the Secretary of Agriculture explaining how the guard was overtaken by a stranger without a punch being thrown or a shot being fired. The man they are looking for is me. I took the guard's soul. I am about to take yours right here, right now in this deli line."

Tim Walsh turned around to look at me. "Oh please, you again? I thought you left for the casting call of The Walking Dead."

My temper flared. "Look Walsh, there must be a small part of your brain that believes me. Even if you don't, is it worth the risk? Give me a name and you won't ever see me again. If not, your son Paul and daughter Madelyn will be seeing me as they come out of the school they attend over on 17th street. I have a son and I would never want to remove the soul of an innocent child but you are leaving me no choice. I have many other responsibilities right now and I am out of patience looking for this Mendace character."

Walsh moved into my personal space. "Listen to me, Freddy Krueger. If any harm comes to my family, I'll use every resource I have to find you and make sure you rot in an unmarked grave with your eyes being fed to the nearest crows."

"Walsh, you have zero chance of ever finding me. I have authorities in countries across the globe trying to lock me up. It will never happen. Now, give me a name or watch your children suffer without a soul. Every day when you wake up your conscience will remind you that your job took precedent over keeping your family safe."

Tim Walsh yanked me out of line and to the corner of the room. There were five others in the line of the tiny corner store. There was a dull light coming through the large window in front of the store from the overcast afternoon. I was shoved up against the window near the entrance. Others in the store were now glaring our way.

"Look asshole, one last time. I don't know who Jason Mendace is. I don't. I told you that before. All I know is, we get paid from a corporation run out of Florida. It's called The Rhawnhurst Associates. Now, git outta here and stay away from my family. If I ever see your face again, I swear next time you'll be face to face with the deadly side of my Smith and Wesson."

I could hear the store manager barking from across the other side of the counter, "We don't want no trouble here. Take your beef outside, before I call the cops."

I offered reassurance to the shop owner. "Not a problem, sir, I got what I came for." With that, I bolted out the front door and back into the shadows of a hazy day in Washington, D.C.

Researching the corporation in Florida was not hard for my assistant, Peter. Florida has what are called, "Sunshine Laws", which makes most information, public information. The corporation was run by a guy named, Robert Lentz. The mailing address was in the same area Congressman McAdams resided, so I drove over to his office to speak with him about Lentz.

When I arrived at the Congressman's office, the staff was racing everywhere. His assistant informed me, only after persuading her how important it was to speak with him, that McAdams was being detained for questioning at the FBI's office. I charged over to the building where he was being held, to see if I could help in his release.

After arriving at the FBI office, ro one would even admit McAdams was in the building. I asked to speak with my friend Agent Nesstor. He pulled some strings to allow me access to speak with Congressman McAdams. I was led into a small white room with two chairs that sat on opposite sides of a small table and a clock high up on the wall. The congressman was led in moments later where he sat on the opposite side of the table from me. He was in street clothes that looked as though he had been in for more than a day. He looked haggard.

"Cale, they think I murdered some history teacher. It's a set up. I wouldn't murder anyone. My lawyer will be getting here later today, but this is all because I was investigating something. I kept asking questions about money and what one specific fund is being used for in the nation's budget."

"Who is setting you up George? Why would they set you up for murder over a budget item?"

McAdams moved forward in his chair. "Desmond Danker, they think I murdered him. He's been investigating the same things I've been. He had a theory that the budget item is allocated to pay for children born out of wedlock by high ranking politicians. It's hush money, Cale. I can't prove it and I'm not even sure it's accurate. But it got Danker killed. There are some very important people who want this messy business to all go away. What better way than to frame me for the murder of the only other guy investigating it?"

"I'll see what I can find out for you, George. But another reason I came over here was to see if you know a guy named, Robert Lentz and some company named, Rhawnhurst something?"

McAdams practically jumped from his chair and into my lap. "You gotta be shitting me, Cale. Lentz, Lentz is the guy who pays the bills for Mendace? Now I know the President is behind all this crap! Lentz is one of the money guys connected to President Morrison. Ah man, this guy's bad news, Cale."

I sat with Congressman McAdams until my visiting rights ended. He filled me in about Lentz, Danker and what he knew. By the time McAdams was finished weaving his conspiracy tale, I knew I would be on the next flight to South Florida to acquaint myself with one, Bob Lentz.

Visiting Florida gave me an excuse to drop by and see my mother and father. It had been many months since I had last seen them. My mother griped the moment I saw her, "Caeles, that wife of yours doesn't feed you right. If you would visit your mother more often, I can give you the strength you're going to need now."

I explained to my mother without much success, "Mom, uhm, Kalani was kinda frozen in time if you remember and I have been traveling since she started to feel herself again. Besides, we have not been home since she was unthawed."

My father's approach was different. "They couldn't have picked a finer leader, my son. I'm very proud of you." It was nice to see my parents for a day, but I had much to do. I asked if they knew Lentz since he lived in the same town. In fact, they had. It turned out that Lentz owned one of the larger restaurants and night clubs in town. "The food's not as good as your mother's but I give her a break once a week or so and Lentz's place is one place we eat."

Downtown Boca Breezes, where Lentz had his establishment, was bustling with people meandering up and down the sidewalks. People were looking in shop windows, stopping in the Irish pub for pints of beer, while some of the remaining patrons were finding their way by Lentz's place for a meal. It was easy to spot Mr. Lentz. He was in the front bar telling jokes and giving away a free shot of whisky to anyone who could tell him what he shot in his round of golf earlier in the afternoon. I guessed, "Eighty-one."

"That's exactly right. Now who the hell are you? I've never seen you here before," Lentz proclaimed.

"I am a friend of George McAdams. We have some private matters to discuss, if you don't mind, Mr. Lentz."

Lentz looked at me with a crooked eye. "Georgie was a good kid, now he's all mixed with investigating some budget item. I told him a hun-dert times to let it go. I warned him that place would take his soul, but no, that kid thinks he can handle that town."

I chuckled under my breath. "I can assure you the Congressman McAdams has his soul intact. In fact, I would not be so sure he committed any crime. His soul is actually pretty clean. I doubt he has done any wrong in Washington. Now, would you like all your customers to hear the rest of our conversation, Mr. Lentz, or can we move somewhere more private?"

Lentz frowned then attempted to stare me downs. "What did you say your name was, pal?"

"I didn't, Mr. Lentz. But if you would like to step away to somewhere more private, I will tell you."

"You know what? I'm gonna show mercy on you. Maybe you don't realize that you don't come to the home of Bobby Lentz and tell him where he must go and what he must do. I'll go someplace and hear you out, but it betta be good."

"I don't mean any disrespect here, Mr. Lentz, but please."

He took me to a back office. A rather large gentleman, standing over six foot four and didn't weigh an ounce under three hundred pounds followed us in and closed the door behind us. Lentz offered me a seat. He strode to the other side of the room to his desk. He sat down leaned back in his black leather chair where he fired up a cigar.

"Cubans. They sure know how to make a fine ceegar. Now, start spilling your guts why some stranger would walk into my place and pretend like he can tell me what to do. And don't start yapping me some sob story about McAdams. I warned that punk to back off his investigation many times. He just didn't know when to quit."

"Mr. Lentz, I am not really here about McAdams. Although, the longer I look into your soul and listen to you speak, the more I think it is very possible you have something to do with his circumstance."

Lentz sat forward in his chair and attempted to scare me with his tone of voice. "You listen real good, punk. I ain't got nuttin to do with George sitting in that FBI office. Yea, I know all bout his troubles. Now, you got one last chance to tell me who you are and the real reason for you being here, if it ain't about our dear friend."

"My name is Cale Novo. I am here about a fellow by the name of Jason Mendace. The records indicate you pay the bills for his internet service. I would be willing to wager you know his real identity. What can you tell me?"

"I can tell you that you have exactly thirty seconds to leave this place and never return. If I ever see your shadow in my doorway, my associate behind you will take you on a one way ride to the local waterway. Do we understand each other?"

Lentz attempted to convince me about how special he thought he was, but he had no idea, who I was. He was about to find out. "Mr. Lentz, do you believe you have a soul? Better yet, do you believe your associate behind me does?"

"You got fifteen seconds."

"Then I suggest you answer me in those precious seconds, Mr. Lentz."

Lentz waved his arm and snapped his fingers to the hulk like man lurking behind me and pointed at me. "Yeah, I am a firm believer I have a soul. Now, your time is up."

As his associate latched on to my shoulder, I stood up. I turned in his direction and looked deep into the big man's soul. He may not have been on my list but after a quick peek into his soul, he should have been. I looked at the hulk's not so distant relative in the eyes and spoke loud enough so Lentz could hear. "I am sorry for what is about to happen. Maybe when I have the time, and you repent for your sins, I will return your soul."

The big man reached into his jacket pocket but I didn't give him an opportunity to go any further. I grabbed hold of his arm and cast off his soul to the Surrounding of Souls. He too must have believed in his soul, because he dropped to the floor. The brute was motionless.

I turned towards Lentz. He was digging into the side drawer of his desk. "Mr. Lentz, sit down, or what happened to your associate will happen to you. Now you are on the clock. You have exactly ten seconds to tell me who the real Mendace is or your soul is mine for all eternity."

"What the hell just happened to Oscar?" I now had Bobby Lentz's full attention.

"I took his soul, Lentz. I know you thought you were the most powerful man in the room, but it is time you reconsider your strengths and start answering my questions. You are down to five seconds before you find your soul on the shelf ext to Oscars."

I could already start to feel my body shake. I knew I had to act quickly.

Lentz opened up like a piñata on a kid's birthday party. "Jason Mendace is not a he or she, but a series of people. The person who writes most of the stories is some kid, looking to make favors with the Washington politicians. One of the President's cabinet members feeds this kid, Simpson, the information they want written on his blog. Simpson writes the stories under the name Mendace. In exchange, he gets tips on real stories that he writes under his real name, Josh Simpson for a Washington paper. He's a young kid trying to make a name for himself as a journalist. There is one other who writes a blog now and again, but Simpson, that's who you're after. Now please, don't hurt me."

Lentz was visibly shaking in fear. Either that, or I was shaking so much now, it was me rocking back and forth. I attempted to stand and make my exit. "Lentz, if I find out you are lying to me, I swear, I'll return and rip out your soul and not think twice."

I almost tripped over the soulless man on the floor. I heard him groan as I reached for the door knob. I knew he was still alive as I returned to the shadows.

Tracking down Josh Simpson would be an easy proposition. He wrote for the largest newspaper in the Washington area. I showed up at the front desk in the lobby of the newspaper building claiming I had a story but could only offer it to Simpson. Within minutes, a kid who didn't look like he even had to shave on a daily basis was standing in my shadow, acting as eager as a rookie ballplayer seeking his first base hit.

"Ok, mister, I'm a busy guy, whaddya have for me?" I stood there looking at this punk kid thinking he's really not making a good first impression with his attitude.

"Mr. Simpson, or should I call you Jason Mendace, we need to go somewhere more private."

"I'm not going anywhere with you, dude. You got something to say to me, then let er rip, otherwise, I got real news to dig up. And you can shove that Mendace bull crap back up your ass, cause others have already tried to make that one stick."

I was tired. I wanted to head home to California and leave the soul stealing career behind for a few weeks. I wanted to grab up my family and enjoy life again. This kid pushed me over my line of being patient. I no longer cared to make one hundred percent certain he was my target. He would be my next stolen soul.

"Ok, Josh, so you're not Mendace, my mistake. But you need to follow up on the story about the congressman being questioned over at the FBI for murder. He didn't do it. He was investigating a budget item and I believe the President or possibly Speaker Corbin has set him up for murder. It could be your biggest story yet, if you care to be a real journalist and connect the dots."

The punk kid, who takes five days to get a five o'clock shadow, again laughs at me. "You came over to my work place to tell me that McAdams is being set up for murder by the President of the United States? That's supposed to be your big story? Get outta here before I have security toss you to the street."

"Josh, you will look into this story for me. I consider George McAdams a friend. When you decide to work for me, I will return your soul. Until that day, consider yourself just another lazy journalist, missing a soul."

He turned to walk away but as he did I grabbed his arm. He yelled for security but it was too late. I instantly removed his soul. I watched Josh Simpson bend over at the knees as if he was catching his breath. By the time security made it to the front lobby, even my shadow had disappeared.

14

"Elder Stella was inflicted with a gunshot wound on a mission. It's not certain he will survive, Elder Novo." Those were the first words heard from my assistant Peter, upon my return from Washington. He concluded with, "We will need to replace him on the Council if he doesn't survive."

I immediately ran over to the office of Brandon Bink, who I assumed assigned Elder Stella the case. "What were you thinking, Bink? First you send my wife on a dangerous assignment soon after she started to feel healthy, now you send an old man into a dangerous situation. There must have been a better way to handle things."

Bink fired back. "Elder Novo, let's be very clear about something. I am given a list of souls to be taken and I have thirty three people I can choose from to complete the task. I don't have a list of gun owners or how dangerous the mission might be. Everyone was on assignments and my case load was getting backed up. Elder Stella volunteered. The soul he was to remove was of an elderly bank robber who was accused of his crimes but jumped bail and fled to Spain. The guy was reported to have coffee at an outdoor café every morning. It should have been a two day trip. Elder Polus looked over the assignment and assumed someone on the Council could handle it."

"Guess what Bink, it's never easy. You try finding these people and getting within proper range to remove someone's soul."

"Well from what I understand, Elder Novo, you must be pretty good at it, because you took a couple extra souls on your last trip." Just what I needed, lip from Brandon Bink. "No one else on the Council leaves for an assignment unless I know about it, Bink, that's a direct order. We can call it your Soul Directive."

Bink stood defiantly, blocking my path to the door. "You get your Soul Directive signed by the remainder of the Council and I'll consider it. Until then, I suggest you do your job with the same level of competence as I do mine." I really wanted to fire Bink from his duties but we were shorthanded and the guy really did do his job well.

In speaking with the members of the Council, we had to start reviewing possible candidates should Elder Stella not survive. One option was to bring back Charon Orcus to the Council but I immediately voted no. I had two others who agreed. There was still a movement to bring him back to power. Our Council was a divided mess. I also couldn't get my decree signed where I had to approve any elder permitted on a mission.

I couldn't even get my grandfathers backing. "Caeles, it's a rare time when one of the Council steps out on an assignment. You're the only one still capable of taking on even the easiest of thefts. I wasn't aware Elder Stella was taking on a mission. Had I known, I would have done our best to persuade him to decline."

It was getting to the point where I had no idea why I was chosen to be the leader of the Council. I couldn't get any of my ideas passed as law, or my ideas to be taken seriously. Most of the staff was borderline belligerent and two Council members made it perfectly clear they wanted Charon Orcus to return to the Council, despite my objections. They also didn't hide the fact they also preferred Orcus to return as our leader.

The following day, Kalani returned from her assignment. She looked healthy and was happy to be back in the field removing souls. I was fully aware we were shorthanded but I still wanted her to take a vacation before heading out on her next case. I convinced her to return to California with me for a couple of weeks with our son, Nic.

While at home, Kalani and I discussed the declining numbers among our soul stealers. She floated an idea to see how I would react. "Cale, I think the next opening on the Council should be filled by a woman. It might encourage other women to step forward. Women, who have the ability to steal, yet choose not to pursue our highest calling."

"Maybe, but our charter does not allow for women on the Council, my dear wife. Besides, the last thing I need right now is to be lobbying to install my wife on the Council."

I immediately realized I would be eating a cold dinner alone. I was also being presumptuous with my thinking. I think the cold meal I would be eating later was a bargain compared to that stare my wife throws my way when she thinks I am being a chauvinistic pig, or worse.

"Let's get one thing straight, Cale. I mighta been frozen in time for a few weeks but my brain isn't stuck in medieval times, like yours. Maybe I didn't expect you to jump at my idea but I also thought by now you would hear me out before jumping to conclusions. I wasn't talking about me. I met a woman who is one of us in the compound, while I was recuperating. We hadn't met before. Bink informed me that she is a highly successful stealer. Plus, she doesn't take a few extra along the way, like you seem to do."

My beautiful wife was never at a loss for words. I knew my next words needed to be precise. It also occurred to me that being a leader meant keeping an open mind to all ideas. After all, I was being critical of the Council for not listening to me and I was doing the same thing in not allowing my wife to speak her mind.

"Ok, you're right, Kalani. Please tell me about this woman you met. I find it odd our paths have never crossed, but tell me about her."

"Well, my dear husband, let's not forget, you and I never met in the compound and neither of us had any idea we were both soul stealers when we met in Hawaii. So don't assume you know everyone of our disciples."

My loving wife never missed an opportunity to make sure she made her point, sometimes with a twisted edge taking a piece of me with it. She continued.

"Her name is Tasha Timmons. She rarely visits the compound and, unlike you, she doesn't have half the world's authorities capturing her on video cameras. She has little family and relishes taking souls. Unlike you, it never crosses her mind to give em back. Bink tells me she's very efficient and even more private."

"It sounds to me like she would never accept a position on the

Council, Kalani. Why would someone so private and happy in their career want to change?"

Again with the stare before she continued to complain in my ear. "Cale, sometimes you speak and your brain isn't functioning. Did it occur to you that maybe she wants the power the Council would provide her? Did it occur to you that maybe she sees the possibility in being a role model for others? No, of course it didn't because you've got your narrow minded point of view that you love to hang on to. Plus you rarely take the time to think, before you speak."

Kalani had pushed my limits of wanting to be polite. "Talk about someone speaking without thinking! Who's the one who's tried to introduce the idea of us returning souls after decades, if not centuries? Who's the one attempting to rediscover our true mission on earth? Who's the one attempting to bring our disciples back from the brink of extinction? I love you dearly, but sometimes you don't give me enough credit for all the times I do in fact think beyond my little shell. And you know it."

"You're right, Cale. I apologize. I was just all jazzed up in meeting Tasha. She's the first female soul stealer I've ever met. She's such a cool lady and I wanted you to keep an open mind, that's all. I didn't ask her if she would even consider a position on the Council. I didn't think it was my place. But I've got her number and she's expecting your call. I told her that the leader of the Council was making a point in meeting the remaining stealers and she was next on the list.

Another stare. This time Kalani moved closer and offered me a soft kiss on the lips as she made her way to the bedroom. She slowly turned with one last stare and comment.

Don't mess it up, big guy. You got my blood pressure all out of whack so I'm going to lie down. Order yourself some pizza for you and Nic."

I'm sure even fifty years from now, she will always know how to get the last word.

Later that evening and with only two slices of pizza left in the box, I stretched out in my favorite lounge chair to enjoy a basketball game with Nic. The phone rang. It was Agent Elliot Nesstor on the other end.

"Cale, we got problems, buddy. I need you back in D.C, right now."

"No chance, Elliot. I'm taking a few days with the family, enjoying some long overdue down time. I will get there in a couple of weeks on my way back to the compound."

Nesstor became more insistent. "Cale, this is no game. My boss matched your image from video cameras from when you came to see McAdams in our office to the film they had on you when you did whatever you did to that kid reporter. Don't forget, Cale, he also met you back in New York at that prison with me. He knows I know you."

I attempted to calm Nesstor. "So what, Elliot? So your boss has me on camera grabbing the kids arm, big deal. I did not kill the kid. There is nothing he can do to me. Besides, he will never find me."

"You're not understanding me, Cale. The kid's not written a blog since you zapped him. Very powerful people want the kid to produce. My boss is using me as bait to find ya. If you don't return that kid's soul, I'm getting axed. My boss doesn't believe in your soul taking abilities, but I do. He knows we keep in contact and you feed me leads. He doesn't care what you need to do. He doesn't even care what you did to that kid, but someone is putting a ton of pressure on him to find you and fix that kid. Someone out there believes you're real and that someone must know the kid is Mendace. Fix the kid for me, Cale, or I'm toast with the Bureau."

"It is not that simple, Elliot. There is a process I have to go through to return a soul, and there are no guarantees the kid's soul will even return with me. I won't bore you with all the steps, but it is not like I blink my eyes and rattle my brain and make it all better. I'd like to help you, but I really can't do it this time. I will make it up to you next time I find a real juicy case. I promise. I will make sure you get credit for the arrest."

"Cale, please, if you don't make that kid right, my career's over. The only job I'll be able ta git will be breaking up squabbles between blue hairs on deaths door playing mahjong in South Florida. I've done you tons a favors over the years, you owe me."

"Yeah, I hear that a lot. Ok, tell your boss I will try to return the kid's soul. However, in return, you have to get a peek at the McAdams file and specifically see if there are any remarks about Danker. If you can look into that for me, I will do my best to restore Simpson's soul."

"Nesstor started to laugh. "You know what? You may have given me a few big breaks along the way, but you really are a major pain in the ass. How's that soul stealing wife of yours?"

"She's the same, ripping souls and making me order out for pizza. I'll see you in a couple days. Oh, and tell your boss, he should be careful what he wishes for. He might not like it once Josh Simpson gets his soul returned. Simpson's going to owe me and his task will be to find out who is setting up McAdams. I have a feeling it might be the same people who are pressuring your boss to get the kid back writing his blog."

I spent the night tossing and turning doing my best to rest. I knew Kalani wasn't going to take the news well that I was about to return another soul. I had convinced her to take time off to spend with the family and now I was the one running off again. But this was the life we chose.

I decided to visit the Surrounding of Souls from my home with Kalani watching over my body. If my body is disturbed during the process, my own soul could be lost forever. Kalani knew the risks every time I attempted this process and made sure all the doors were locked and the phones shut off. Nic was at his tutoring lesson.

My mind was at peace as my wife stood guard. The spirits lifted my soul to a busy intersection in the center of an unidentified town. I could see two cars, both front ends smashed into each other. It was a mangled mess. A man dressed in a dark suit, red silk tie, white shirt and polished shoes came out from behind the car closest to me. As he came closer, I noticed the blood dripping from his forehead.

"I am the gatekeeper of The Surrounding of Souls, what brings you here?" The bloody man asked.

"I'm the soul of Caeles Novo. My mission is to find the soul of Josh Simpson and return it to his earthly body."

The man moved closer. I could now see blood seeping from

under his jacket.

"That won't be possible. Joshua should have been in the front seat, not Jeffery. He cheated life once, I will see to it, it won't happen a second time."

"Fate has its own way," I responded. "May I ask who you are, Gatekeeper?"

"I'm Jeremiah Simpson, the driver of the dark blue sedan over there. I am also the father of Joshua and Jeffery. I switched Jeffery and Joshua in their seats so that I could help Jeffery with his homework on our way home from school. A drunk driver hit us and I was killed along with Jeffery. It's all my fault Jeffery isn't alive today."

I was running low on time. The spirits were about to lift my soul back to my earthly body. "Mr. Simpson, I am sorry for your loss, but there is no reason to lose two sons. I can restore Josh's soul and make him whole again. It's why I'm here."

"Joshua will be staying here with me. He never could appreciate what he had in life. My two sons may have been identical twins but they couldn't have been more different. It was Jeffery who had a future. I took that from him. No, you can have the soul of Jeffery, but I'll never release Joshua's soul. Be on your way."

"Mr. Simpson, it can't work this way. Only the soul of Josh can be restored to his body. Please, as a father myself, I would be horrified to lose my son. But you have a chance to turn Josh's life around. This might be what he needs to live a better life."

My body was aching for the return of my soul. Time was

short. The gatekeeper appearing as the father of the two boys moved even closer. The stench of death was wafting everywhere.

"Take the soul of Jeffery and put it in the body of my disappointing son, Joshua. Should the time arise when you find a human worthy for a soul as gifted as my son Jeffery, I will allow you to return the soul of Joshua to its original body. You may move the soul of Jeffery to continue in another earthly body, until that body ceases to exist. Jeffery's soul, nor mine, will ever be at peace until Jeffery has lived a fruitful life. My decision is final."

As the spirits were lifting my soul and returning it to my earthly form, the soul of Jeffery was attached. I was given little choice. Nesstor is a valuable asset and friend. I needed to protect him.

The next morning, Kalani and I flew to National Airport where Elliot Nesstor picked us up. I brought Kalani along since in the past when I'd restore a soul, I would need to recuperate. I can no longer be that vulnerable to the world after restoring a soul. I have too many searching for me. Elliot knows firsthand the powers Kalani has and the lengths she will go to protect me. I trusted Elliot, not his superiors. Kalani would ensure my safety after restoring Simpson's soul.

We were taken to a small apartment building more than thirty minutes from the monuments and museums that dot the landscape along the nation's capital. Elliot assured us there would be no interference from his superiors. Time would be given to restore a soul back to Josh Simpson. Kalani and I would be free to leave after the task was completed. Elliot had never lied to me in the past, but he could have been lied to by his superiors.

Kalani and I walked around the perimeter of the building and the adjacent street. In our line of work, not only do we have devices that pick up signals from radio transmissions, but we both have developed a keen eye for traps over the years. I had little choice but to trust Nesstor since the longer I retained two souls, the more I was putting myself at risk of hurting my own. Everything around the area seemed innocent.

Agent Nesstor led us into a small lobby where we took the elevator up to the third floor. We walked down a narrow hallway till he had us stop at the third door on the left. He knocked on the door. He knocked again. Josh Simpson opened the door wide enough to see his face.

Elliot spoke first. "Mr. Simpson, I'm agent Elliot Nesstor, we spoke on the phone two days ago. This is Mr. and Mrs. Novo. They would like to speak with you. May we come in?"

Simpson's eyes were dim. His baby face pale, his speech slow. "I dunno, Agent Nesstor. I'm not into seeing guests right now. The place, I got stuff all over. No place to sit really. Come back when I'm feeling better, will ya's?"

I took the lead. "Josh, we met at your work place a week ago. I can help you feel better, but I need a few minutes of your time. Please, nobody cares about how your place looks, but I promise, I can make you feel better."

"Why, you some kinda doctor? I dunno. I been feeling down for days. Besides, I don't remember meetin you."

As Simpson started to close the door, Nesstor shoved his way in. He pushed Josh onto the sofa. Nesstor called for me. "Hurry, Cale. Do your magic and let's get outta here."

Simpson refused to settle down. He made every effort to break free from Nesstor's clutch. The much stronger Nesstor was doing his best impression of a ranch hand roping a calf for branding. "Come on, Cale, zap this kid, hurry!"

Kalani stood there laughing. "Yeah, hurry up, Cale, and don't miss. I'd hate for the kid's soul to er d up in the sofa pillow or worse yet, in Elliot."

Nesstor stood straight up and let go of Josh. "Holy shit, Cale, is that even possible?"

Kalani did her best to torture poor Elliot. "Yeah, why? Cale didn't tell you? He's only maybe seventy-five percent accurate with his aim, Elliot. If I were you, I'd duck."

Simpson now runs down the hallway screaming, "Somebody help me, vampires broke into my apartment. I'm being attacked. Help! Help!"

Lucky for us, most people work in the middle of the afternoon. Only one person on the hallway could be bothered to check the commotion. An elderly lady poked out from behind her door. "What's all the noise about? I'm tryin to watch Oprah. Do I need to call the police?"

Nesstor flashed his badge at the woman still in her long nightgown, "It is ok, Madam. I've got things under control. Please, go back into your apartment and all will be fine momentarily."

Kalani yells, "Yeah and do it fast, cause I'm the head vampire and I'm a hurting for some fresh old lady blood."

Nesstor grabbed Simpson just as he attempted to step inside the awaiting elevator. He then put a cloth against Simpson's nose and mouth and rendered him unconscious. "That'll shut the little prick up," Nesstor said with delight.

We all moved back into the tiny apartment. "Ok, Cale, do whatever it is you do before people start snooping around or the old lady calls the cops."

"Elliot, I've only restored a soul and few times. I've never tried it with someone knocked out. What did you do?"

"Don'cha worry bout how I do my job or what I slipped em. Just give the kid his soul back. I need him back at his computer in the morning or my boss is going to be all over my ass and yours."

Kalani and Nesstor stood guard at the door. Sirens were now within ear shot. Relaxing my mind was a chore under these conditions. Nesstor started to tap his toe. The sound went through me as if I was front row at an AC/DC concert.

"Elliot, every tiny noise throws me off. Can you control your Buster Browns, please?"

Kalani took another shot at Nesstor. "Yeah, the louder it is in here, the better chance Cale has at missing his mark and that thing could go bouncing and land up about anywhere."

"Maybe its best I wait on the other side of the door," Nesstor quipped.

Kalani latched and bolted the door as Nesstor left for the hallway.

"Be quick about it, honey, we're about out of time here," Kalaini warned.

I focused my best and released Jeffery's soul into the body of

176

Joshua Simpson. I didn't like the idea of not being able to speak with him once I restored a soul but Kalani was correct. We were out of time.

Kalani and I both scrambled out the third floor window and down the fire escape to the window on the second floor. Lucky for us, the window was not latched and no one was home. We went down the stairwell to the first floor and out the back door of the apartment building. The sirens we heard had gone past the building and on to wherever they were intended.

We will never really know for sure how much Elliot Nesstor knew about the other three men who were spying on us in the area. Maybe Elliot had enough faith that we would never be captured. Kalani could hear the men breaking down the door as we were escaping out the back. She had been monitoring them in her earpiece the entire time. She never heard Nesstor speak with them. She also never heard the three say anything that would indicate they were even associated with Elliot. But she knew exactly how much time we had and that we were being set up. I'm sure we were to be detained once Simpon's soul was returned.

Our people are like a fine art photograph. Everyone looks at the highlights and think they see the image. However look deeply into the shadow area. That's where you have to look and where we thrive.

15

Once back at the compound, I found my way to Brandon Bink to check on Kalani's next assignment. I wanted to ensure she would be given one I deemed relatively safe and close to our home. I still wasn't convinced she was back at full strength. It was time to flex my power as leader of the Council, or resign. These men may have more seniority but their policies have almost wiped us from the earth. Change was coming or I was going.

The report on Elder Stella wasn't encouraging. He would survive the bullet wound but he had lost too much blood. The transfusion was with blood matched his A positive analysis, but his blood couldn't be duplicated with blood from a local blood back. In the short term, Elder Stella had lost his ability to see into another's soul and remove one. Should he ever regain enough strength to take on the stress of being an advisor to the Council, we would consider it. However, his era of being a full time member of six had concluded.

The first Council meeting upon my return started out as so many had been before, a low tolerance of my ideas. Nothing I said was being taken seriously. I sat gazing around the room at paintings of past Council members on the egg shell colored walls wondering why I was squandering my time. It was time to assert leadership or go back to stealing broken souls fulltime. Kalani and I had been very competitive in the past about who could steal the most souls in a year. Maybe it was time to bring back our friendly competition and relieve my boredom sitting in a room with four old men rehashing the same tired concepts.

I interrupted the tiresome speech of the four. "With all due respect fellow Council members, my ideas are going to be considered with more sincerity immediately, or my time here has ended. You all turned to me for leadership when I banished your past leader. If you all think I intend to sit here, eat fine food, drink fine wine and aspire to be a leader in name only, you are mistaken. I am not that person."

As usual my grandfather was first to speak, "Elder Novo, we do consider all your thoughts as having immense value."

Who was he trying to fool? "Possibly, but not enough to implement them? No, here are my terms to carry on as a member of this Council. You will take my proposals more seriously starting with my Soul Directive. It will state that no Council member can leave on an assignment without my approval and it starts immediately. I am also going to meet with one of our own, Tasha Timmons, about a possible replacement for Elder Stella. I will then fly to Washington to check on Simpson, then on to Texas with an agreement in my hand signed by this Council that will allow Dr. Grayson Winfield to have blood samples from many of our disciples. He will use the samples for research to help restock our bloodlines. He will create more sou stealers from our disciples who want to steal but have not been able to complete their training. In exchange for his efforts, should he succeed, he will no longer be banned from our compound and will be accepted back into our fold. These are my terms and are not debatable. If you accept, I will stay on as leader of the Council. Should you say no, consider it my resignation."

"Outrageous," was the first word I heard from Elder Polus. "You have done nothing but bring turmoil to this Council room every time you enter it. I knew from the first time you stood before us in your youth, with your ridiculous rants, you were trouble."

"Now, now, Elder Polus," Elder Rex said. Elder Novo does make some valid points. It's a fact that our ability to keep up with the backlog of broken souls is impossible with our shrinking number of capable soul stealers. We shouldn't be so quick to dismiss him."

"He did just fine when he would take souls and move on to the next one," Elder Robus stated. "Now the fool gives back the ones he's taken. I agree with Elder Polus, let him resign. We don't need anyone giving us demands to remain in this Council. His votes count no more than mine or yours, Elder Rex. Why give him power over our assignments?"

"For one, maybe we have grown too old and foolish to know our own limitations like our dear colleague, Elder Stella," my grandfather stated. "Think about what he's asking for here. Not one of us has gone on an assignment for years. I don't see any of us going on one in the future. Secondly, he only wants to meet with this Timmons woman. And lastly, so what if he offers a few blood splatters to Doctor Winfield?"

"You really aren't thinking this through, Elder Spia," Elder Polus retorted. "If Winfield has our bloodlines, think of the damage he can cause us."

I needed to calm the room. "Gents, Winfield has not even heard my terms. You are all getting upset over very little. If you cannot even agree to these minor demands, what future do I really have as your leader?"

The room went silent except for a few quick, low tone grumbles. Robus sat back in his chair crossing his arms with a look of defiance. Polus looked skyward refusing to look at anyone else on the Council. The other two looked at me waiting on something. What, I was not sure of, but dissention filled the room leaving me with little else to breathe.

"Since it seems clear the four of you do not like the idea of me controlling when you can go out on assignments, let's go another way. I have no issues with taking on assignments. I certainly can fill my requirements. Let's pass a law stating all Council members must steal a minimum of four souls a year or your seat on the Council is revoked or suspended until you fill your quota.

Elder Polus again voiced his displeasure with my suggestion. "How dare you suggest I no longer help in our survival. I have for decades been loyal and dedicated to all tasks put in front of me. But there comes a time, even for us, our bodies can no longer tolerate the complexities of stalking a broken individual and removing their soul. Quotas are unacceptable."

"That is exactly my point, Elder Polus. The time has come for the four of you to focus on rebuilding our future and not leaving here on a whim because Bink has a backlog of souls. I am attempting to protect you from yourselves. More importantly, I was bringing what I thought should be a simple unanimous vote to this Council. You are proving no matter what I suggest here, it will be voted down. It is for that very reason, I resign."

"Wait!" Elder Rex raised his voice louder than I had ever heard it. "It's time to accept the fact our time is nearing its conclusion. We have known this for decades, yet we struggle to hang on to our power. And to what end? If we allow Elder Novo to resign, we are doomed to lead our people into extinction. I'm not claiming Elder Novo to be our savior, but I am claiming we have been assisting in our own demise."

Elder Spia, my grandfather concurred. "Four of us have been on this Council for close to a century. During that time, our agents have declined by over seventy percent. We've watched as others have wed pure human bloodlines, thinning our gene pool. We all agreed it wasn't our responsibility to create laws demanding our lines remain pure. But we have paid a sacrifice for our leniency.

Elder Polus again fought back. "Are you suggesting we are not only lazy but negligent?"

"I'm suggesting we have ruled in a time of decline and did little to reverse its effects. If we allow Elder Novos to abandon the Council, our ruin will only accelerate. We may have acted in haste in appointing him leader, but to ignore his small demands now would be carelessness."

Elder Rex spoke again with a demanding tone. "I know Elder Novo would be doing me a favor by keeping me secure in this compound. I demand a vote on the law entitled Soul Directive which gives the authority of the leader of this Council to approve any assignments of Council members."

The vote was four to one in favor with only Elder Polus dissenting.

Elder Rex spoke again after the vote. "Let's forget all this nonsense about resignations and who controls what assignments. I for one have long retired from removing souls and so has everyone else on this Council, other than Elder Novo. This should have been an easy vote."

The room quickly cleared out with the first of my suggestions made into law, on the books as HC13001, The Soul Directive. Without another Council meeting scheduled for weeks, it was time to visit with Tasha Timmons, Josh Simpson and Grayson Winfield. I was also given a new assignment.

Peter sent me a copy of the personnel file on Tasha Timmons for me to read while on the airplane to meet her. I could see why Kalani was impressed. Tasha was born in Canada, but like most of us, her family moved around the world. She studied at Princeton, Harvard, Cambridge as well as the Moscow State Technical University. She was fluent in English, French, German, Italian and Russian. Tasha also understood some of the Scandinavian languages. By her height and weight listed in the file, she stood taller than most women but petite. From her photo pinned inside her file, I could see she had strawberry blonde hair that frames her face. The report also claims she had a tattoo of a small skull with wings on her inner thigh. She had stolen more souls than anyone over the past six months and had been in front of the Council over the years for questionable behavior. She was single with no permanent living address on file. I didn't want to read too much into the report. I wanted my own impression of her to determine if she would make a strong candidate.

We arranged to meet in Stockholm, Sweden, at a place on the waterfront called Pontus by the Sea. I immediately recognized her from her photo and with a friendly smile waved her over to my table.

Despite traveling the world and eating in many different places, this restaurant was different. It was fighting to have an upscale look with elegant tables and chairs yet the walls filled with bookshelves and old tattered books. The others section was filled with smaller weather beaten wooden tables and an open air, lovely view of the sea. I was struggling attempting to decide if I should grab a Hemingway novel off the shelves or sip my espresso and enjoy the view.

As Tasha approached, it was uncomfortable at first. Neither of us would sit with our backs to the door. We had to swing the rustic brown table and deck chairs to make her feel at ease. Luckily, she had eaten there a few times while on assignment and the staff recognized her.

With broken Swedish she quickly ordered for us both. Settling back comfortably in her chair, her hands folded on the table in front of her, she smiled and waited for me to disclose my real reason for our meeting.

I smiled back at her. As her file had indicated, she carried herself as a strong and accomplished woman. I leaned forward on my seat, resting my arms on the table and began our initial meeting.

"Miss Timmons, my wife Kalani, was very impressed after meeting you. She thought it best that you and I meet. Thank you for agreeing to meet with me here. I usually do not like to interfere with someone while on an assignment but this was the most convenient time for me."

"Let me set the record straight from the beginning, Mr. Novo.

Just because I'm single doesn't mean you and your wife can take advantage of me. I'm not into any kinky style swinging. Your wife was cute and all, but it's not my thing."

"I have no idea what my wife said to you, but I can assure you, I am not here for perverse reasons. It is strictly for business."

Tasha Timmons peered back at me with eyebrows arched, "Uh huh, they all say that in the beginning and then I find myself drunk and naked in some hotel overlooking the Paris skyline. I know your type too well. Pervert."

I sat there watching the boats pass by, confused over what Kalani could have said to this woman to bring on this type of reaction.

"Miss Timmons, are you aware of whom I am? I am the leader of the Council, Elder Caeles Novo."

"Mr. Novo, that's a fancy title, but it doesn't give you any special rights or privileges with me. I'm here out of respect for your title, but if you think I'm going to be the stuffing in your cookie, count me out. If you really want to talk business, I'm all ears, but if not, then I'll assume this meeting is over."

I was growing more perplexed by the moment. "What on earth did Kalani say to you?"

Her jade colored eyes now stared back at me with a hint of puzzlement.

"Your wife told me that she was really impressed with me. She also stated that you both could use a woman like me because she couldn't think of having another man rule her, she wanted a woman. She said that you had a lot of control over the situation and that you would soon be looking for a strong woman for the top position. Pervert."

I had to laugh. I imagined it was an easy mistake to make.

"Miss Timmons, possibly I can see your confusion, but I am not a swinger, nor is my wife, so please refrain from assuming you know why I am here."

Tasha shrugged her shoulders and crossed her arms along her chest "Well, I must admit, you didn't seem the type in that stuffy suit and tie practically cutting off your air supply. But then again, what do I know about what your type looks like in day light."

"Tasha, that's enough. This conversation will end and end badly if you don't allow me to tell you why I am really here."

"You're right. Possibly I'm showing poor taste. What then do you and your wife really want from me?"

I took a moment to allow the air to clear. After a long sip of my tea, I answered with a profession sounding voice. "My dear Kalani believes it is time for the Council to be represented by a woman. She thinks you would be the perfect choice. I am here to see if I concur or not. I am considering adding your name to our list of candidates. As you may or may not be aware, Elder Stella was struck with a bullet on assignment and had to resign his position on the Council."

Tasha's eyes squinted. "No, I hadn't heard that, I'm sorry. But you must be joking, right? You think I'd be a good candidate to sit up there with artifacts from the last century? Do you really think you control something or someone? No one controls me, and I wouldn't let the Council members watch my goldfish."

This woman was really starting to annoy me but I trudged on. "I had the same reaction you are having right now, Miss Timmons. I think those men have ruled long past their capabilities to lead. It is why we are looking for people like you. I want you to take some time and think about what it means. Serving on the Council is our highest calling."

"Robbing souls then on to the next person is what I do, Mr. Novo. I don't wear suits, and I don't like to control others. I take from my subjects and do my job. That's my true calling in life."

I needed to change the direction of a conversation that started poorly and wasn't getting much better with time. "Please, I want you to think about it. And on a totally different topic, I also want to know why you aren't married or want to start a family? Our numbers are dwindling, we really need more like you to produce offspring and start a family. We need all our kind with your ability to keep our bloodlines strong."

Tasha pointed her finger at me. "I knew this was about getting me butt naked in some seedy hotel. What's wrong with you people in that compound? Every time I visit, Bink is peeking down my blouse and asking me out on dates, and now you. For a moment there, I really did think this was about me joining the Council. I can see it was always about your sexual fantasy. Pervert."

My patience had run out. "Get over yourself, lady. If you're not interested in being on the Council then fine, but the other question was merely because we're attempting to find ways to restore our numbers. Heed my words. Soul stealing is a lonely and largely thankless duty. It's nice to have someone you can relate to and cozy up with at the end of a mission. I have the one I cozy with and that's Kalani. There's no room for you in our bedroom. But if you change your mind about the Council, let me know."

I stuck her with the check and left quickly. Our meeting had not gone as planned. I called Kalani to let her know I didn't think Tasha was ready to serve on the Council. It was a brief conversation since Kalani assumed I turned Tasha away from wanting to serve. I was in no mood to be taking any crap from my wife. It was time to head to Washington.

16

No one knew how Josh Simpson might react to carrying his brother's soul. Our historian had no knowledge of it ever being attempted in the past. I needed to check on Josh to make sure I had not made a dreadful error. My hope was that Josh's mind wouldn't corrupt his twin brother's soul, now residing in Josh's body. Possibly the new soul would win the inner battle that was likely to happen between body and soul.

I assumed the authorities weren't still watching Simpson, but I wanted to keep a safe distance to be sure. I didn't alert Agent Nesstor I was in town as an extra precaution. I didn't think Nesstor would help in having me captured, but it was possible his phones were being tapped. His boss knew we stayed in close contact.

In following Josh around for two days, I learned he took public transportation to and from his office. The second day, I followed him to the subway station after work. We both walked down several steps in a well lit stairwell with hundreds of other eager workers heading to and from work. There were also a few people looking for spare change or others passing out leaflets.

Josh was dressed in blue jeans, sneakers, a well worn black sweater and an Orioles ball cap. He was easy to track since most others in the subway station all wore your standard Washington attire of fancy suits. The majority of women draped themselves in dark colored pant suits or expensive looking skirts and blouses. Josh looked every bit the young, slightly disheveled, just out of college type, lounging around town.

I moved closer as he jumped on to a subway car and sat next to him.

"Josh, don't be alarmed. I am not here to harm you in any way. We have met twice. The last time we met was in your apartment when I told you that I could make you feel better. Do you remember me?"

"I do. Don't' try anything funny or I'll stop this train and call for security."

"Relax, Josh, honestly I am here to check on you and ask for your help."

Josh gave me a startled look. "Me give you help? Why the hell would I ever help you?"

"Because I am the one who gave you back a soul and made you whole again."

Another startled look from Simpson, "You are a frigging lunatic who needs serious help, that's who you are. I've been studying judo since you attacked me. I suggest you move away before I hurt you."

"Josh, you are not going to hurt me and I am not going to hurt you. I know you are trying desperately to make a name for yourself as a reporter. I also know you wrote that blog credited to Jason Mendace. I know about your father and brother killed in a car wreck. I know all about you. So listen to me closely. Congressman McAdams is being framed for murder. I am too busy to prove it myself, but I am positive something is going on. I need you to investigate that story for me."

"The guy is guilty. There is no story. Like I said, you're a freak and I don't want you anywhere near me. Now get out of my face."

People sitting near us were taking notice that Josh was getting upset. I needed a way to calm him and make him interested in digging up the story surrounding Congressman McAdams.

"Josh, if I were you, I wouldn't believe a word of what I am about to tell you either. However, the reason you felt ill for a while then recovered and possibly even feel differently is because you were lost. You had lost your soul. All I can tell you is that with the help of your brother and father, you have been given a second chance to do right with your career. You don't need to be a shill for the President and report lies and half truths about his opponent in the upcoming election. I am telling you, this story about the Congressman will make a name for you. One you can be proud of."

"Look freak, stop talking about my dad and brother. You don't know them. They died a few years ago, so stop acting like you just spoke with em."

"I won't attempt to convince you of anything, Josh. You will either look into the story or not. However, let me leave you with one last bit of information. I am sure you remember the time when you were fifteen years old and your house was robbed. Your brother didn't lock the door. You knew he was going away on a trip with friends that coming weekend. He was afraid he wouldn't be allowed to go over his forgetfulness. You had both been warned about locking the door since it was not the first time you two had left it open after school. You took the punishment for your brother by telling your father, it was you who left the door unlocked. You were grounded for a month. Your father now knows it was your brother. He asked me to tell you he is sorry he didn't press your brother harder for the truth. Everyone assumed it was you from the start."

"No one knows the truth expect me and my brother Jeff! Who told you about that?"

"Your bother Jeff is much closer to you now than ever before. And by the way, your father knows your brother paid you a hundred dollars from his birthday money as a bribe so you would lie."

Josh Simpson sat there with a stunned looked. Moments later, the train stopped at his destination. Josh gathered his bag and stood with the others waiting for the door to open. Just before he got off the train, I left him with one last plea.

"Help Congressman McAdams, Josh. Your father is watching."

The door opened. People scrambled. Josh got off the train but watched me through the window as the train pulled away. I disappeared back into the shadows.

Next stop was to Texas to visit with Doc Winfield. I wasn't sure how he would take my proposal but if he truly was a healer as he professed, then possibly he would help. I also wanted to check to see how Nurse Simon, sometimes lady of the evening, Rose and on part time librarian, Isabella was doing.

I arrived on a rainy, blustery day in Texas. It reminded me of Winfield's personality. I didn't have much time in Texas, as I was already late in starting my next assignment. I had limited faith the Council members would be working on solutions to our real issues. If Winfield rebuked my offer, I had no other options at the moment. It was essential I had him consider it.

Nurse Simon greeted me as I entered through the medical office front door.

"Heeeey, Mr. Novo, right? I surely wasn't expecting to see you. But for me, you're always welcome. I still don't know what you did the last time you visited, but I feel so much better. You here to see Doctor Winfield? I'll tell him you're in the waitin room."

"Hi, Nurse Simon. Yes, I came to see Doc, but I also wanted to check up on you. Do you remember if the person who took your photo the day you became ill has returned to see Doc Winfield?"

"No, can't say I've seen her."

"Her? Last time you told me it was a man! Was it a woman?"

"Oh, I'm sorry Mr. Novo. My head was so mixed up last time you were here. It was like I had a bad case of the flu and I just couldn't think straight. I wish I could remember. Surely, I do. It could have been a man, maybe a woman, it happened all so quickly. I only remember feeling like my poor head exploded from my body seconds after that photo. I was barely in the room more than ten seconds after those photos were done. I only remember they had a baseball cap on and were all dressed in black. I never did see a face. Doc had me walk into the room with the camera all set up. Someone was standing behind that silly camera and bam, they took the pictures and down I went. Doc pulled me into the other room and I never did see the camera person leave."

Nurse Simon giggled, "Come to think on it, I aint never seen the photos neither."

I smiled. "It's ok. I am just happy you are feeling back to normal. Now if you don't mind, I would like to see Doc Winfield."

Moments later I was being led down that long office corridor I so despised. At the end of the hallway would be a man I still wasn't sure I could trust. I had little choice. The only good part of the walk was being escorted by Nurse Simon and her cute wiggle. I also took in a whiff of her Channel No. 5 that would drive most men to their knees. I was quickly left staring at a man scowling at me behind his messy over sized desk, as menacing as his horrible smelling aftershave.

"Well lookie here Nurse Simon. It's El-Dar Novo. The man must want our help darling, else I know he wouldn't be fixin to come to Texas just to say hey. Now would you, Novo?"

"That's what I like about you, Winfield. I've never known you to be wrong. Yet. So, yes, I am here for your help. Does that surprise you?"

Winfield waved Nurse Simon away and offered me a seat.

"I know it's not about your perty wife, Novo. Word's gotten back to me she's one healthy filly back out there doing what you people do. I also know my good ole daddy is still confined to his quarters pissing and moaning at anyone who will listen. So it's not about him. So why travel all this way to see me, eh cowboy?"

I took a deep sigh then offered my proposal.

"I need your help. In return you will be granted full access to our community, our compound as well as receiving a full apology from the Council for any accusations in the past. It will be signed by the Council, written and signed by your father with his full admission to everything you told me."

"Hell, Novo, weren't you supposed to already have gotten that letter for me the last time I helped ya? You think I trust a darn word that you utter?"

"I did what I could the last time, Doctor. But, you told me that you are a healer, did you not? I need your powers as a healer for us, right now."

"Why'd you really come here, cowboy?" Winfield sat up in his squeaky chair, staring me down.

I took another deep sigh and rolled my eyes. I was upset Winfield seemed closed off to my motive for the visit. I hoped persistence would pay off.

"I need you to discover a way of keeping our blood lines intact. We are a dying breed and you are one of the world's leading researchers on blood disorders, even if this fine looking office says otherwise."

Winfield took a sip from the bottle of water stationed at the corner of his desk. He smacked his lips in my direction. He knew exactly how to raise my blood pressure, only this time I wouldn't allow him to push me emotionally. Yet, I suspected he would try.

"You come prancing in here uninvited, eyeing my best girl's figure, insult the way my office looks, promise me nothing I damn care about, and expect me to help you? You need to gallop on outta here, Novo. Cause your time's up."

"Sure Doc, I knew you couldn't do it anyways. It's one thing to pretend like you're a real man of medicine, a healer I think you called it. It's completely another thing to actually be responsible for a cure and help your own people. I knew you were all talk. Good day, Doctor Winfield."

I stood up and started walking for the hallway when Winfield spoke up.

"Oh, so you think that half ass attempt at messing with my medical skills will be enough to get me to help you, Novo?

I stopped in my tracks and turned back to look in Winfield's direction.

"No, I really don't think so, Doctor. However, I do believe you are lying about not caring about approval from our kind. It's important to you. I am positive you believe you are a brilliant man who feels he was shoved off to some out of the way location asking for grants and hand outs to continue your research, so you can do what you do best. That upsets you, looking to others to fund your research, beyond your patients. Despite having articles written about you for your advancements in medicine, you can't get your father to say good work, son. No doubt that eats at you every single day and if you did this for us, you would be able to shove it in everyone's face. And you know that. But your disrespect for me and our people won't allow it. After all, you have your pride and an ego the size of Texas Stadium to look after, isn't that right?"

"Well damn, cowboy. Now that your perty wife is walking around and talking you think you can push me around? Hell, I could damage you boys far more than you realize. Well, I got news for you, Novo, ya'll is history. Now go fade off into a dull sunset on a tired horse with no water. You and your ilk are done, El-Dar Novo."

This was one time Winfield was not going to get the last word.

"I don't curse, Winfield. Ever. But you my good doctor are pure chicken shit. I'm willing to bet that you have helped others with your research that you disagree with, yet still heal them. But for us, your own blood, your family, you turn your back. I offered you a real chance to make your father and community proud. You could have helped continue a tradition started thousands of years ago, but your disdain for me got in the way. I guess you're not as smart as you thought you were. Good luck, Doc-Ter Winfield."

As a parting shot leaving the facility I barked at Nurse Simon, "Your boss is a coward."

I felt like I had wasted almost a week of my life. Tasha Timmons was too independent to be on the Council in my mind and Winfield surprised me to some degree. Then again, Tasha did remind me of myself in not wanting to obey the Council. Winfield was another matter. I thought attacking his desire to please his father would work, but I was wrong. It was time to allow the other members of the Council find a replacement for Elder Stella and think of another way of creating soul stealers. But next on my agenda was doing what I was really trained to do, steal a soul.

17

The latest assignment was close to my parent's home in South Florida. It involved a real estate agent with a dark soul. Chad Davidson was a tall, slender native of Boynton Beach. He was more famous around town for less than one minute in high school, then he was for putting together millions of dollars worth of real estate transactions.

Chad grew up in a middle class family. His dad worked as the butcher for the Publix market in Lantana while his mother worked as a guidance counselor for the Palm Beach County School System. He had two younger siblings.

All through school, Chad was an overachiever. His parents pushed him to keep his grades high enough to be a regular on the honor roll. He was never in any trouble for sampling drugs or late night drinking. Because of his height, he was awkward around girls, but his sense of humor more than made up for his gangly style.

His ambition in his teen years was to one day be the general manager of a sports team, preferably in the NBA, though any sport would do. His bedroom wall was pinned with sports memorabilia. Every March during spring training baseball, you could find my next target scouring the back fields looking for autographs. He was the first person to ask Cliff Owens to sign his baseball on the sweet spot.

Despite craving to be a top athlete, Chad knew his place on a team. He was willing to do whatever it took to participate on teams. Because he was well over six foot in length by the time he reached high school, he was made a reserve on the varsity basketball team his second year. He was not the best shooter, nor was he known for his ball handling and passing skills but he could rebound the ball from missed shots. That alone would garner him some playing time during games.

During his senior year in high school, Chad Davidson's basketball team won their regional championship and earned a trip to the Lakeland Center for the Florida State Championship. They won their first round game and found themselves in the Championship game on an early Saturday evening. He had broken his leg early in the season and was not yet back in basketball shape. Cleared to play a week earlier, it is still difficult for anyone to play after being shut down for eight weeks.

He watched from the bench, cheering on as his team mates battled in a back and forth, the contest tied at fifty two when Kyle Sharples fouled out. Junior Moss had already fouled out earlier in the final quarter which left Chad Davidson the only big man remaining on the bench. His leg was fully healed but he had barely gone full out in practice. There was no time to be concerned for his leg. He was instantly tapping the scorer's table checking into a tied game with less than one minute to play.

After checking in, he was lined up as the opposing team had

two free throws at the opposite end of the court from his team bench. The first shot was up and in. Chad leaned on his leg double checking his confidence. He was ready to leap high should there be a rebound.

The second shot was up. Focused squarely on the ball as it ricocheted off the opposite side of the rim from where he was standing, the other team had come down with the rebound. Rather than bringing the ball back out for another play, the big man on the opposing team went up for a shot. Chad jumped as high as he had in months, maybe ever, as he swatted the ball away and off into the friendly hands of his point guard, Tony James. The final team timeout was called by coach, Justin Orozinsky.

There may have been less than a thousand fans in the arena but the crowd was overwhelming with their enthusiasm. The instructions from Coach O were barely audible. Not all of the team was aware what play was to be executed as they walked back on the court. Chad asked Tony where he fit into the play.

Tony told his big man, "Just go stand at the top of the key and don't move."

The ball swung side to side across the court more than once with the big guy standing almost motionless as the time evaporated from the clock. Less than ten seconds now remained with the home team down a point.

As the scoreboard showed seven scant ticks left, Tony dribbled close to his big man to screen off his man and fired up a hurried shot. Chad's only instincts were to find his way to the basket in desperate search should there be a rebound. The shot fell off the left side of the rim right into his waiting hands. He came down with the ball and within an instant back up, shooting the ball only to have it fall an inch short.

Chad jumped again, this time tipping the ball back at the basket less than a second before the final horn blasted. Everyone watched as the ball fell through the goal on Chad Davidson's tip for the winning score. Half the crowd roared in victory while the other half watched in disbelief.

Standing on the podium, accepting his gold medal along with his team mates and school officials, the surprised hero would later tell me that he had no thoughts of college, a future career in sports management or even graduating high school at that moment. His only thought was how he now understood why athletes talk about selling their souls to win a championship.

Chad went on to the University of Miami and earned business degrees in management and economics. While earning his degrees, he gained a contact within the front office of the Florida Marlins baseball team. He worked with the Marlins as an intern for one year.

After graduating from college, he was offered a job working in Jupiter, Florida, where the Marlins and St. Louis Cardinals held spring training. Both teams also had minor league clubs who used the facility all summer long. He would be the assistant to the general manager of the stadium. It wasn't his ideal job of actually running a major league club, but he thought it would be a stepping stone for future success.

The following spring, the traveling secretary for the Marlins contacted Chad and asked him if he would obtain a real estate license. "We have players moving in and out of the area all spring and summer. I need someone in the area that can help me find places other than hotels for all these guys and their families to live. Are you interested?"

He jumped at the idea thinking it would be a great way to prove his worth to the major league team. He was later contacted by the Cardinals for the same position. Two months later, Chad was a licensed real estate agent. His dad thought it was a great back up plan since he kept telling his son, "God ain't making any more dirt. Use that to your advantage."

Over the course of several years, Chad became a huge asset to the Marlins and Cardinals. Although he was not officially named as general manger of the stadium and surrounding fields, he knew the position better than anyone. He would fill in at any job when needed, including selling hot dogs. He became so valuable, neither the Marlins nor Cardinals wanted to hire him away from the stadium. He was such a huge asset to both teams.

One of his responsibilities was to attend Chamber of Commerce meetings, Kiwanis Club meetings and any other civic group that would allow him to speak. He was there to promote the idea of spring training baseball, as well as minor league baseball in the region. He did it so well, many of the local politicians leaned on him for economic reports. Chad would do surveys of local hotels and restaurants during the spring and summer. His goal was to see what the economic impact was to the local economy, because of fans flocking from out of state.

He started to realize his ambitions were being stifled in what he now perceived a dead end job. Even if he eventually moved into the general manager position, it was not working in the front office of a professional team. It was a close second, but not what Chad had envisioned as a goal. He sent out resume after resume, always being frustrated with his responses.

He again went to the Marlins and Cardinals but neither club had a position for him other than a low level job reducing his already meager pay check, with no access to his real ambitions. He called the presidents of both teams one last time before finally resigning his job at the stadium.

Chad went to work for a local real estate office and quickly discovered with all his connections from the stadium and local groups he met over the years, he had a built in clientele. It was not only an easy transition but a lucrative one. He was soon earning a comfortable living working in real estate. Eventually, his skills were better suited with commercial deals in finding locations for start up businesses, as well as investments. He worked with some of the ball players who had played in the area as minor leaguers, now making large contracts as major league players.

Chad married his long time girlfriend. The couple soon had their first child. Life was pretty good. That was until the phone call. I suspect it was one reason I was assigned to remove my next targets soul.

It had taken me weeks to find Chad Davidson, the first time.

As I walked up to him, I sensed relief. It was as if he was expecting someone to seek him out.

"I'm surprised you Federal boys took so long to find me," Chad articulated.

"I am not with any police agency, Mr. Davidson. I have my own agenda for wanting to find you. May we speak privately? We need to discuss what has happened to your soul."

We sat at a poolside bar in Freeport, Bahamas. It was only the two of us situated at a small circular table with two shaky aluminum chairs. Chad blended perfectly with the tourists adorning a colorful shirt covered with a flowered design. His wet hair, swim trunks, flip flops and towel draped across the back of his chair made me believe he had just finished a swim in the nearby hotel pool.

I had the impression he wanted to cleanse his conscience to a jury before even being charged. He had me listening to his life story, his basketball heroics and all about his young family, without me offering much of a reason why I wanted to meet with him. I wanted to make a final determination if he deserved to lose his most prized possession, his soul. So I allowed him to ramble on about his real estate accomplishments, his struggles in his career, until finally, I cut him off.

"Mr. Davidson, I am here because your soul is dark and I want to know why. I would assume it has something to do with the hundreds of thousands of dollars that is now missing from the company escrow account, but I want to hear your side of the story."

"Did my wife send you?" my target asked.

"No, I am not here to return you to your wife or even find the missing funds. I will leave that to the proper authorities. I can however tell you, that if you do tell me where the money is and why you possibly stole it, I will go easier on you. It is always best to repent."

"Yeah sure, pal, and I was born yesterday. I tell you where the money is, you go and grab it up, then leave me here with my dick in my hands being sent off to prison. Fat chance."

The waitress came over to ask if we needed any refreshments as I glared at Chad Davidson. All I could think about were all the responsibilities I now had. I wanted to finish this job and get on with my life.

"Mr. Davidson, I really do not care if you tell me the exact location of the missing funds even if you do know. I want to know why your soul is so dark. That is all."

"What's the deal, pal? You been up pounding a few too many Budweisers, watching horror flicks in the room and now you think you need my soul to steal?"

"Last chance, Mr. Davidson, I have a direct line on my cell phone to one of the top FBI agents. Even if he does not care who you are, he will know who does. Tell me what I need to know and I will be on my way. You can get back to enjoying the view."

Chad eyeballed a beautiful girl making her way around the edges of the pool. He took a sip of his drink and started to tell me more about why I was assigned to track him down.

"Like I was telling ya. I know lotsa people. So one day, this guy from an outta state construction company gives me a shout on the phone, ya know. Said he got my name from someone at the Chamber of Commerce. He wants to know if I got some weight with any of the Palm Beach County Commissioners and the zoning knuckleheads. I tell him yeah. So, next thing I know, I'm the point man for putting together a deal to bring two more major league baseball teams to Palm Beach for spring training. Makes good sense, right? I mean I gotta track record with the local business people, politicians, and the baseball people know me. Seemed to make sense to me at the time," Chad stated with a soft smile.

My foot started tapping the ground as my blood pressure rose.

"Mr. Davidson, get to the point. Did you steal money? Did you beat your wife and kid? I want to know why your soul turned dark."

"Relax, pal, I'm almost done. Maybe I exaggerated a tiny bit. The construction guy, he hires me to help find a site for the new stadium. I spend days calling all round and looking at my plat books, trying to find enough raw dirt for the guy. I get hold of this old fruit farmer wanting to retire and sell his property. So, I get the old man to sign an exclusive to only sell the land through my company. Bingo, even if I don't sell it to the construction boys, I got a new listing. So I'm a happy camper. But then I get to thinking and things get weird."

I enjoyed viewing the crystal clear water off into the distance. I enjoyed even more gawking at the few remaining beauties in bikinis around the pool but Chad needed to finish the story.

"What got weird, Chad?"

"Well, think about it. Who builds a stadium on spec? I mean what if no one wants to move in? Why is some outta state guy calling me before anyone else? I'm thinking maybe the local politicians were all in with this deal. The state had to be kicking in some funding too. I mean the construction company is the one calling the shots before anyone even admitted to having funding. What's that all about?"

"Get to it, Chad, my time is valuable and you are about out of it."

"Well, I don't know how much you know about our commissioners but we got more than one cooling off behind bars. I come to find out this whole thing was a slam dunk from the beginning. One of the commissioners knew he had the funding but didn't want to put the contract for the stadium out for bid, like the law says. So, they made it look like the construction boys was the ones driving the deal, so they could build it without bidding the job. That's some pretty sneaky shit, eh?"

I had to take a moment to digest Chad's improbable story. I wanted to ask one last question more out of curiosity, now that I endured over an hour of this guys story telling.

"Where's the five hundred thousand dollar deposit on the land sale, Chad? I have also been told that's not the only escrow money missing from your company's bank account."

Chad called the waitress over and ordered another drink. He spied the same view I looked at moments earlier, before scratching his forehead and finishing his story with a rushed tone.

"Pal, I still don't know who you are. You could be a cop. You could be anybody. All I'll say is that when I found out the fix was in on the bids, I felt like I was being followed. So I figured I'd lay low over here a while. Whatever happened to the missing money, I ain't got a clue."

His story was plausible but still, I made it very clear to Chad I thought he was not being truthful. All of a sudden Chad changed his entire story.

"Ok, here's the deal. My wife's got cancer real bad and we got medical bills coming out the whazoo. I needed some of the money to pay off my bills before they took my house. I asked for another sixty days till this land deal closed but the bank refused. They could see I was gonna be making some serious coin from this deal but no one would help us out. My wife knows where all the money is. Go find her."

Now his time was up. He was done lying to me. It wasn't my job to find the money. Why was I sitting and listening to this nonsense? As I reached over to take his soul, the waitress delivered his drink.

My target about to lose his soul, stood up. "I gotta visit the boy's room. I'll be right back.

Chad used the waitress for a screen the same way he had set one for his point guard in basketball. I couldn't remove his soul without making a scene in front of the waitress or worse yet, removing hers. I followed him down a narrow concrete walkway between a shower room and the outside wall of the hotel. I could see the sign for the men's room at the end of the walkway. I watched him enter but waited several feet down the breezeway allowing myself to suck in the fresh sea air. Next thing I knew I was sitting on the ground hearing unfamiliar voices.

"Can you hear me? Go slow. Some kid whack you with dis conch shell. We are sorry, sir. Now try to sit if you can."

I tried to focus on who was speaking but my head was throbbing. My eyes wouldn't fully register to my surroundings.

"One of de ladies saw de whole ting. We know dat boy. He made trouble here before stealing from the peoples. We caught eem but your money is missing in de wallet. We will give you a free night in de hotel. Please accept our deepest apologies."

I could now see two people dressed in blue sport jackets.

"Who are you, what happened," I asked.

"A local boy hit you with dis conch shell and took your wallet. But one of de ladies coming from da shower saw da whole ting. She gave a good description and watched where he ran to. Our security camera had eet on de monitor too and our security man caught him. I am Pierre Dussuant, one of de mangers here. Dis ees, Doctor Wallace. You have been out for many minutes, sir. Let de doctor check you for concussion, please."

It wasn't until the next morning I could function properly. The hotel staff had given me a beautiful first class room to recover overnight. The next morning I went searching for Chad Davidson but he checked out. I took a flight back to South Florida once my head stopped pounding. What a couple of weeks I just survived. I had three goals and essentially failed with all three, Tasha Timmons, Doc Winfield and now Chad Davidson. I needed my mom's home cooking.

18

It's amazing how your perspective changes with some sleep and a belly full from mom's home cooking. Chad wasn't going to escape me for long. One of our disciples, who didn't have the ability to steal souls, but helped us track people, was Anne Surrey. She was better known as "Lurking Annie". She worked in the banking industry and could track people using bank records.

From my initial research on Chad, I knew about his basketball heroics. Anne found an offshore account that was set up recently using the name Lakeland5453. That was the place and score of the championship game. After money was withdrawn from an ATM machine at a hotel in Freeport, I was off to see if my target was now there. He was. As soon as Chad took money from that account, anywhere in the world, Anne would inform me.

While reading the morning paper, my dad read me part of a story from the local section.

"Paper says another commissioner is stepping down to spend more time with their family. The reporter is suggesting that maybe it's connected to the stadium deal that's being delayed. A local builder was in front of the commission wanting to know why the stadium wasn't out for bid. Didr't your guy say something about that, Cale?"

"You know what Dad, even if Chad was telling the truth on this one, he did have a dark soul. I don't want to believe all the ones on our lists are mistaken. I know we had a few who shouldn't have been on the list lately, but I think that has all been taken care of once Orcus was removed as leader."

"I don't envy you, Son, just be careful. People shouldn't lose a soul over trivial matters."

The story did give me pause to investigate the report more. I wasn't however going to change my mind, once I found him again. I was going to take his soul. But now my curiosity was getting the best of me. I stopped by to visit with Mrs. Davidson.

"I am sorry to bother you again. We met recently. Do you remember me? I am Cale Novo. I was here looking for your husband."

"Yeah, I remember. Did you have any luck in finding that bum?"

"I did. I don't know where he is now, but I did find him in The Bahamas a few days ago."

Her reaction wasn't what I expected.

"That bastard! He's been promising me trip to Nassau for years now and he goes there without me? Wait till I get my hands on him."

"Uhm, actually it was in Freeport. The reason for my visit is to ask you about two things. One. How is your health doing? Also, your husband claims that possibly you have banked some of the money from a recent land deal he was working on. I am not looking for the money. But be warned, if you do know where it is, possibly the police will be the least of your worries. I suspect Chad is wrapped up in something larger than either of you realize."

The woman stomped her feet and crossed her arms in small fit. "I knew he got his shorts all in a wad and ran out on us. It's got nuttin ta do with any missing money. I'm betting he doesn't have it. I know I don't. I took some money from our account last month and ran off to Vegas for a week. I didn't tell Chad. After our son was born, I couldn't deal with life. When I got back, I made up some story that I might have cancer and that I needed some mommy alone time for a few days. I blew a ton of our savings shootin craps. Now, he thinks I got some guy on the side. I swear, I don't, and I don't have cancer. I just couldn't take listening to our baby cry night and day and his daddy not lifting a finger to even change a diaper. I ran away so now he's doing the same damn thing. Trust me. He'll be back after he makes me suffer a few days. He's probably blowing the rest of our cash. He's probably shootin craps right now just to spite me."

I stood on this lady's front step, wondering why on earth I bothered to care to check on this loony bin of a family. Her story was so dumb, it was likely real. I thanked her for her time and went back to my parent's home for another home cooked meal.

"Winfield is looking for you. I believe his exact quote was; tell Novo to git his boney ass in front of me, pronto." That was a message left for me by my assistant, Peter. Since my latest target was nowhere to be found, I was off to Texas.

After arriving at Doctor Winfield's office, something was not quite right. The patient in the waiting room was not a surprise but it was the way Nurse Simon was acting. I knew quickly Rose had appeared and was working in the front office.

"Hey sugar, Rose hasn't seen you in a while. The doctor will see you soon. I'll let him know you're here."

"Rose, why are you working here?" I asked with an inquisitive voice.

Rose looked at me with the same naughty smile I had seen before. "Rose has no idea what you mean, sugar. I may not be who you're looking for, but I sure do know how to take very good care for people. You just make yourself at home."

I watched patiently for over an hour as Rose took care of patients and answered the phone. Finally the door to the hallway I despised walking down opened. "Follow me please, Mr. Novo."

Nurse Simon and her soft voice had returned. Her wiggle was a treat as I was being escorted down the hallway. "How are you feeling Nurse Simon?" I asked as we made our way past the waiting rooms and scale on the right side of the hallway.

"I'm feeling just fine, Mr. Novo. I don't know if I told you or not, but I'm fixin to go on vacation soon. Doctor Winfield told me that he will be away for a couple of weeks and I deserved a little break. We were planning on going away together later this summer but he told me he didn't think he could go with me right now. So, I'm gonna jump on some little ole airplane and get myself a nice tan all over my body. Don't cha think that's just a fine idea?"

My heart missed a beat. All I could think about was Nurse

Simon on a beach somewhere covered in oil. That was until I heard Winfield growling at me, "Sit your ass down, cowboy. You got one shot at making this right. Don't miss."

I sat my ass down and did my best to focus on what Winfield had to say. But I did take one last peek at Nurse Simon as she made her exit back down the hallway.

"Novo, I surely don't blame you for looking. But I swear, if you ever touch that filly, my finest shotgun will be put to good use. Now you wanna hear what I have to say or don't ya?"

I sat back in my chair. I wondered if Winfield really didn't observe when his employee became different personalities. I had seen all three at one time or another in his office. Was it possible she only showed herself to me? I stared at Winfield and offering him a nod of my head, waiting for him to tell me why I was summoned back to Texas.

"Cowboy, I don't declare you to be the sharpest tool in the bin, but maybe you did hit a nerve with me. The way I see it, there are two kinds a leaders. There are those who put themselves in position to lead and then there are the ones installed by others. My mind's still rattling round trying to figure which one you are. Either way, maybe you aren't as dumb as you look."

"Gee, thanks so much Doctor Winfield. I declare you are much smarter than you look too."

I wasn't really sure why I felt it necessary to dig back at him, but I did. The frown on his not particularly handsome face was enough to give me an internal snicker.

"May I continue, Novo? As I was saying, I'm trying to figure out if you really have any power to make my offer happen, or you're just a mouthpiece for the old men on the Council."

"What's the offer, Doctor?" I said with testiness in my voice.

"You done listen close now. I'm only gonna say this once but I'll go real slowly, in case you don't comprehend so well. I'll work on seeing if there is a solution to making more soul stealers through changing the DNA in ya'lls bloodlines. I ain't making no promises other than I'll give you my word, I'll do some research on it. But there are rules to my helpin ya."

I sat there waiting for his rules as he continued slowly.

"First rule. I git to go inside your sacred little palace and see my daddy eyeball to eyeball. Since he won't come see me, I'm fixin to go see him. Second, any experiments I do with blood, it's dun with your daddy as my personal lab rat. I know he can't steal, so he's the perfect choice."

His offer was disturbing but why should I have expected any less from this man. "I'll get you inside our compound, but are you insane? Do you really think I'll allow my father to be used as a common lab rat?"

Winfield smirked. "Some think I am a bit crazy, yep, El-Dar Novo. Now let's see how much of a leader you really are for our people. You have my daddy imprisoned. I think it's only fair I get to use yours to help save our people from extinction, don't you, our exulted leader? And for the record, I don't like being labeled as chicken shit. Let's see who plays chicken now."

I took a moment to gain my thoughts before responding. "Even if I were to agree to your rules, Doctor, there are no guarantees my father will play along with your little tests."

"Oh but he will, cowboy. Don't you see the irony in all of this? My daddy lost his ability to take souls cause he didn't trust his only son. But your daddy, well come on, cowboy, he always trusts you. Don't he? And you came here asking me for help, so you must trust me. Don't ya? Me and my daddy, we wore the black hats for a while now. It's time we got to share the white hats with the Novo family."

Winfield leaned all the way back in his wooden leather chair putting his feet up on the desk. He gave me a monstrous look and laugh usually reserved for Vincent Price movies.

"So, what's it gonna be, El-Dar Novo? Are we making plane reservations to go visit my dear ole daddy? And let's git some blood samples, starting with you and your daddy? Or maybe you need to run back to your people and let em all know when it comes to being a leader; you're really a pile of chicken shit."

How do I trust this man? There has to be a better way of discovering why our numbers are shrinking. Despite our bloodlines being thinned out, some should still have the power to see into others souls and steal. We needed answers.

I sat there agonizing, wondering if I should allow this man to use anyone as a lab rat, let alone my father. But then again, if he doesn't run tests on our disciples, who could he run tests on? Was it possible to offer our powers to anyone not from our heritage of the original one hundred? The Council certainly would have difficulty approving his research. But I was confident we could strike an accord to keep both sides pleased.

"I will take you to the compound, Doctor. You may visit with your father for one day and one day only. I will supply you with blood samples from all our remaining soul stealers as well as some who failed in removing souls but have our bloodlines. I can't guarantee my father will submit to your testing until I can speak with him. That's the best I can do."

Winfield removed his feet from his desk and sat erect in his chair. "You got one hour to get your daddy to agree. Till then, I don't move."

"I'll talk with my father. But until then, get your bags packed, we are heading across the globe."

My father not only agreed to the testing, he jumped at the idea. He wanted to assist me so badly the risks didn't matter to him. I did my best to explain that Winfield wasn't to be completely trusted, but it didn't matter. My mother was not pleased at all, but she also knew my father's desire to help me restore our people.

I soon found myself heading to our compound with my cautiously welcomed passenger. The Council was very guarded in allowing father and son to be reunited inside our headquarters but I think their curiosity won out in the end. After all, maybe Elder Charon Orcus would admit his failings when he had to face his son in person. It was a chapter in our history we needed to bury.

Our compound was built hundreds of years ago. It is located in Southern Europe, more than a two hour drive from a major airport. It is surrounded by hills with luscious landscaping. We have continued to build homes over time but we are running out of room within our confines. Part of the area is surrounded by a wall, the rest borders on steep hills.

It appears like any small community in the area. Since it was built so long ago, few ever travel past it, attempting to do more than deliver mail. There are twenty homes on site with one large building that houses our Council room, our library, a conference room, a few smaller meeting rooms and a residence usually reserved for the leader of the Council. The homes are reserved for other Council members and their families as well as trainees and a few staff members.

We keep it well maintained but don't like it to stand out against the other local communities. Some of the locals suspect suspicious activities with no evidence given. It's all hearsay at the local markets. We keep to ourselves and never cause any commotion for the local authorities. We pay our taxes and don't bother with others, so they don't bother with us. After several generations, our home has become an accepted part of the landscape. We have kept it non-descript for a reason.

Traveling with Doctor Winfield was long and quiet. Kalani bought me a pocket sized device that stored music on it. She was way ahead of the gadget market than me. I did my best to tune in my favorite songs and tune out my traveling partner. He attempted more than once to bait me into a discussion over the merits of our work but I refused to participate. I was more than aware of his disregard for our mission on earth. It was one reason why I was unsure if in the end, he would attempt to assist us or harm us. Part of my strategy in allowing him to meet with his father was so that maybe, Elder Orcus could convince his son, our work still had merit.

We arrived after close to twenty hours of travel with the added time change. We both desired a good night's rest. As anxious as everyone was to get his meeting over with between the two men, being refreshed was the better option.

The following morning after a large breakfast of eggs, pancakes and fresh orange juice, I was ready to face the day. My ever insistent assistant, Peter, was constantly in my ear about making sure everyone met in the conference room at the appointed time. Our original schedule had the Council meeting with Doctor Winfield to sign an agreement outlining how much time he anticipated it would take for results as well as a budget to complete his task. It allowed him access to blood samples as well as our agreement to meet with his father. But the schedule had changed. Originally Elder Orcus decl ned to meet with his son, but once we told him we would no longer offer him a home or any type of financial support, he agreed to a short visit. We also had to agree not to further punish him or his son for anything that might be disclosed in our meeting.

When I arrived at the Council room, the four other Council members were seated as well as former member, Elder Stella. Charon Orcus wandered in looking very casual as if he was on his way for a day at the beach with his shorts, sandals and collarless shirt. I had never seen him look so casual. He sat on the side opposite of me and two other members of the Council.

Grayson Winfield was then led in by Peter, who was mumbling about how no one is ever on time. Winfield sat next to me. He was dressed in a fine suit with not one hair out of place. I could sense the tension as the doc took his seat. Winfield slowly sipped some water from the glass in front of him, before staring directly at his father.

I started with a greeting and an acknowledgement this was not intended to incriminate anyone. It was purely as a request from Doctor Winfield to meet his father face to face in exchange for the doctor's assistance in possibly determining why our numbers have been deteriorating so quickly. Everyone was quiet, until Elder Orcus spoke up.

"Why'd you come such a long way, Grayson? There's nothing here for you any longer. At one time you were a brilliant physician with a bright future. You tossed it all aside. You never agreed with our cause, plus you attempted to ruin me, while pretending to be helping me."

Winfield clenched the end of the arm rest of his chair. I could see his body stiffen as the tension increased even more in the room. He began to respond. "For one thing, my dear ole daddy, I AM a brilliant physician. For another, you are a lying sack of cow manure. I never once made you drink a damn thing, nor did I make that potion in the first place. You stole my notes. You know you stole my notes, now you have no one to blame but yourself. Well, that and likely that chemist ya'll employ, your buddy, Chamoun. My guess is the two of you messed with my research long enough for you to become an impotent fool."

Orcus remained calm and answered back. "I will die with the truth. As far as Chamoun, he didn't need to help. You tried to make a drug to help us live twice our usual life span. You failed. It was your screw up and I'm the one paying the price for it. If these blasted fools think you can help them, I'm only happy I won't be in charge when you fail, again. Now, if that's all you have for me, good day, Grayson."

Charon Orcus got up out of his chair to leave the room but not before Grayson Winfield spoke his mind.

"I knew you wouldn't be man enough to admit the truth,

Daddy. You failed me as a father and as a leader. I can go home now knowing you will go to your grave a spineless liar. You might have your soul back, thanks to me, but it's going to be destroyed again before you die. You really are a miserable ole coot. Good riddance to ya."

Orcus gave his son that same monstrous look Winfield offered me a few times back in Texas. At least now I knew where it came from. Orcus exited the room.

I allowed Doctor Winfield a moment to regain his composure wanting to offer my condolences over his father not being more understanding. But then again, I had been in front of the Council many times over the years. I knew Charon Orcus never had acquired sympathy for others.

I made an attempt at offering empathy for him. "I truly am sorry you came all this way, Doctor, for so little. I do believe you that your father stole your notes and brought his pain upon himself."

Winfield would have none of it. "If you think I give a rat's ass about anything you think, El-Dar Novo, than you're dumber than a fox who can't find the hen house. I wanted to give that man one last chance to come clean before he died, but he didn't take the bait. He can rot in hell now for all I care. I know the man I am, and that man is a much better one than my father."

The other members of the Council remained quiet until Elder Robus spoke up and flung our previous agreement across the table to Doctor Winfield. "So, Doctor, you will be leaving us then and starting your research? We will start to round up the blood samples. Please look over our agreement and initial next to your name."

Robus was cut off by Winfield with a tone I was all too familiar with now.

"Another horse's ass speaks to me as if I should care. Ya'll just don't get it, do ya? Hell, even if I did come up with sumtin to make more of you antiquated swindlers, then what? Ya'll been at this for over two thousand years and for what? Tell me. There's more pain and suffering in this world today than ever before. I watch as mindless robots strap bombs to their bodies and murder innocent people. Have you people ever stopped any of that lunacy?"

I interrupted Winfield's rant. "Now hold on. We do all we can with our limited resources."

"Do you really, cowboy? I see horrible, disgusting people walking this earth and ya'll take the souls of guitar players and embezzlers. Ya'll don't go after the darkest of souls. Ya'll go after ones in nice locations, like it's a long vacation for your bunch. Our people believed in the mission. Now we pay the expenses on this place and all your travels so we can live longer on this despicable planet for another few years. So what?"

I responded to Winfield again. "One of those people we've kept alive longer is you, Doctor Winfield. You will be able to see great medical advances over the course of your lifetime. You can create medical history! I am sure many in your profession would love to change places with you."

Winfield pounded his fist on the table. "To what end I ask you? I save people from cancer so they can walk into some shopping mall on Christmas Eve only to have their heads blown off by a lunatic? And what ya'll people doing bout' that? Why you're off to Hawaii chasing a small time drug dealer."

"You're being very unfair with us Doc," I retorted. "Many of those lunatics you speak about don't have the darkest of souls before they do horrific damage. We don't predict the future. Also, we are constantly put in dangerous situations. Oh yeah, it's easy for you with your microscope playing footsie with your nurse while we attempt to remove as much injustice as we can. If you want to remove the worst of the worst then go visit Bink and take an assignment. Otherwise, honor your word and help us figure out a way to restore our numbers. Better yet, remove yourself from benefiting every time we take a soul. You had your chance to be on this Council one day and make these decisions, but you chose another path."

Winfield pounded his fist again. "That's where you are so wrong, El-Dar Novo! I was never given a chance because my father lied about me. Then your precious Council tossed me outta here like a horse with a broken leg."

Both the doctor and I took a few long breaths. Everyone else was motionless for close to a minute before Elder Rex spoke up. "Doctor Winfield, we can't go back and correct the past. Since we share most traits with humans, we are vulnerable to mistakes. It's hard for me to judge if you no longer believe in our cause because you were shunned, or because you never learned to understand who we are and our mission on earth. Either way, I would like to remedy the situation. I am not asking you to remove souls as Elder Novo may be suggesting. But extending a hand with the understanding we need each other. Let's start there, can we?"

"Ya'll really don't see the big picture here, do ya? You can't rid the world of assholes looking to harm others or themselves. You can have thousands of you people and evil will still exist. Give up, boys, the clock dun run out."

Elder Rex responded back. "Doctor, our mission was never to rid the world of evil. Our mission was to remove souls of others who no longer could see the beauty in this world. I'm sure you remember from your teachings, there cannot be good without evil. We fully understand evil will always exist. But we are only using the talents given to us from the heavens above, just like you. So the choice is yours. We can all work together in continuing our mission, or you can return to your office. I will speak with Elder Novo in assuring you he won't contact you again, should you decline to assist us."

19

Jamaica wasn't the smartest place on earth for me to venture since Nesstor had to free me from being arrested the last time I was on the island. Doc Duvaliar's murder was still unsolved, which meant the authorities still believed I was involved. I used one of my many aliases to gain entry through customs. I entered the country presumed to be on a business trip, which for me, was true. More money had been withdrawn from the same account that was used when Chad was found in the Bahamas.

I checked into the finest hotel in Kingston. If he wasn't in Kingston, I would check Montego Bay. Being in Kingston offered me an excuse to go back to visit the office of the Custos Rotulorum. This was the "Keeper of Roles", where Doc Duvaliar informed me our book of secrets was usually stored. The only person who had access to remove the book was either Doc or someone in his immediate family.

After Doc was murdered, I didn't know where the book might turn up. I was hoping maybe someone in Doc's family would return it back where it was stored on the island. When I asked the gentleman behind the desk if he knew of the book he replied,

"You are second one to look for book. Dis ees not library."

I was more than a little surprised anyone else knew the book was stored at this location. "Who came looking for the book, sir?"

"I don't ask names", the man replied. "Pretty lady, tall one, but she not from here. Never seen her on de island." I did my best to get a better description but he refused to elaborate. I thanked him and was on my way. This would be another task added to my laundry list of chores, finding this book. Inside the pages told the tale of our history and how to take and retrieve souls. By reading the pages it wouldn't allow others to take souls without our unique abilities. However, it was still not something I wanted unaccounted for on earth. It was very curious how anyone else even knew it had gone missing.

I drove past the bank where the money was withdrawn from the account I suspected Chad Davidson was using. I then looked for the closest hotel near a beach in the area. When I discovered it, I went inside and walked around the pool deck and beach. For some odd reason, Tasha Timmons was stretched out on a beach towel and lounge chair at the edge of the pool. Not only did I think it prudent to say hello, I was curious why she was in Jamaica and not on assignment.

I walked over to where she was stretched out in a lounger with her face looking directly in the sun's direction on a partly cloudy day. I couldn't tell with her large sunglasses covering her eyes, if she was awake. I moved into a position where I blocked the sun from her face.

"Good day, Miss Timmons. What brings you to Jamaica?"

She removed her glasses with little urgency, slowly wiped her face with the corner of her towel and let out a long yawn before speaking. "Is there any particular reason why someone would be blocking my view? Especially anyone who dares to think they know me."

Her act was starting to wear thin with me. "That's enough, Tasha. It's Cale Novo. I noticed you and thought it proper to say hello. I also wanted to see what you were doing here. Shouldn't you be on assignment in Europe?"

Tasha put her glasses back on and let out a deep sigh. "Please move, Mr. Novo, you're blocking my view. And if you must know, I'm on holiday. You being on the Council must realize we're permitted a respite now and again. I generally use my time tanning my body and flirting with men who think they have a prayer in seeing beyond my tan lines."

Refusing her demands to move, I continued my investigation. "Yes, I enjoy a break now and again myself, though it has been a while for me. I do find it curious however that you are here on the same day a long legged woman showed up over at the government building, looking for a very special book. Is that purely a coincidence?"

Tasha again wiped her forehead with the end of her towel. "Do all you Council boys speak in riddles? What book? Maybe you've been in the sun too long, Mr. Novo. Or possibly you're still suffering from being beat up by an unarmed child in the Bahamas."

Our second encounter wasn't going any better than our first. "What have I done to deserve your rude behavior? Be careful, Tasha or I'll speak with Mr. Bink about having you chase dark souls all over war zones, until you learn some manners."

She removed her glasses this time with more urgency. Tasha Timmons then moved her lounger into the position enabling her to sit straight up and down. "For one, you're still in my sun. For another, I'll go wherever I'm assigned. I told you, it's what I do. And make no mistake; I'll be the best at it in the most horrible of conditions. In fact, better than you are while chasing petty criminals around the tropics. And, I won't get knocked out by little boys and their sea shells."

I was done taking lip from this woman. "I don't know what you've heard and from whom, but I was accosted from behind by a known criminal. I have three stitches in my head to prove it. That aside; I too go wherever my assignment directs me. I apologize for interfering with your prep work for fraternizations with the local men later this evening to boost your already over inflated opinion of yourself. I won't make the error in attempting to get to know you better in the future. Good day, Miss Timmons."

She stood up from her lounger and rested her towel on her sun burnt shoulders. Her face was now within a short distance of mine. Her icy stare was one I would expect from someone as dangerous a thief as her. Tasha rolled her shoulders back pushing her chest ever closer to mine.

"I'm considering allowing my name to be entered into the open spot on the Council. I can't wait to annoy you at every turn. You have very thin skin for a leader. I suggest strongly you keep your emotions in check. If not, others will exploit it. Good day to you, Elder Novo."

Tasha walked away and back into the direct line of the sun. Her back was glistening from the sun glinting against the oils on her body. Her pace was quick but with a feminine touch. Her wiggle was not as pronounced as Nurse Simons, but I noticed a few heads turn to look her way as she made her way through the sliding glass doors of the hotel's back entrance. I reflected on our chat as she walked away. Despite the large irritation she was now becoming, I had to admit, her words did have some merit.

After my verbal exchange with Tasha, I was back on my original mission, find Chad Davidson and remove his soul. I spent two days looking for him in Jamaica with little success. The only record I could find of him was a credit card payment for purchasing fuel at a marina. None of the major hotels had him registered. I decided to head back to Florida until Chad resurfaced.

The next morning after arriving in Florida, the local newspaper reported a story about how the missing escrow funds had been found. The report claimed the deposit check for the land deal, along with three other checks were found in a folder in the real estate broker's office. The real estate broker who managed the office where Chad worked, claimed, "It was an unfortunate oversight." It was also being reported in the story that the State of Florida was adding fifty million dollars to the project to keep spring training baseball alive in Palm Beach County. The land deal would again move forward, however the construction contract would be put out for bid.

If Chad's not an embezzler, why was his soul so dark?

I asked Anne to do more digging into the bank account being used by Chad. It was associated with a Bahamian corporation by the name of "Island Transport Service". The company shared an address with a law office in Nassau. That was about all she could uncover, other than there had been activity on the account he day before in Nassau. I headed off to the Bahamas in search of the elusive Chad Davidson.

I checked myself into a fine hotel on Paradise Island then made my way over to the attorney's office listed in the records. Located on the second floor of a wooden building along Bay Street, I took the creaky outside steps up the side of the building to see if anyone was in. There was one window, partially open, next to a door with the name of the law office on it. No sign of any transport service. I knocked on the door. No one responded. I attempted to enter but it was locked. Peering through the window, all I could see were three desks with papers on each, two wooden filing cabinets, and a fan oscillating from side to side across the small crowded room.

Disappointed in not finding anyone, I ventured over to the hotel where the money was withdrawn from an ATM machine. Chad was a registered guest but had checked out earlier in the morning. I asked around if anyone from the hotel staff recognized my subject and if he had ever stayed there before.

"Yes, we see Mr. Davidson many times in the summer. He stays one night and leaves de next morning, many times. He is welcome guest over de years."

The hotel manager kept on offering information, "He is boat captain, takes people fishing on de weekends. Very nice man." He showed me on a map where the local marina was located. Off I went.

I showed Chad's photo around the marina and asked a series of questions attempting to find Chad or possibly a boat he might be working on in the area. Finally, one man told me he knew Chad but that he was known mostly as the "Transport Mon."

The man who knew Chad was the marina manger. He looked to be in his late sixties with very dark skin, short curly grey hair, a white tee shirt with the sleeves cut off, jeans in need of washing, and a cap with sweat stains across the top. He appeared very fit for his age with large biceps and an attitude to match. After I peppered him with a few questions, he turned the tables on me.

"Who send you looking for Transport Mon? You must be friend of friend to get on boat. You know someone?" The man removed his cap and wiped a hard day's work from his chin.

My curiosity was piqued. "I am a friend of Mr. Davidson. He told me to meet him here and he would take me on his next trip out."

I assumed by his facial expression the marina manager wasn't buying my tale.

"If you know Transport Mon, then you know when he sails and where to get ticket. Now go."

I tried one last time. "I went by the lawyer's office but no one was there. I couldn't get a ticket. Can't I pay when I get on the boat to go fishing later with Chad?"

"You pay at de office for all trips, now go," the old man barked at me.

I went, but not far. I moved up on the hill with my binoculars waiting for my target to appear. He had to be near. I had stolen enough souls to sense when I was close to finishing a mission.

As the afternoon sun fell across the inlet, my target was

dropped off in a car by someone I didn't recognize. Chad got out of the car, removed a few things from the trunk and greeted the old man I had spoken with a few hours earlier. He handed the marina manager an envelope, then walked over to a boat where he dropped off a cooler and a few orange life preservers. I now assumed the boat would have passengers. Soon after Chad checked in, the marina manager drove away. It was my time for action.

I made my way down the hillside and into the marina past several boat slips. I hadn't noticed the name of the boat my subject had boarded until I was a few feet away, "The Transport". I could hear my subject whistling a tune below deck. I became uneasy about charging down below when I noticed a handgun in a holster sitting on a side sofa. I decided to call out for my target rather than risk startling him and finding myself with a bullet wound on a boat preparing to head out to sea. After a few calls from the dock, Chad appeared and asked.

"Can I help you? If you're looking to join us tonight, we're full. Maybe next time, pal."

It was now dusk and hard to recognize faces from more than a few feet. I didn't think Chad realized we had previously met until he moved closer. Once he did, he reacted by offering a quick smirk.

"Hey, I know you, don't I? You were that guy in Freeport talking all crazy about wanting my soul and looking for some money. I told you already, I don't have your money. Now if you will excuse me, I have a charter leaving in thirty minutes."

"What kind of charter business do you run?"

Chad looked at me and smiled. "The kind where I get paid, really well. Look, if you're gonna arrest me for something, just do it. I know I didn't steal any cash. After you ran me down, I called my wife and she told me she doesn't know what the hell you are talking about either. And thanks by the way, she's all pissy now, cause she thinks I'm down here gambling. So either show me a badge and take me in, or let me get back to getting this boat ready to sail. I got work to do."

"Do you believe you have a sou , Chad?" I asked.

He became agitated. "I believe I'm about to pick up that friend of mine over there that stops people like you from asking too many questions of guys like me. Any minute now, my guests will be arriving. The last thing they wanna see is a strange face asking stupid questions. So you can either turn around and leave, or become my bait for the trip."

I took one last look. His soul was dark, maybe not from stealing money but he was a lost cause. I slowly moved closer and responded, "I'll let you get back to it then. Enjoy your charter." I held out my hand and he shook it. A soft grimace came across his face as if he had heartburn. I removed my hand from his palm and moved to a safe place where I could recover from removing his soul.

As I was walking down the pier a few people passed me. They ranged in ages from a young child to a man who looked to be in his fifties. Each had a small travel bag in their hands. I was starting to feel the effects from taking Chad's soul. I didn't have time to see if they got on his boat or not.

I headed back to South Florida the next morning for one last home cooked meal before returning to the compound for meetings about filling our open Council position. The following morning, I was packing my suitcase and giving my mother a send off hug when my dad called me into the back room where he had the television blaring the news.

"We are standing on the pier at the Lampman Marina in Key Largo, Bill. The Coast Guard has just brought in a boat with three suspected illegal aliens attempting to enter South Florida. As you can see just to my right, is the captain of the boat. He is being taken to the police station for questioning. He has been identified as a South Florida man by the name of, Chad Davidson. The reports are still sketchy at this moment but the others on the boat claim that the captain lost all sense of direction and never found their promised drop off point. We have learned there were four other men on the boat who jumped off the watercraft sometime during the early morning hours. The Coast Guard is searching for those men. When I find out more, Bill, we will get back to you.

"Thank you for that report, Maryanne. That was Maryanne Hill with a breaking story about a boat possibly attempting to smuggle people through the Florida Straits. We will have more on this breaking story later in the broadcast."

My dad almost came out of his seat yelling at me, "Did you hear that, Cale? That's the guy. That's the dope you've been chasing. It musta taken him sometime after getting zapped before it affected him."

"I know dad but I saw those people walk past me. I'm responsible if something happened to them. I should have done a better job in taking Chad's soul in Freeport when I had my chance. I really blew it this time. I've been too lenient and wanting to see the best in people."

My father got out of his lounge chair and walked over to me. He put his arm around me attempting to console me. "This isn't on you. You didn't put those people on the boat and you weren't responsible for their safety."

I didn't want his consoling. I knew the truth. "Had I grabbed that guy's soul last week when I had him in the chair next to me, Chad never could have captained that boat."

I walked around with guilt all day long. It only got worse when it was reported that two of the men were found by police on the beach near Key Largo. The two survivors informed the police that sharks had taken the other two men as they struggled to swim to shore.

I wasn't sure I would ever recover from knowing I had a hand in killing two people. Taking a soul from undeserving people was one thing, knowing my failure led to innocent people dying was another. I would never give anyone the benefit of the doubt ever again. My desire to take souls and take quickly was now surging in my veins.

20

Upon returning to the compound, I was escorted directly into a meeting with the Elders. Elder Polus was as usual the first to confront me. "We're taking a lot of heat from the search committee to appoint a woman to our Council, Elder Novo. Even the budget committee has reported a loss of revenues this year due to a declining membership. We believe promoting a woman will encourage more to seek our abilities once again. We should consider all options."

Personally, I wasn't opposed to having a woman on the Council, but I didn't know of one who would be a good candidate. I sat back listening to the debate back and forth among the other four elders at the dais until finally my grandfather, Elder Spia, broke the news to me.

"Elder Novo, I realize you won't appreciate the pace at which we worked while you were on assignment, but the four of us met with Miss Tasha Timmons. She joined us before her holiday. We along with the search committee interviewed her for several hours. We think she would be a strong contributor to the Council."

He was absolutely right. I wasn't thrilled that Tasha was interviewed without my knowledge. Nor did I agree with their assessment. "I have spoken with Miss Timmons twice and neither time did she come across to me as a level headed individual who could handle delicate matters. She's a straight ahead, take no prisoners type of person. We need thinkers not bullies."

The elders started fidgeting in their seats and giving me a look of disappointment. Once again Elder Polus was first to challenge me. "Elder Novo, you are the one who brought her to our attention in the first place. Besides, we have very few options available to us. She is one of only a handful of women who have the ability to see into and take a soul. I want to bring this to a vote."

The other three elders voiced opposition by grumbling and swiveling in their chairs. I watched and listened to the men argue about how the process should work. It was difficult to get the usual six member Council to agree on anything. I hoped it would be easier with five, but it wasn't. It was a recurring theme for me of traveling the world, stealing souls, only to return to the Council meetings and frustrated that the entire hierarchy was a complete waste of my time. I could walk the streets and look into souls. I could take all the souls I wanted. I could survive. Who could stop me? Why did I need a Council to pick them for me? But I was a member of a rare society, one I wanted to protect.

Finally I stated, "Ok, that's enough from all of you." I'm out giving my life to our cause and you guys can't figure out how to take a simple vote after all these years? You want a vote then take a vote."

My grandfather again tried to explain but I was barely

listening. "Elder Novo, we had an agreement among us that you as leader of the Council would be the one to call for a vote on the Timmons nomination. We didn't want you to feel blindsided upon your return. We wanted you to be comfortable in calling a vote after knowing she was thoroughly vetted by the search committee and the Council."

"Fine," I replied, "If it's really my choice, then no vote." Again the room erupted with cat calls and growls not only from the elders but also a few members in attendance. "Did the Council or the search committee bother to interview any other women or men for the position?" I asked.

Elder Polus raised his voice and looked directly at me. "We did what was in the best interest of our members. Now call the vote!"

Again I brought up the question. "So am I to assume that's a no, Council members? You didn't bother to open the position to all possibilities? Everyone agreed that Miss Timmons was the best candidate without even bothering to interview even one other individual?"

Silence filled the Council room. The four elders on the dais were each looking in separate directions. I did my best to make eye contact with any one of them. I looked out into the audience where the chairman of the search committee was seated in the front row. Jackson Albury at least had the decency to look me in the eye, but only offered a shrug of the shoulders.

Elder Rex commented while looking at the few sitting in the audience. I suspected the words were intended for my ears only. "Our members have made it clear that history will prove our choice was prudent, not only by adding a woman, but the specific one chosen in Miss Timmons."

I relented. The vote was called and Tasha Timmons was the first woman inducted as a member of the High Council. The vote was four to one with my dissenting vote. With no other official business to discuss, the meeting was adjourned.

I called Tasha to congratulate her. Her response was typical Tasha. "Five men to one woman, this hardly seems fair for you guys. By the way Elder Novo, between you and me, all I had to do was show up for my interview, bat my eye lashes, flash some cleavage and those old farts couldn't wait to vote for me."

"Tasha, I hardly think that's the reason they were so quick to want you on the Council. If I were you, I would value my service to our disciples more than wearing a short dress. From what I was told the members were clamoring for a woman on the Council and you were first on the list. And for your record, flashing your lashes and shaking body parts won't help sway me with any future votes. So don't bother trying."

Tasha chuckled in the phone. "Never underestimate me, Elder Novo." I could hear her laughing harder as she hung up the phone. I was starting to realize she only wanted to get under my skin with her comments.

For the next several months I stole many souls. No longer was there a concern if the Council made a mistake in the selection process. I was rarely involved in selecting dark souls. I left that up to the four older members to review the files. Most times I didn't even look into my target's soul before removing it. I again took my position as the preeminent taker of souls on earth.

I worked mostly in the western half of the United States as did my wife. Kalani and I, along with our son, Nic, spent much of our time back in California. Kalani was still working very hard as well.

We considered having another child but it was difficult for a few reasons. For one, she enjoyed her career as a soul stealer.

Another reason was that years earlier when I met Kalani, she was on assignment to steal the soul of a drug cartel leader from Hawaii. Kalani was born and raised in the Hawaiian Islands and knew the area well. She was abducted by the drug dealer and was injected with drugs for many days. I saved her from the cartel but since then, conception has been difficult for us. Doctors aren't sure if the drugs are the reason or not. Lastly, with all the hours each of us travel, creating a family nucleus can be challenging.

Many of our disciples chose family life over soul stealing, including my own mother. There was also an extended time when Elder Orcus discouraged two soul stealers from marriage, including my own relationship with Kalani. Our people have also been thinned out over the generations from mating with pure humans. Try telling two people in love, they can't marry and raise a family, because their bloodlines don't match. You don't.

That's why I did all I could to get Doctor Winfield, who is one of the world's leading experts on blood cancers, to work on discovering the secrets of our bloodlines. He was given blood samples from our soul stealers, along with many who have direct bloodlines, yet never developed the ability to steal. I wanted to know why and if the ones who claim not to have the ability really do, like my mother.

Winfield was also given samples from a few who had the ability and lost it, like Kalani's uncle. There were three soul stealers who could take a soul, yet couldn't see into another's soul. Our bloodlines were a disaster. The Council realized it was a huge gamble to give someone like Winfield our blood, but we were desperate. We had thousands who were descendants from the original one hundred from one side of the family, but not both sides, due to marriage outside our kind. We continued to support all of them by allowing them a longer life every time we removed a soul. They don't live as long as the pure blooded of our kind, but their lives are extended beyond normal humans. We now had so few with the ability to see into another's soul and steal, it was a huge drain on the few of us remaining soul stealers. Once the last of us is gone, so would be our mission.

It was believed for many decades, that I was the only one who developed the power to restore a soul. That was until I removed the soul of Paulo Kapono, a dirty cop, who had taken over the drug cartel in Hawaii. His soul was later restored. It's still a mystery who did it.

After Kapono's soul had been restored, I gave all the information I had about him to Agent Nesstor, with the FBI. Bringing down the cartel became Nesstor's first big bust, and cemented our future working relationship. He and his agents arrested Kapono in Hawaii along with others in a drug sting. One of those others arrested was my wife, Kalani. No one is sure what she was doing there. I bargained for her freedom from the FBI, but since that day there was always a level of mistrust I had with her.

Kalani did admit to working for Kopono in taking souls for the cartel. It was designed to ward off any competitors trying to work their way into the drug trafficking business in Hawaii. She claimed to have done it for the money, to support her dad's medical clinic. She has long denied she restored Kopono's soul. I try every day to believe her, but the doubt remains.

I was reminded of this because my wife's cousin, Aleka, came for a visit. Aleka was a soul stealer as well. Since our travel schedules were so difficult enough for Kalani and me to have more than a few days together, seeing her cousin was a rare day. I hadn't seen Aleka in many years. What struck me as we picked her up from the airport was how similar she looked to Kalani, from a short distance. As she aged, she looked more like Kalani.

While Aleka was visiting we did many of the things tourists do in California. One of those was a trip to Disneyland. What struck me while strolling through throngs of sweaty people and misbehaving children was the reaction of Kalani and Aleka when I peered into a passing dark soul. I would watch Kalani's neck turn a few times looking at the same dark soul. However, so did Aleka. She is listed as one of our three who can steal souls yet, not see into one.

In order to sit on the Council, you must be able to see and steal. Despite being what many consider our highest honor to sit on the Council, I suspected there were some who did both, yet claim they couldn't. This way they could never sit on the Council. Not everyone wants to sit through endless meetings arguing with five others who can't decide on simple procedures, let alone matters of great importance. I had always suspected many with the power to see and or steal, hid their ability to shirk their responsibilities to our people. I now added Aleka to that list. It also opened her up to the possibilities of restoring Kapono's soul. If she could see and steal, having the ability to restore souls was far more likely.

A few days after Aleka left, Congressman McAdams tracked me down on the phone.

"Cale, for weeks now, this young reporter, Simpson, keeps hounding me for a story. I'm not sure if you heard or not, but my trial is over. It was ugly but proved positive. The thing is; Simpson is obsessed with finding more of a story than I believe exists."

I interrupted the congressman. "What's the problem with the press trying to actually do investigative reporting? Let him do his job, George."

There was a moment of silence before the congressman continued. "Well the real reason for my call is to ask you if you did something to Simpson. He claims some spiritual vampire visited him from time to time and threatened him unless he gets to the truth. That sounds like your handiwork. Am I wrong?"

"There's nothing wrong in helping out a friend now and again George. Let the kid do his job."

I could hear the frustration in George McAdams' voice. "Cale, I appreciate you wanting to help me. You were one of the very few who stood by me. I get that. But I'm trying really hard to revive a career, any career. I don't need some reporter running around telling the world, I've unleashed the underground zombie world on him to prove my innocence. Please, Cale, whatever you did, don't let this fall back on me. I'm having enough trouble finding a job and having anyone believe my side of the story. This kid could harm me beyond repair."

I attempted to ease his mind before we ended our call. I explained to the congressman a little bit about what happened with Simpson and that he was the man behind many of the stories promoting President Morrison under the pen name of Jason Mendace. I admitted for a time, Simpson had lost his soul but a soul was returned to him. However for his penance, Simpson was to get to the truth behind the congressman's trumped up charges. George still wasn't thrilled with my methods, but I told him, they are the only methods I knew. We would be in touch.

The following weeks were spent sitting in an Iowa courtroom. Mark Wells was accused of murdering his girlfriend and her six month old child. It was such big news for the rural farm community, they had to move the trial over to the next town and sequester the jury.

For months I had been stealing souls and not thinking twice about it. This one would be no different. But with the heightened security around the trial, it was difficult to reach my target. I sat patiently, hoping I would be able to make contact without an extended stay.

It was difficult listening to the testimony concerning the murder of an innocent woman and her child. But after a few days, I thought I had figured out the real crime. I wasn't convinced many in the courtroom did. I didn't think the defense team or the prosecutor knew what was truly going on. I knew the judge didn't or she would have tossed out the case.

I had run across parents who took the lives of their children before but this one added another layer of deceit. I listened to all the horrid details of multiple stab wounds suffered by the woman and child. The evidence pointed towards a crime of passion. I listened as the prosecutor did all he could to tie Mr. Wells to the crime scene despite the lack of physical evidence. It was such a shock to the small farming community; someone had to pay for the crime. Even if the evidence was unclear who the perpetrator was, someone would pay.

Steve Oliva was the jury foreman. When the judge asked for

the verdict to be read, Steve replied, "Not guilty." The people sitting in the courtroom let out moans of disapproval. Mark hugged his defense team while the judge thanked the jury for their service. I stalked my target. The trial was over and everyone would be allowed to go back to their normal lives. No one would be held accountable for the lives of two innocent people, at least not in a courtroom setting. However, justice would be served.

I waited just outside the courtroom for everyone to exit. Some on the jury left with sad faces while others left with smiles. As Steve Oliva was leaving the courtroom, I asked for a moment to speak with him.

"Very clever, yet very risky. Mr. Oliva."

He stopped in his tracks with the smile now removed and stated, "I have no idea what you're jabbering about. Now if you'll excuse me it's been almost a month since I've seen my wife and kids. I've got some catching up to do."

I'd waited for days for my chance to strike my target. He wasn't going to get away that easily. "How did you convince those attorney's that you didn't know Mark Wells or the victims? That was an obvious lie, Mr. Oliva. And how much did you have to pay the clerk of the courts to call your name for jury duty for this case?"

"I didn't pay off anybody." Oliva said as he hurried towards the exit.

"You didn't pay her off, I agree." I told Oliva. "After your mistress had the child, she kept coming after you for more and more, telling you that she would expose you as an adulterer. Didn't she? Your reputation with your wife and high standing in the community would never hold up against the scrutiny. When she came to you asking for the hundred grand, that's when you finally snapped. I saw the photos and rage. I know what you did, Oliva. You killed that woman and your child."

"Get away from me, creep," Oliva told me. He then yelled for security.

I grabbed his arm, looked deep into his eyes, took a moment then ripped out his most prized possession. Oliva fainted on the spot. As security arrived, I told them I saw him staggering toward the exit. I informed the armed guard I could tell Oliva was ill. I explained I was only attempting to help. With all the ensuing commotion, I started to look for Mark Wells.

Wells and his attorneys were walking towards me, laughing. I walked up to Mark and congratulated him by shaking his hand. "I'm not sure if it was a bigger risk for you or Oliva? Either way, I find it reprehensible that you knew about the extortion by your girlfriend. After she was murdered, you went after Oliva for hush money. You took the payoff knowing that if you lost the trial, you could try to expose Oliva as the real killer. It was worth a one hundred thousand dollar gamble to you. I found the deposits in your offshore account. You lucked out getting Oliva on the jury and being a jury foreman to sway the votes, but unlucky for you, I have Anne. She finds hidden bank accounts for me."

Both of Marks' attorneys pushed me aside and warned me to leave Mark alone. It was too late. I had his soul too. Wells was not scheduled to lose his soul. I wasn't sure Mark Wells even knew his dead girlfriend was extorting money from Oliva until I watched the testimony. I had no idea that was the reason Oliva's soul was so dark. Not until I sat in the courtroom for several days. I only knew I was assigned to take the soul of Steve Oliva.

I watched several times as Oliva acted as if he knew Wells with a nod or offering eye contact at key moments in the trial. I noticed the women jurors weep at the sight of the graphic photos. However, not only did Oliva never cry, he turned away. It was as if he didn't want to see the horror a second time. That's when I started digging into Oliva's past, more than what was in my file. Anne discovered four payments to an offshore account set up for Mark Wells starting three months before the trial began and ended the day the trial started. The attorneys representing Wells were paid for from a corporation that was traced back to another corporation owned by Steve Oliva.

Steve Oliva owned several farms across Iowa. He was on several boards of directors, was a past school board member with a sterling reputation. The victim, Lee Ann Rodrick, was a waitress in the coffee shop where Steve had lunch multiple times a week. The police questioned people in the coffee shop, but I was the only one to follow up with the waitress who quit weeks before the murder. She admitted to me that Lee Anne confided in her that she was extorting money from Oliva to buy her silence. I figured if I was stuck in Iowa, why not solve the murder? I didn't know for sure all my assumptions were correct until I looked deep into Oliva's eyes, then his soul. I knew then. Then I asked myself, why I took the soul of Mark Wells too? His soul was dark too and no doubt would eventually show up on our list. Why make an extra trip to Iowa?

21

"That file was assigned to me. I swear." I sat at the dais asking myself, how was I supposed to sit in judgment over someone for taking an unassigned soul when I took more than my fair share? Not only that, but the accused was Aleka Kono, my wife's cousin. It would be a losing battle since this was the second time Aleka had been accused of taking souls not on our list. Her punishment was to stay in our compound for three days and take a refresher course on our rules.

The first night of her punishment I met with her for dinner. "What really happened, Aleka? Tell me why you took that guy's soul. Did he harm you? Did you use your own judgment

Aleka seemed annoyed by my questions. "I told you at my inquiry. I didn't take any soul that was not assigned to me. I don't know why no one will believe me, especially you, Cale."

Her tone rang of sincerity but something wasn't adding up. "Aleka, I checked with Bink and our reports. Nowhere can I find any record of that soul being assigned to you. That soul has never even been reported by any of our spies as even being damaged. I want to believe you. But there is no evidence to back up what you are telling us. I'm sorry. Take the course and I'll look into finding a way to make our system more accurate."

Aleka wouldn't let it go. All during dinner she ran through the exact time and place she received the report from Bink. She told me she couldn't prove it because she burned the file just after taking her target's soul, as we are taught. After an hour of listening to her story, I thought I would take advantage of her truthful mood.

"Be honest with me, Aleka. Can you see into another's soul? I noticed when we visited Disneyland, you turned your head almost at the same time I did when a dark soul passed by. I find it hard to believe it was a coincidence, that many times."

"Dang, I knew I was being too obvious," she told me. "I try to shut it off but I can't all the time. Ok, fine, I can see. I lied about it because I hate coming to this compound. It gives me the heebee jeebies. I was afraid later in life I'd be assigned to be a lookout for dark souls, or worse yet, a candidate for the Council. Politics ain't for me, Cale. I just wanna steal souls for a few more years, then retire and start a family. I love what I do, but not forever."

This was now a recurring theme. Too many of our disciples no longer saw it as an honor to do what we do. Maybe our bloodlines weren't as distorted as I originally thought? Since Aleka was being forthcoming in her answers, I kept prying.

"What about your dad? He claims he stopped being able to take souls many years ago. Do you know if he can still remove souls?"

She took a long pause measuring her response. "I don't know, Cale. All I can tell you is that for two years my dad worked for this company in Honolulu that got us tickets to the Pro Bowl. You know the all star game for the pro football players. Well this one guy, who was a running back for the NFC side, after the game we were invited to a party with the players at the hotel. The running back kept hitting on me. My dad asked him to stop but I guess the guy was drunk, who knows. But later on he grabbed my arm and tried to pull me into the bedroom. I whacked the jerk and let out a plea for help. My dad freaked."

I sat listening to Aleka's story. I didn't like where this was going but I kept quiet. She continued.

"Well my dad, he eventually calmed down. He starts acting like everything is hunky dory, just an honest mistake on the guy's part. Minutes later, he asks the running back if he can take a photo with me and him. My dad zooms in real close, so I know he's only getting the player in the frame. I knew my dad once stole souls by taking photos, like many of you older guys did back in the day."

I laughed at her comment of us "older guys" and asked her to continue.

"My dad clicked the photo. I saw it after it developed. It was only of the players face. I wasn't in the photo at all. This guy was an all-star running back for many seasons. The next season, he fumbles four times in his first game and dropped every pass thrown his way. He got worse and worse till he was benched. The doctors claimed he came down with some sort of ear imbalance. Maybe he did. Only my dad knows if he can still take a soul or not."

Aleka and I sat for the rest of the evening discussing her goals in life. We then talked about what we could do to make it easy for her to raise a family and continue to be a soul stealer. We didn't come up with any permanent solut ons but I do think we eased her mind into thinking it was possible to raise a family and continue her work for us.

One more Council meeting was on the agenda before I could go back to doing what I did best. At that meeting, I suggested we changed our education curriculum. "There seems to be a misconception among our members that you can't have a family and still be an active participant in our mission to take damaged souls. I believe we need to add a ccurse in the training period that eradicates that myth from our kind."

My words were met with opposition from Elder Polus. "Our education system is the finest in the world. It's worked for over a century now with our members becoming some of the finest scholars across the globe. Are there any of our institutions you don't want to change, Elder Novo?"

It wouldn't be a Council meeting if someone didn't want to challenge my logic but I continued to make my point. "Elder Polus, I agree with you one hundred percent. We do have an incredible education system that does manifest itself into our disciples being placed in positions of power and prestige across the globe. But you are making my point for me. Our mission is to take damaged souls. Our mission is not to become world leaders. We have done such a fantastic job at creating world leaders in science, education, politics, banking, they don't want to travel around in dark alleys taking souls any longer. They want to lead in their chosen career paths."

Again, Polus objected. "So we should dumb down our education because we are creating world leaders?"

"Of course not, Elder Polus," I stated. "I am only suggesting we teach our future soul stealers to embrace having two lives. Think about it. Who has access to more dark souls than crime fighters or jail wardens? How easy would it be for police officers when arresting someone for viscous crimes to put on the handcuffs and take their soul right then? I am sure I can come up with many more examples but we must change with the times. We are a dying species."

The remainder of the Council stayed away from our disagreement until Elder Rex offered a motion to set up an education committee to review my idea. The motion passed five to one with Polus as the lone opposing vote. It wasn't ideal, but I was hoping it would at least get the process started.

After the meeting, Tasha Timmons asked for a moment of my time.

"Elder Novo, we've gotten off to a bad start. I'd like to apologize for my part of the tension between us. I do think your ideas have merit. I can also see now you want our people to thrive again as soul stealers as well as possibly another career. We'll be serving together for a long time on this Council. Let's try to do it with the understanding we are very different people but with the same goals."

I was shocked with Tasha's request but pleased. "That sounds good to me, Elder Timmons. Thank you for your kind words. By the way, I'm curious. Why did you really want to be on the Council? I can see now your meeting with Kalani was not purely by chance. And the timing of you being in the compound when the other four were looking to make a decision; I realize that was not a coincidence either. You manipulated your way on the Council."

Tasha winked and smiled. "I don't know about you, but I do my best work when I'm on the top." She turned and left the room allowing me to hear a faint giggle.

Months passed with little done about forming a committee. I wanted the younger generation to start their training with the understanding they could have a family or personal life and still fulfill our original mission. I called Peter several times for updates and asked him to push the others to move on my agenda. He claimed he relayed the information several times. I didn't want to fly half way across the world every time I wanted to check on the status. I certainly wasn't short on frequent flyer miles.

I grew weary from all the soul stealing I was doing. I also started to lose a grip on what I believed. Much to the displeasure of the elders, in my past, I would take my time and track my targets. I actually cared about these people about to lose their soul. I wanted to find something good in all of them. I wanted them to be candidates for a second chance in life.

My first stolen soul was a piano player. The guy likely committed more than one murder but I tried desperately to see goodness in the guy. I wanted to be able to restore his soul one day. I went to see him perform not long ago. He still played the songs from decades gone by but not with nearly the passion from the first time I heard him play. He's older, no doubt. But I do wonder sometimes what he could have done with his life, had he not had his evil side and retained his soul.

When I restored my first soul, I was convinced that was my calling in life. I knew the Council made a mistake in taking the soul of Dylan James. The guy was the perfect candidate to have his soul restored. I was happy I did it. But now I second guess it all.

I'm not responsible for all the world's ills. I can only control what I do. If others can't appreciate all they have and lose their soul, who am I to decide who gets a second chance?

Doctor Winfield asked if I would drop by his office the next time I was in Texas. I asked Bink for an assignment in Texas so it would not be a wasted trip to the area. Harley McShane would be my next target after visiting with the Doc.

For the first time after arriving at Winfield's office, there was no trepidation. The man couldn't hurt me, or my family. There would be no favors in either direction. I wasn't sure why he wanted to meet with me but any anxieties of the past were gone.

Nothing had changed about the front office. Nurse Simon still greeted me with her friendly demeanor and cute wiggle down that long hallway. Only this time, I saw all the things hanging along the way in a different light. I noticed awards and accolades in matching picture frames, lining up bearing witness to Winfield's success. I saw him as a leader in medicine, not my nemesis. I eventually made it to that familiar office and was asked to take a seat by Doc Winfield.

"Well, if it's not El-Dar Novo come to visit us again. I do trust you like our steamy weather this time of year?" Winfield's tone was not as combative as it was in the past. "Well, I know you being the busy executive and being the big time destroyer of people's lives with that soul stealing thing, you don't have lotsa time to sit and wait on what I gotta say."

He may not have been as combative but he knew how to push my buttons. "Doctor, you asked for a visit, so here I am. I appreciate the work you are doing for us but please get to your point."

Winfield interrupted me before I could say more. "Relax, Novo, I wuzz just trying ta make some small talk before dishing out my findings. I'm not the most social a critters, so sometimes I don't start conversations so well, like you polished talkers. But you sit back and listen ta what I do know."

I sat back in my chair with an open mind and let him proceed.

"I think ya'll is a bunch of lazy two timers. I took long looks at them three hundert blood samples ya'll sent. I might have found a reason why more of ya'll don't steal souls. The samples from people with ancestors who hadn't procreated inside our bloodlines in over a thousand years are missing sometin. But I did find a unique gene in the DNA of the ones who did stay loyal ta our bloodlines. I don't reckon I've ever seen that gene in all the years of studying human blood. I'm a thinking that's the key to having the ability to soul stealing. If my tests are accurate, I'd say close to fifty percent who claim to be soul taking neutered, well, they might be lying to ya. Cause them boys, well, they got that gene."

The more my mind ingested what he had to say, the angrier I got. "You mean like you, Doctor Winfield? People who can remain true to our mission but decided to pursue other careers? Admit it, Doc. You can take a soul just as easily as I can."

Winfield closed his eyes then looked to the ceiling and rubbed both hands across his face. He then lowered his head, opened his eyes and placed his hands back to his desk before offering his rebuttal.

"I dun told ya many times, cowboy. Doctor Winfield is a healer, not a destroyer. I don't know if I could take a soul, it ain't in me to try. Yes, I have the gene. I looked. But never once have I tried to remove anyone's soul. What you do is pure evil. It's a big reason why I never liked you. You're too damn good at what ya do."

I had to laugh at his comment. "Is that a compliment, Doctor?"

"Novo, I wuz brought up just like you. Hell, my daddy was the leader of ya'll till you practically killed da man. So, I do know why you do what you do. You wuz brainwashed from the time you'ze a youngin. I git it. But that was never fer me. The first time I started ta learn about fixin people rather than taking from em, I knew where my heart wuz. Oh yeah, my daddy was more pissed than a Cowboys fan on a losing Sunday. But I had ta be my own man. Sure, it was ok for everyone else's boy ta run off being some kind of hero, but not this here Grayson."

Listening to this man tell me how he was so righteous and I was brainwashed was not sitting well with me. "Why are you helping us then? If we are such destroyers of men's souls, why do this for us?"

Winfield stared at me. He smirked and said. "There are many things I ain't, El-Dar Novo. But one thing I am is a man a mah word. I know it took a lot on your part ta git me in ta see mah daddy, one last time. I tried ta make peace with the old coot. I surely did. I wanted him ta see me for the man I had become. Hell, there might not be anyone alive who knows more about blood cancers and research then me. But because I never followed my daddy ta the top of the Soul Council, for that I'm chastised and lied about? Well, I dun told ya'll, I'd look at blood samples and I did. My work is officially dun. My debt ta ya'll is paid."

Winfield sat back in his chair and let out a deep sigh. I felt like he was letting go of something. His shoulders slumped and I noticed a small frown. He was never the friendliest of creatures, but this was a different body language. One I had never encountered with him in the past.

"Doc, I sense either sadness or maybe relief from you. I want to believe all you have told me. But I am still not sure I can totally trust you. I still do not know who took Nurse Simon's soul. I want to make peace with you, but that is still a mystery to me. You claim you despise others who take souls, yet someone close to you lost hers till you made me restore it. Please explain what happened with her."

Winfield sat up in his chair, folded his hands on his desk and calmly responded. "I gotta tell ya, cowboy. Her losing her soul was just as big a shock ta me, as it was ta you. You can believe what you like, but I had nuttin ta do with that filly losing her soul. At first, I thought she was sick. I never did think on looking inside her soul. Then I did. It was missing and all of a sudden, you show up. I figured I'd use that ta my advantage. So I told ya a little white fib. In the end, you got your family back with my help and I got to stand in front of my daddy one last time."

"Something is still not right, Doc. Nurse Simon told me that someone came here at your request and took some very provocative photos of her. She told me she felt ill soon after. I know you were taught that some of us still take souls by snapping a photograph. Are you telling me that was a coincidence too?"

This time he let out large belly laugh. "Cowboy, I bet ya didn't know ole Nurse Simon has a dream ta be a model in Paris or in some men's magazine. Hell, I paid some local photographer ta take some shots for a portfolio she wanted to start. That's all. I know she's not running off to be some high fashion model, but I wanted to put a little twinkle in her eye for her birthday."

I was now more confused than before I walked into his office. Winfield wanted me to believe that close to half of our disciples had the ability to pursue our mission and didn't. He wanted me to believe it was pure coincidence that his nurse lost her soul right when I needed help from him. He then insisted I restore it before he would help me. The man always did make my head spin.

"Doc, I really do appreciate your help. But are you sure about this unique gene? Some of us carry it and some of our species don't? You believe that the ones who carry this gene should be able to steal souls? And for the ones who don't carry the unique gene, how do they still live longer lives?"

"El-Dar Novo, what I believe is that some in your group, the ones who do carry that gene, likely have all the same abilities you do. If they don't have the gene, I doubt they do. But you can test it on your own daddy. He's got the gene. So does your mamma. How do you think you got your abilities, cowboy? For living longer, well I suspect they don't live quite as long and fer the rest of your answers, I'ze still a doctor and researcher, nutin more."

For the first time ever, I was leaving Winfield's office believing he was sincere. We actually shook hands and smiled at each other. It entered my mind this would be the last time I ever crossed paths with Doctor Grayson Winfield.

As I turned for the hallway, he offered one last thought. "Caeles, I've met some of the finest scientific minds in the world. Some quit because of what they might find. Some quit because the pressure was too much on them. Some quit because they decided to travel and spend time with their families. Some went on to achieve great advancements in medicine. Just because you have the gift or the ability to do something, don't mean that's your calling in life. Good-bye mah friend."

Winfield was right. I gave him a wave of my hand and made my walk down the hallway with a heavy heart from all he told me. The front office had two people waiting and Nurse Simon was on the phone. I waited until she hung up before leaving so I could say my goodbyes to her as well.

"I am not sure I will be back, Nurse Simon. So please take care of yourself. Here is my number in case you ever need me. And do say good bye to Rose and Isabella for me."

Nurse Simon took the card with my number on it and slipped into her bra. She gave me a soft smile and said. "Oh, I'm sorry to hear that Mr. Novo. But if you are ever in the area, please give me a call. Maybe we can have lunch or something. Plus one of these days you must tell me who this Rose person is. I've had to change my home number twice because people keep calling for Rose."

I smiled back. "Will do, Nurse Simon. Take care of Doctor Winfield for me. He might not be such a bad guy after all." I took a few steps away from the front counter and started to open the front door when I heard a remark from where Nurse Simon had been standing.

"Hey, sugar. Rose takes care of everyone, including you. You go on about your business. I've told you before. Rose has everything under control."

I looked back at the front counter and smiled. I knew Doc Winfield still had no idea who he had working in his front office or in his bedroom.

22

After the revelations from Winfield, I knew I had to investigate his findings. Believing potentially hundreds of our disciples had the ability to execute our mission and chose not too, was unnerving. Harley McShane, my next target, would have to wait.

I felt angry. I felt betrayed by my own people. How could they not understand we had a mission on earth handed down centuries ago? It was never about collecting seats on stock exchanges or being mayor of anywhere, USA. Our mission was to remove souls from people, who no longer for whatever reason, appreciated all that was given to them. I wanted to rip out the soul of everyone who didn't see that our sole mission was handed down from generation to generation.

It would have been nice to live in the same home with my wife and child most days. It would have been nice to go on nice vacations with them and live a peaceful life. But responsibilities were etched in our DNA. Our mission must endure. The idea from Winfield of being brainwashed annoyed me. I wasn't brainwashed. I was trained to live my life as mapped out centuries ago.

My parents weren't expecting me. It wasn't a planned trip. However, after Winfield told me my father carried the gene allowing him to take souls; I had to discover the truth. My mother sat patiently with me in the back room of their home until my father returned from his golf game. The moment he arrived, I stood up and pounced with my words.

"Didn't you think Doc Winfield would discover you're a freeloader, like so many others who carry our DNA?"

My mother jumped in to defend my father. "That's enough Cale. Your father's a good man. He had his reasons. Show some respect."

She wasn't going to push me around. "Of course you'll defend him. You're a freeloader off my hard work, just like my father. Why? Why did you both hide this from me? I'm a soldier for our cause. I live day by day, fighting to survive, removing broken souls, fighting members on the Council, risking my own life returning souls, for what? Tell me, Dad. So you can become the oldest man to win the United States Open Golf Championship?"

My father put his golf bag down and moved across the room. He stood next to my mother and started to speak with a soft voice.

"You already know your mother was told to watch over you and nothing more. You were destined to lead us one day, Cale. Her mission was to make sure you grew up strong mentally, spiritually and physically. I would say she did a fine job. Look at the leader you've become."

My body gave out. I was too emotionally charged to stand any longer. I started to cry and sat back down. My dad took a pause before he continued.

"As for me, I took souls. Yes, I had the power. I don't know if I still do, but as a young man, I did. I finished my training and went on my first mission. I met your mother during training. I made a promise I would return to her a better man after I stole my initial soul."

He moved to a chair across the room and sat down. My mother sat in the chair beside him. My dad's hands started to shake slightly. My mother clasped her left hand with his right. He continued to speak but it was obvious by his voice, he was now very upset.

"He'd been playing in the park with his children. When I snapped that photo and my first ever subject fell to the ground, I was overwhelmed with joy. I had no pity for the man. It didn't matter to me that his children wept because they thought their father had just died. My shadow covered him for several minutes until help arrived. I knew it was time to leave the area. But the sheer power I felt, it was nothing like I felt before. I had an uncontrollable desire to do it again. So I did. I picked out a random person walking the streets and I dropped him. Again I stood over him with rage. I don't know why."

My father started to cry. It was the first time I ever saw him cry. He sunk deep into his chair and covered his face with a pillow. My mom gently rubbed his leg and started to speak.

"Cale, the Council punished your father severely for his actions. He was required to retake some of his training. It was several months before he was given another task. The same thing happened again. Your father is not a man with inner rage. He's a good decent man. Some are not destined to have the power over others. They need to be controlled. The Council assigned your father the business of building homes. He built homes for our members as well as the general public. It was your father's way of paying his debt to the Council and our people. Don't think poorly of him. He may have our DNA, but stealing souls wasn't something he could control."

There wasn't much more to say. I remained for a quiet dinner with my parents and left the next morning. It was the only time in my life I felt sorry for my father. He told me so many stories during my training of how he wanted to be good at soul stealing but never could. He told me he never had the power. I see now it was the power of self control he was lacking.

Harley McShane was now once again on my radar. He was well known within his rural Texas community. He had run for local office three times but lost each time. Harley was always the first to volunteer for any school or chamber functions. The locals always knew Harley's politics were the opposite from theirs. It didn't deter him from being very outspoken. It also never got him elected. But he was appointed to the local elections board. Harley's career was as a computer programmer from his home. I knew he would be an easy target since he was in the public eye so often.

When I arrived in Texas I got a call from Aleka Kono. "Cale, you asked me to call you if I had knots in my tummy about any assignments after I felt hosed by the last one. Well, I was assigned to some rich dude in Tokyo. As I was about to jerk his soul, I took a quick peek. His soul was spotted but nowhere near as dark to be on Santa's naughty list. My report said this guy was whack. I tripled checked to make sure it was the right guy. Something ain't jiving cousin."

"Ok, sit tight Aleka. Do not do anything until I can find out what is going on." She gave me the name of her target and other information in the file sent from Bink. I also told her to send me a copy of the report signed by Brandon Bink. Peter was my next call. He was to ask Bink to pull a list of all the assignments for any soul stealer currently on duty.

Peter sent the list within a few hours. Twenty seven were officially on duty. Aleka was marked as being on vacation. Oddly, so was I. I contacted the other twenty seven. All matched the names to the list provided by Peter from Bink. I called Aleka and told her to head home until I could figure out what was going on with her and me both being marked on holiday, yet receiving assignments.

The following morning I searched for Harley McShane. He never left his home all morning. My time was short. I knew it was now unlikely I would take his soul until I could find out if he really was on the list or not. But I needed to at least see the guy to see if he carried a dark soul. I decided to knock on his door and use on my favorite aliases. I wasn't really sure how I would get information from the guy when he answered.

"Good afternoon, Mr. McShane. My name is Special Agent John Latens. May I ask you a few questions?"

He made it so much easier the moment he opened his mouth. "I knew you government types would be around! I swear. I didn't do it. I tossed everyone one of em in the trash. Please you must believe me."

I looked into his soul and believed him. He didn't have a dark soul. But now I was curious why the confession with just a hello on the doorstep.

I asked to step inside. He obliged. McShane asked if I wanted any refreshments but I refused. He invited me into his living room where I sat on his sofa. He sat in a chair across the room. The room was well kept. It had a big screen television, a few chairs and the sofa. He sat there, wringing his hands. I was hoping he would continue telling his tale but he didn't. I had to pry it out of him. I figured I would act like I knew all about his sad saga. "So, Mr. McShane, how long ago did you toss them in the trash?"

"The night of the election: a few weeks ago. My neighbors, they all know my politics. I was shocked when I was appointed to handle the voting ballots. If those suckers showed any signs of being messed with, I would be tar and feathered. There was no way I could do what that man was asking of me. He wanted me to hand in the ballots he gave me, not the real ones. You must believe me, please."

I wanted to calm his fears. He was obviously very scared by the nervous twitch on his face. I kept digging. "Do you have a name of the man who asked you to alter the votes?"

"No. He came up to me in the parking lot a few days before the election as I was leaving the grocery store. He told me he would supply me with new ballots. If I didn't switch them with the ones I was supposed to take to the main counting station, something really bad would happen. But I swear. I didn't do it."

"I assume the ballots were for the Presidential election?"

"Well, yeah, Agent Latens, but I don't think that's what was going on with this guy. The vote for President in Texas was always going to be a blowout. There was no way a few ballots from this town could change a thing. But for the local congressman, well a vote here and there could change it all. The districts were redrawn recently and it was supposed to make this area a more balanced election."

I sat wondering why I would be assigned to take the soul from a guy who didn't fix an election. Plus he had a relatively clean soul. He looked too terrified to be doing anything but telling me the truth. From all my years of training and chasing criminals, this guy didn't have any attributes of being a real criminal or a broken soul.

"What happened in the election, Mr. McShane?"

"You don't know? I would think you would know that before banging on my door. The incumbent won by less than one hundred votes. Maybe you are too busy with your job, Agent Latens, but me, I'm a political junkie. I live for elections. I don't like it, but the President's party kept control of the House of Representatives by six members. With four hundred and thirty five voting members, a six member majority ain't squat. My guys thought they could win back the House but they didn't. I sure hope you vote, because one or two votes really do make a difference sometimes."

"I apologize, Mr. McShane. You are right. I travel so much and get assigned cases, I don't always have the time to pay close attention to all the details of who I am chasing. But I do my best to make sure only those who should pay a price, do. One last thing before I leave. Do you have a description of the guy who asked you to swap the ballots?"

He took a deep sigh then wiggled his nose. "The guy had a slight accent. Not sure, but I think maybe Italian. He was tall, olive skin, dark hair. The one marking I won't forget was this small tattoo on his neck, just behind his uhm, right earlobe. I really couldn't make out what it was cause I was so afraid the guy was going to mug me. The second time I saw him, when he gave me the ballots, I was too scared to look the guy in the eye. I took the ballots, dumped them in the trunk of my car until the night after I dropped off the real ballots at the counting station. Sorry, but that's all I know. But please, I swear I did the right thing. People all like me here despite usually being on the opposite side of most issues. I can't let them think I cheated in an election."

"Here's my card, Mr. McShane. If the guy with the tattoo or anyone else approaches you again, please call me."

I was escorted out the door. Was it a coincidence I was asked to remove the soul from a guy who didn't steal an election? Maybe me taking his soul was the bad thing that was going to happen to him if he didn't replace the ballots? There were too many unanswered questions for me to take this guys soul.

Time for answers, it was a long flight back to the compound but one that was necessary. Bink was locking the door to his office when I arrived. "You're not heading anywhere just yet. Open the door and your files and let's find out what's going on here."

"What brings you back home so soon, Elder Novo?" Brandon Bink asked with an inquisitive voice.

"The report I received from Peter is inaccurate. We need to find out what's going on in your system." I was tired and cranky and made sure Bink knew my mood by the tone in my voice.

Bink logged back into his computer. He pulled up his database and mapping system showing where all the members on assignment should have been. We matched the list Peter sent me to the one on his screen. His screen had me in Texas and Aleka in

Tokyo, not on vacation as my list indicated.

"Mr. Bink, I was sent to Texas to remove the soul, from what I can tell, a hardworking decent citizen. I'm not sure how he got mixed up in some voting fraud issue but that's for another day. I thought you checked your list closer now, so mistakes like this don't happen?"

Bink turned his head sideways, squinted one of his eyes and frowned. "I don't understand it myself, Elder Novo. But I've told you in the past. I don't have anything to do with who gets picked by the Council or the committee to lose a soul. I'm sure you've seen the lists from the search committee that's passed along to the Council for final approval? Once the Council signs off on it and hits my desk, I assign the tasks. I don't ask questions."

"Is Eve Longer still the head of the search committee?"

"Of course she is, Elder Novo. She's had that job longer than I've been doing this one. Word around the compound was that she and Elder Orcus had a thing for each other. Have you ever seen the photos of her when she was young? I can see why the big guy would want her close. But it's all rumor of course, I didn't say anything." Bink said with a smile.

"Something is still not right though, Mr. Bink. The list Peter sent to me, I was marked as on vacation. It had Aleka Kono on vacation too. Yet on your screen, we were both clearly on assignment. We need to look at upgrading your system. We also need to review the process of the search committee."

Bink twisted his head and frowned at me again. "Elder Novo, I didn't give Peter any lists. I was wondering where you got yours from. I was too afraid to ask."

"You sure Peter didn't come asking you for a list, maybe five days ago?"

"I'm very sure, Elder Novo.

I left Bink's office wondering how Peter got his list. I tracked him down having dinner with Elders Polus and Robus. Peter explained that when I asked for the list, Bink was away for the day. He asked for the most recent list from Elder Robus who confirmed his story. It still didn't answer how I was marked for vacation along with Aleka but all three declared the list given to me was from a different program than the mapping database I witnessed in Binks office.

"Sorry, Elder Novo, but I'm not familiar with Bink's computer system. You were recently on vacation the same time with Miss Kono, don't you remember?" Peter tried to ease my mind I was getting upset over a clerical update. I wasn't as convinced and called for a Council meeting for the following morning.

"Fellow Council Members, our system of determining broken souls is as broken as the souls themselves." The meeting began with me agitating the other members right away. Only Elder Timmons was not present since she was stalking her latest target. It would take too long for her to return for one meeting. I continued offering a motion. "I move that we don't take another soul until this entire process can be examined."

Elder Baruch Robus reacted quickly. "Damn you, Elder Novo, why do you insist on showing up and trampling our traditions?" I could see his puffy face turning red with every word. "Our way of choosing damaged souls has worked for centuries. We try to be perfect, but every system has flaws. Why can't you ever leave well enough alone?"

I took a few moments to see if anyone else on the Council would speak but no one did. I decided since no one else would take up my cause, I would continue. "I don't expect our system to be perfect, Elder Robus. However, in this last round of assignments alone, at least two out of twenty nine were not souls on the level of removal status. Perfection is one thing; however this is either incompetence or a flawed selection process."

My motion was ignored as all the other members wanted to speak from the dais. It didn't matter what the topic was, it seemed they all wanted to say something for the official record. It gave Elder Polus enough time to search our laws and cite that anytime a motion to stop taking souls was offered, a full Council must be present. They tabled my motion for a later date.

After everyone spoke their mind and the official meeting concluded, Elder Polus stood up from his chair and walked passed me. "Our system works exactly as planned, Elder Novo. I suggest you come to terms with the fact that you will never win this battle."

Maybe he was right. Between the four older men on the Council, they had served for over four hundred years combined. I hadn't served two years and Tasha sat in on one meeting. It was so difficult to change anything despite knowing our system needed some tweaks. I had threatened to quit before, but I hated to consider myself a quitter. Possibly once the four of them died, or were too weak to remain on the Council, I could find more like minded members to sit and see things my way. That had to be my only solace for the time being.

23

Mexico can be a beautiful place in the summer but not where I was heading. One of our newest trainees failed to remove the soul of a man suspected of being the largest breeder of dogs trained for fighting each other. It's rare we send out a second soul stealer but I was told his assignment was given out in error. He wasn't ready for such a tough task. I could add that to the list of agenda items for the next Council meeting.

My journey took me to Mexico City. I would spend the evening hours learning my latest toy, a GPS unit. It was a brilliant device but my first time using one. This would be my last task for a few weeks. Kalani called a few days earlier. We were going to spend a week in Hawaii once this mission was complete. Sleep was difficult later that evening thinking about my wife in a bikini on white sandy beaches. Eventually my eyes got heavy and the last thing I remember was peering at the clock reading past two am.

Soon after falling into a deep sleep, Mikeal Sano came to me in a dream. He warned me of pending danger. The first time he ever appeared was to introduce me to my wife. This was not as friendly a visit. "Fighting dogs take many forms," was all I could remember of his words after I awoke. Preparing for a potentially dangerous day, I struggled to get dressed.

The report Peter gave me had the coordinates of where Pablo Valenzuela was seen fighting his dogs. The main fighting area wasn't far from his well-armed ranch. I was told the fights were outside in a valley and started mid-afternoon. I left early in the morning to find the location since it was more than a two hour drive outside Mexico City.

Not being completely familiar with the new GPS system, I hoped I was in the right location after arriving. It was a desolate valley surrounded by cascading hills in the distance. There were few trees. Wind whipped through the vast wasteland creating a giant dust bowl. After getting out of the car, I walked around looking for signs of previous dog fighting. There were a few poorly constructed pens made from chicken wire and a wide circle built with small stones. I could see a few footprints not blown away from the wind as well as dog droppings. In the distance, a lone crow picked at a carcass of a dog that was on the losing end of a battle.

Leaving my car parked nearby was not a smart idea, so I got back in the car and drove over a mile away and waited for activity. Hours later, as the sun started its decent over the side of the hills, darkness found its way across the valley. Either I had the wrong place or the wrong day. Time had come to return to the hotel. I took the small dirt road back towards the main street when I came upon a large tree branch crossing my path. I found it odd since I didn't see a tree in the area. I had no choice but to move it from the road.

The bulky limb was too heavy for me to move alone. I thought about driving around it but on eithe˜ side of the road was loose dirt. I didn't want to risk getting stuck. I tried to move the branch again. It was too difficult. Suddenly, car headlights came towards me.

The car stopped on the other side of the branch. Two men got out. The man who got out of the passenger side called over to me. "Podemos ayudar, you need help?" What a break, I thought. I really didn't want to get stuck in the middle of nowhere all night.

"Can you guys help me move this off to the side of the road, please?" With three men, it only took a few moments to move the heavy tree branch. I thanked them and began walking back to my car. That's when I heard and felt the first shot. I fell in the dirt road face first. I could hear someone walk closer then felt dirt being kicked in my face and hair. From my time spent with the Aborigines, I knew how to shut my body down, appearing to be dead. Despite my heart wanting to race, I quickly slowed my heart rate to almost nothing.

One of the men rolled my body over to be face up. I feared death was imminent. I knew I didn't have time to open my eyes, reach for him and take his soul. Calculating that playing possum was my best defense, I remained motionless. I was kicked in the right side of my rib cage. A second shot hit me in the upper chest. The same man who asked me if I needed help earlier spoke.

"Ciao, Elder Novo. This all could have been avoided had you learned your manners." He then dragged my dead weight body several steps away from the dirt road. After he got me where he apparently wanted to leave my body to rot forever, he yelled over to the other man who had helped us moved the branch. "I did ze hard part, you bury ze bastard. Be quick, we got too rock and roll, mio amico."

It didn't take long before I heard the thug panting as he dug my future home. I was on my stomach and started to breathe slowly. I refused to end my life in this barren wasteland. Every time another shovel of dirt was moved, all I thought about was Mikeal's remark, "Fighting dogs take many forms." The shoveling ended. My body was rolled into a shallow ditch face down. A third shot was fired into my back. "Zat one's for being prick ta Tasha. Good riddance, soul mas-tur."

I gasped for air as dirt partially covered my body. I didn't want them to realize I was still alive but I also needed enough air to continue my existence on earth. The guy who shot me sounded panicked. "We're late, zat's guud enough. No ones gonna find em in dis hell, let's go." That voice would be forever imprinted in my brain.

After I heard both cars drive off, I used the last remaining drop of energy to lift myself from the partially filled, shallow hole. Lucky for me, not only were they dumb enough not to check to see if I was dead, the hole they dug was easy enough to escape. Whoever hired them got ripped off.

The evening sky was filled with twinkling stars. On most nights, I would have enjoyed star gazing but I wasn't sure if I wanted to move much more than getting out of the poorly made grave. Maybe I was too afraid to try. My body ached from the gunshots in my back and chest. No one would hear my plea for help, so I didn't try. My mind raced with thoughts of who set me up and why Tasha's name was mentioned. Whoever was hired to kill me, knew exactly who I was in name and power. I could no longer trust anyone except Kalani and a few trusted confidants outside the compound.

Since I was left for dead by my assailants in the middle of nowhere, I felt secure in stripping off my bulletproof vest. I never failed to heed Mikeal's warnings. The entire time I was on the ground, I prayed the man hired to kill me wouldn't shoot me in the face. I pulled the slugs from the vest, tucked them in my pocket, tossed the vest on the ground and walked the dusty road. I figured it would be much easier to walk under the cool cover of darkness than with the sun beating down. Rest was not an option.

I walked through the night and into the early morning hours until I came across a small town. A large fee was paid to one of the men with access to a vehicle to get me to the nearest hotel. The hotel wasn't exactly five star accommodations, but it offered a clean bed to rest my weary body.

Kalani would be my only contact with the rest of the world, until I could devise a strategy to find my assailants and their reasons for the assault. She was outraged when she heard the news. Her first reaction was to storm the compound and rip out the soul of everyone in her path. That would have been a mistake, but I understood her reaction. I couldn't say it didn't cross my mind as well. But the object was to find out who did this, not have us branded as criminals within our own community for removing innocent souls. It was possible the Council had nothing to do with the attempted murder. Possibly it was a scorned boyfriend of Tasha's. Who knows what stories that woman might have told to make a lunatic with firearms jealous?

Two days later, I made my way across the Mexican/ US border where I checked into a small motel using one of my rarely used aliases. I mailed the best of the bullet fragments to Agent Nesstor, to see if his agency could match it to anything in their databases. It was several days before he had any information, but I received a return call.

Nesstor laughed after our initial hellos. "I'm amazed no one's taken a run at you before, Cale." His voice then changed to a more serious tone. "Forensics ran your fragment through a series of tests and checked every database imaginable. That bullet came from a 9mm handgun. The lab boys tell me they aren't one hundred percent certain but they believe the same gun was used in other unsolved crimes."

"What do you mean they can't be certain, Elliot?"

"We're getting this information from sources across the globe, Cale. Some agencies are not as high tech as us. Each crime is being investigated by the local authorities where the crime was committed. One was a murder of a state senator from Illinois, one a family doctor in California, one an executive from a Russian company that mines platinum and the most recent was a failed attempt on a tourist in Spain, some old guy. The guy in Spain survived the attempt, the others weren't as fortunate."

What were the odds the tourist was someone I knew? "Tell me Elliot. What information do you have on the guy who was shot in Spain?"

"Sorry, Cale, there's not too much to go on here. But they did get a name, a Nathan Stella. The nurse claims in the report this Stella fellow lost a lot of blood and refused a transfusion. He disappeared from his hospital bed in the middle of night. Sorry I can't be more help. The FBI's not working the cases. I just found what I could to try and help ya out."

"Thanks, Elliot. You were far more help than you might think. I'll be in touch."

"That's what I'm afraid of, Cale." I could only imagine what Elliot Nesstor was thinking as he hung up the phone.

The next step was to find out what Elder Stella knew. The last time I visited with him in the compound, he was frail. He never fully recovered from the wound. Exposing Kalani to Stella in the compound was not a great option but was the best.

Patience might be a virtue but not mine. Sitting in a low rent, flea infested building masquerading as a legitimate place to rest was not my idea of fun. I was a powerful agent of the Lord of Life, someone who traveled the globe, moving freely from place to place with few cares. Being subjected to watching vampire movies and thirty year old reruns on television, while Kalani traveled to the compound, was not the best use of my time. My blood pressure rose every time one of those creepy vampires took a soul. They only think they know how to take a soul. I'm the real master soul stealer! But now I'm feeling like a frightened geek on dodge ball day in gym class. Someone would pay for exposing me to this type of fear.

Several flea bites and six days later, Kalani showed up at the motel against my orders. She never did listen to a word I said but I was grateful to see her.

"I know, I know, but I had to make sure my husband was safe. Please forgive me. When this is over, I promise, I have this bikini that will make you forget all about me disobeying you, again."

The woman knew how to diffuse my anger. After she endured my rant about fleas, vampires and the cooking at the local diner, we shared a few moments with the bed bugs under the covers. Life started to come back into focus, until Kalani told me about Elder Stella.

"Cale, Stella is scared out of his wits. He wouldn't tell me who, but I know he not only knows who tried to kill him, but why. I didn't tell him about what happened to you. I don't think he's going to live much longer. He had that grey skinned look of death. The only thing he did do, right before I left, was to whisper in my ear some talk about too much power in the hands of a few being dangerous. He then started hacking up a lung and asked you and me to watch over his grandson, Jacob. He knows something, Cale. But I think he's afraid if he tells someone what happened to him, Jacob will pay the price."

Reflecting on what Kalani told me, I thought about the last time I saw Bink. He implied he never assigned any retired bank robber to Elder Stella in Spain. Someone else gave Stella the assignment with Bink's name on it. He also implied Stella's target didn't exist in our list of souls to be taken. I blew it off. I assumed Bink wanted me to bring up what he implied at the next Council meeting, so I could play the fool on the dais, for all the times I yelled at him. Maybe he really was trying to tell me something. Life was out of focus again.

Being intimidated and hiding away in flea bag heaven couldn't continue. A being with my power and responsibilities was going to attack the day. But first, I had one more call to make. Agent Nesstor wasn't real thrilled about me asking another favor so quickly, but he did confirm my worst fear. Authorities in Mexico confirmed to Nesstor that no one by the name of Pablo Valenzuela owned a large ranch near the coordinates provided to me in my report. Nor did anyone with that name breed dogs anywhere near that location. It was a set up from the start. The men who wanted me dead knew exactly where I would be.

Kalani fought the idea but I decided to travel to the Compound and act as if there was never an attempt on my life. I would turn in my report as if my assignment was successful and see what the reaction would be. Who would want to deny the existence of Pablo Valenzuela?

I demanded Kalani take Nic and stay with her parents for the time being. It wouldn't have been her if she didn't squawk but she relented. The trip to the Compound was scheduled so that I would enter while most were asleep. I didn't fear anything or anyone in the Compound. Guns were strictly forbidden and despite my flea bitten ankles, I was near full strength. No one inside the Compound would dare attempt to remove my soul.

24

"Your reaction said it all, Peter. You look like you have seen a ghost."

My assistant, Peter, who gave me the task of heading to Mexico, and I suspect gave the assignment to Elder Stella to head to Spain, stood in front of me with the blood draining from his face.

"I'm not sure what you mean, Elder Novo. We weren't expecting you back anytime soon, that's all."

As quickly as the color drained from his cheeks, the blood rushed into mine. My head exploded with anger knowing with a moment's glance, someone I trusted would forever be an enemy. Peter may as well have been dead to me.

"Be honest, Peter. What were you promised if you aided in my demise?"

He stood there acting the part of a Greek statue. After a few seconds, his lips moved but nothing else. "I have no idea what you mean, Elder Novo. You were scheduled to be in Mexico, not here

280

in the compound. You caught me off guard, I guess."

My emotions were running the gamut of wanting to jail him for conspiracy to commit murder, to removing his soul, to screaming at the prick for lying to my face. "Yes, I was scheduled to be there, days ago. Then again, I imagine you suspected I would be there for a longer time, didn't you Peter? One last chance to come clean before I rip out your soul, what did they promise you?"

Peter crossed his arms and sounded defiant. "Go ahead. Try to take it, you can't. I hope you enjoyed all that home cooking at Uncle Mel's diner. Your time is done, Elder Novo. Let's face it, if you can't see into another's soul or remove them, you can't sit on the Council. Come on, take a look. I dare you!"

Who was this punk to dare me to do anything? I grabbed hold of his left arm to rip out his soul purely for insubordination but nothing happened. Peter was right. I couldn't see his soul, nor was anything happening. He looked at me with a childish smirk.

"Awe, too bad Elder Novo, or should I call you Caeles from now on? We didn't know what to do when you were spotted crossing the border by one of our employees. It wasn't easy getting someone to follow you to that cheap motel in California. That idiot, Faustina couldn't kill you or Nathan Stella. We had to resort to Plan B."

I didn't want to believe what was happening. I grabbed for his arm again.

"Try again, I really don't care. You'll never take another soul," Peter replied. "Your good buddy, Doctor Winfield, did he tell you about his experiments while he worked here in the compound?"

I lost focus on what Peter had to say. Be careful for what you wish for, was all I could think about while Peter blabbered on about all the experiments Winfield had done in the compound many years ago. I remembered wishing for a time with no responsibilities to anyone but my wife and child. I wanted a life away from all the travel and battling with the Council. That time came without warning. My mind focused back to what Peter was still yapping about.

"I'm shocked. Winfield didn't tell you about his most dangerous experiment? You do know he hates us soul stealers, right? Well, he developed a potion that you have to take a few times, and it takes away your power to see and remove souls. Imagine our shock when Doc Chamoun ran across it in the lab."

How stupid could I have been? Every morning at the diner I would drink the water that didn't quite taste right. The waitress kept telling me all the water tasted that way in the area. I should have been smarter.

"Oh, I can't wait, Caeles. I always wanted to be one of the six on the Council and now I will be. That's what I was promised, your seat unless you agreed to continue our real mission. If not your seat, then I would get the next open one. All I had to do was have people follow you everywhere and be able to eliminate you at moment's notice."

I didn't know what to feel or think. Was it possible I was really done as the leader of the Council and a soul stealer? What did Kalani know? What would they do to her or my son? How does one go from the top of the mountain to the bottom in an instant? And what was the real mission Peter was talking about?

I found out later, when I was summoned into our board room.

Elder Robus, Elder Polus, Peter, Elder Timmons, and for some reason, Charon Orcus were already seated. I took notice of who wasn't in attendance, Elder Spia and Elder Rex. I then glanced at a tall man with olive skin and a small tattoo below his ear lobe sitting in a chair behind the main board room table. I made a point of asking the tattooed man if he had the time. He peeked at his watch, "Just before noon. Why? You got hot date, ex soul mastur?"

That was the voice. The one forever stamped on my brain. That's the asshole that shot me. It's also the man who tried to intimidate Harley McShane back in Texas. It was plain to see now who tried to kill me.

I stood across the table from the others. The fact they filled all the seats on the opposite side made it obvious, I was a team of one. The five pair of eyes staring my way would not intimidate me. I took the only seat situated on my side of the table. Sitting as erect as possible, my chest pushed out, chin up, I stared directly at Elder Polus. I knew I was as vulnerable as I had ever been but I refused to show it. I may have lost the abilities passed down to me from my ancestors but I would never be powerless.

Polus spoke first. "Elder Novo, as you are aware in our bylaws section one, article six it clearly states that only those with the ability to see into another's soul and remove it when ordered, may be a member of the High Council. It has come to our attention that you no longer possess those abilities. Is it accurate to say that you no longer meet the requirements to be a member of the High Council?"

I held my chin even higher. I carefully looked each person in the eye who sat across the table. I slowly raised my right index finger, starting with Charon Orcus and ending with Tasha Timmons. I pointed at each one individually and stated, "If I did, I would own the soul of you, and you, and you, and you and you." I lowered my hand back to the desk and calmly stated. "And when the day comes again that I do, and I assure you all, I will get my ability back, I will own them all."

Each person across the table snickered in their own way. Polus again spoke. "Now then, Elder Novo, there is no reason to sound combative. This is purely a hearing to determine if you are fit to sit on the High Council. I ask you again, do you have the ability to remove souls, yes or no?"

I refused to dignify them with another response. I sat motionless for several minutes before Elder Robus spoke. "I make a motion we conclude this hearing with the understanding Elder Novo no longer has the proper authority to remain on the High Council. Since a majority of the Council is present in the room with four members, I move that we convene as a Council meeting and vote to remove Caeles Novo from the High Council."

I sat there watching this folly unfold as the motion was seconded and a vote was taken to remove me, three to zero with my vote being counted as an abstention. I refused to participate. After the circus show was complete, I looked at Polus searching for answers.

"Why do this Polus? Why not just try to gun me down again? Is that how our last few on assignment were killed? Not really being killed by accident on assignments but by your thug over there?

Polus sneered. "We don't like to kill our own, Novo. I can assure you we had nothing to do with their deaths. As far as you, it would look too suspicious to our disciples if attempts were made on your life again, especially after Elder Stella being shot and in poor health. You have always been a major thorn to the Council but why offer our people a conspiracy?"

Polus then pointed his index finger at me. "You and your talk of redemption and restoring souls. We took each and every soul for a reason. We don't want to restore them. And all your endless drivel at the Council meetings to create more soul stealers. It got tiresome. We've spent decades building what we have now. We could no longer sit back and give you the opportunity to destroy it."

"And what is it that you think you have that's so special, Polus?"

Elder Polus stood up from his chair, looked at me from across the table and stated, "Utopia." He smiled in my direction and left the room.

I then looked at Tasha Timmons and asked her why she played along with traitors being so new on the Council.

"I thought you were onboard with all this, Novo. I didn't know until recently you had no idea what we really do here and why. As for me, I only did it for one reason. I've told you many times. I like being on top. When the so called traitors croak, I'll control it all." She too left the room. Peter got up just behind her with a frown on his face trying to catch up with Timmons.

After Timmons made her exit, other than the ticking clock on the wall, the room remained still for a few moments. Then the man with the tattoo, who I now know as Dante Faustino, their henchman with bad skills, gave me a stare as he stood and left.

Robus packed up his papers and left as well. It was only Charon Orcus remaining in the room with me. I knew all the while his glare was peering my way. I assumed he wanted to see me crumble under the pressure. I refused to give him that pleasure. Finally he spoke.

"I knew one day I would take from you, what you took from me. This was always going to be too much for you to handle, Novo. I knew I only needed to wait my time until you pissed off enough of the Council members."

I was in no mood for his lecture and fired back. "I did what I thought was best for everyone, Orcus. I wanted to restore us to numbers that would not have me and the few left always on duty. I felt we had slipped far from our goals. The Council members and staff have surrounded themselves with material prizes, cutting back on training our soul stealers, with no desire to restore our glory."

Orcus moved his chair closer to the table and softened his tone. "Caeles, our mission changed in the last century. You forget we are almost identical to most humans, sharing all the emotions and yes, their failings. Greed is now our mission. I'm just as much to blame as the others, as is your grandfather and now, Timmons. Think about it. We force many of our members to train here for fifty years before heading out into the world. I am now three hundred and twelve years on this earth and don't look a day over eighty. Did you know I was friends with Edgar Allen Poe? I gave Monet his first set of paints? I wrote a speech for Abe Lincoln? My grandfather assisted Michelangelo? I could go on but I won't."

Learning about the arts was not high on my list at the moment, so I asked Orcus to get to his point. My patience was running low.

"We adapted to our longer lives, Caeles. We realized we didn't need to read about history like our full blooded human friends, we created history. We decided to take our skills and ability to live well beyond our human friends to another level. It's been right in front of your eyes all along. But I will admit you were too good of a soldier to ever realize it. Did you know we control the world's economies? I bet not. We control much of the power base across the world and the big concern you brought to the Council was restoring the soul of a broken down guitar player. It's time you woke up to reality, Novo.

He opened my eyes. I did see our disciples and my place in it, in a different light. I thought about why I had such easy access to information when searching for people. I could get bank records about anyone. I could get first class tickets on airplanes even if the flights were overbooked. I could get information from spy agencies around the world. It didn't matter what I did, I had connections and never worried about money. I assumed our funds were only collected in the form of taxes, even though I knew about our accounts with billions of dollars tucked away. I had never sat in on a budget meeting to really explore our cash reserves. I raised my hand as affirmative when my one time to vote on a budget came up in the Council meeting. I never bothered to read it. I assumed my natural charm got me many things. Was I possibly too self absorbed in my thefts around the world to peek at reality? Maybe I didn't want to know.

Orcus gave me a friendly look and kept speaking. "The guy in Texas, McShane. We knew the election to keep the control of the House of Representatives would be close. Our power base lied mostly with the party in control. We had to make sure they won and did. We fixed the election, Caeles. Maybe that guy in Texas let us down, but others didn't. His penalty for not helping us was you, removing his soul. When you didn't, we knew you were too far gone to keep you on the Council. We still have our souls. It's our consciences we allowed to get dark. You never did. That's what makes you too dangerous to sit on the Council.

Now I was disturbed even more. "Wait, you're telling me we are so corrupted now that we stoop to fixing elections?"

Orcus laughed and sat back in his chair. "That's your big concern? It's rare we go that far, but yes, we have. Caeles, look at who our disciples are around the world. The Chairman of the Federal Reserve in the United States is one of us. The Boards of Directors of many leading computer hardware and software companies are our people. Three Cardinals at the Vatican are tied to us. Countless politicians in countries across the world have our blood. We are the majority stockholder in many of the most profitable companies in history. We own a car company. We own an airline. We haven't found a way to fluctuate the price of oil in the Mideast to our advantage yet, but we're working on it. We are majority owners in several media outlets and telephone companies. We partially control the flow of information around the world. We used all of our knowledge, skills and our place in history over time to control the balance of power on earth. Who cares about a few dark souls? We now train our members to be the best in every industry, not take souls."

I was flabbergasted. All my time around these people and even being the so called leader, it never crossed my mind all the power we had beyond taking souls. Maybe it was best I never knew. If I had, it's possible I would have played along. I ran my fingers across my forehead many times trying to take time to digest all I was learning.

"What about your son, Orcus? Where did he fit into all of this, really?"

"Ha, my son." Charon Orcus declared. "He could have run the world. We trained him with the best minds this planet had to offer. And for what? I begged him to stay. Yes, I asked him to find a way to extend our lives and he revolted against me. We would have paid for everything. One day he will cure cancer. Think about this, Novo. What will people be willing to pay for a drug that cures cancer? Oh we so wanted to corner that market. We could have sold the patent to drug companies and made billions."

I stopped Orcus and asked him. "Are you telling me that your son has a conscience? He wanted to do it on his own, on his terms and offer to heal people without paying a huge fee?"

Orcus shrugged his shoulders. "The man is brilliant but stupid. If I heard how he's a healer and not a stealer one more time, I might have ripped his soul out myself."

"What about the soul of his nurse? Do you know who took it?" I asked Orcus.

He scratched his nose and looked out the window. "I was told Faustina took it to rile you up and have you take Grayson's soul. It was a set up to get you off the Council, but I don't really know for sure. I only know that son of mine could have had everything. Now, who knows, looks like that twerp assistant of yours will fight it out with the Timmons woman. They can have it. My time is about up. I'm only happy I lived long enough to see you lose it all, like me."

25

Charon Orcus left me alone with my thoughts. Over the next several hours, my life passed in front of me many times. I reviewed every soul I had taken. Many I couldn't remember their names or why their souls were taken. I began to question if possibly they had a product that competed with a company we owned and possibly not a soul worth removing. Was it a politician who could defeat the candidate chosen by our people to win? After much soul searching, I realized even though I had lost faith in our current leadership, I didn't lose faith in our real mission, sent from the heavens.

The ticking clock on the wall informed me that I hadn't moved in close to eight hours when my grandfather, Elder Spia entered the room and pulled a chair next to mine.

"Cale, no doubt you're disillusioned and angry. We didn't wake up one day and decide to install our disciples into high ranking positions around the world. It happened naturally. When much of society cut their funding for education, we seized the opportunity and placed more emphasis on learning business applications and ways to support our cause. Once our people stepped into the arena of fighting for jobs, they crushed the competition at entry level positions. Their egos took over and they quickly moved up the ranks. Our disciples had fifty years of education compared to at most sixteen to twenty of our human counterparts. Even our weakest minds found ways to succeed."

I knew he was right. When I was fifty years old, I still looked the part of a teenager. I knew so much more about the world and acted much more mature, because I was. By then, I had already traveled the globe, been a chess and poker champion and lived with ancient civilizations. Pure humans could never compete with us for jobs while we still looked young. But I was taught I only had one job in life, to steal souls. Certainly not run the New York Stock Exchange.

"I don't understand, Grandfather. Do all these people realize what a rush it is to steal souls? Do they even know what our real job is here on earth? That it's not to cure cancer?"

My grandfather tried to explain. "They all had the same training as you. But over time, some were asked to get involved in local communities. Many found it easy to assume leadership inside companies. The Council realized we could profit from our strength in education. It snowballed from there. That was never our intention, it just happened. I could have fought it more but I too got caught up in wanting to dominate society."

The intensity of my anger grew. "So I was just some shiny token in your game that ran around taking souls of the competition so all of you could sit here and profit? I gave my life to something I believed in, not so you could all wear the best suits and eat the finest foods, stay in five star hotels and live like kings!"

We both looked at each other until my grandfather spoke again. "I saw where this was all heading decades ago. So did others. It's why I shielded your real abilities and identity from the Council all those years. I knew you were sent to change our ways. Mikeal came to me in a dream and told me, you were the one. I watched you from a distance but helped you develop into the strong leader that still burns inside you. I still believe you are the one to change it back to our past. But it won't be easy. These are now powerful men and women with executive positions in life and beautiful families. They have become accustomed to all the earthly trappings of success. They aren't going to trek down dark alleys chasing criminals. "

I wanted to rip out his soul, but I no longer had the power. This was the second time in my life, my grandfather told me how special I was, the chosen one. Yet he kept secrets. Once again he tried to convince me my destiny was to lead our people back to our original mission. Only this time, I know they're fat and happy.

"Cale, so many times when you were here in the compound, I asked to speak with you. Think about it. I wanted to explain to you what you were up against. Every time you made a motion in the Council room, I cautioned you for various reasons. I know you think it was only to dismiss you. I can assure you, it was so you could see what you were really fighting. I asked you several times to visit me, so we could discuss matters regarding our future. You were always too busy, off on the next mission, you would say. Don't condemn me until you stare at yourself in the mirror."

I pointed my finger in his face. "Did you know they wanted to kill me?"

"Of course not! Do you really think I would have approved? No, when I found out, I was furious. I immediately resigned from the Council, as did Elder Rex. The thought we would kill our leaders was all either of us could handle. No, I looked the other way in allowing them to buy up companies and stop worrying about taking souls long enough. Once they decided to start killing people, especially my own flesh and blood, I quit. My time on the Council is over. My time on earth is waning. I'm sorry I didn't press you harder to come and sit with me. I hope you will forgive me, but I swear, this Faustina character and his dealings, no, I never knew about any of it, including trying to kill Stella. I knew Polus was upset with Elder Stella but I never thought our leaders would try to kill anyone."

The following morning I packed up all my belongings from my living quarters and put them in storage inside the compound. I was determined more than ever to remove everyone remaining on the Council. I didn't know how but I would find a way. I felt naked without my power to remove a soul. I had never carried a weapon but I thought about learning how to shoot a gun. I didn't know what would be lurking around each corner. I didn't suspect anyone would take my soul. If they wanted to, it could have been done in the conference room with ease.

I knew my people's Achilles heel. I knew how to destroy them. I might not have been the most observant when it came to all the commerce that was going on around me, but I did know how to attack a soul stealer. I was an expert in knowing what made them tick. But first, I needed my power back. If Doctor Winfield could make a potion to remove my powers, he could make one to restore them. That would be step one. Step two would be to use the leadership's arrogance against them.

I called Kalani from a pay phone away from the compound on my way to Texas. I told her all that happed inside the board room and she was again full of rage. Keeping her from heading to the compound was a small miracle. As strong as she was, she was no match for the members inside the compound. She might have been able to remove a few souls on the way in, but getting the Council members would be near impossible.

It was one thing to remove my abilities but the arrogance in thinking because they controlled much of the world's economy, that they controlled me, was a huge mistake. Kalani and I had planned for our retirement. We knew how easy it was for bank records to be seized but they didn't know we planted several coffee cans filled with hundred dollar bills in hidden locations. I had the training like them, but I learned how to live off the grid. They would all pay with their souls.

Two days later I was back at Doc Winfield's Texas office. I never thought I would return, but there I was. This time I watched behind me and changed routes many times. I did all I could to be sure I wasn't followed. I walked in the door to find Nurse Simon sitting behind her desk.

"Good afternoon, Nurse Simon, I need to speak with Doctor Winfield, it's an emergency."

"Well hello, sugar, Rose sure has missed seeing you. How you been?"

"Rose? What are you doing here? Where is Doc Winfield?"

Rose got up from behind the desk, walked over and put her arms around me. She offered a very loving hug, then whispered in my ear.

"I told you, sugar, Rose would take care of everything and she has."

MICHAEL CANTWELL

FROM THE AUTHOR

Many authors claim they were born with the passion to write. Not me. My desire to write didn't start until I had already begun my first novel, an event that didn't occur until well beyond my fifty-second birthday. With each passing day my desire to improve at my craft grows. I now have a passion for writing. Maybe this can be better it developed at a later age since we draw so many stories from our own life experiences and people we've met along the way. I don't believe I would've been able to write these stories twenty years ago. But I can't look back and worry about the past. I can only look forward and appreciate each and every person who has a passion to read and thank the Lord above for allowing me the talent to express myself in this manner.

Anyone who has ever attempted to use words to create characters and plot lines can relate to how personal this experience can be. It's a humbling experience when someone tells you they enjoyed your endless negotiations with your own mind; what the reader sees as simple word choice, is anything but. I would encourage you to find your passion, no matter your age, or perceived ability. I never considered becoming a novelist, yet here I sit putting the finishing touches on my fourth novel, with a fifth already in the works. Never allow anyone to tell you that you can't reach your goals in life.

I want to thank my wife of over thirty years and my three wonderful children for putting up with all the time I spend glaring at the computer screen. I also want to thank my writers group, beta readers and my passionate readers for their endless support.